THE
WHITE
ROSE

∾THE∾
WHITE
ROSE

AMY EWING

HARPER TEEN
An Imprint of HarperCollinsPublishers

HarperTeen is an imprint of HarperCollins Publishers.

Library of Congress Cataloging-in-Publication Data
Ewing, Amy.
    The white rose / Amy Ewing. — First edition.
        pages   cm. — (Jewel ; 2)
    Summary: "After the Duchess of the Lake catches Violet with
Ash, the hired companion at the palace of the Lake, Violet has
no choice but to escape the Jewel or face certain death, so along
with Ash and her best friend, Raven, Violet runs away from her
unbearable life of servitude"— Provided by publisher.
    ISBN 978-0-06-223581-7 (hardback)
    ISBN 978-0-06-241475-5 (int. ed.)
    [1. Fantasy.   2. Courts and courtiers—Fiction.   3. Slavery—
Fiction.]   I. Title.
PZ7.E9478Wh 2015   2015005626
[Fic]—dc23   CIP
                                                              AC

Typography by Anna Christian
15 16 17 18 19 PC/RRDH 10 9 8 7 6 5 4 3 2 1
❖
First Edition

For my mother and father,
who always believed

~ *One* ~

THE ARCANA IS SILENT.

I stare at the small silver tuning fork, nestled among the jewels scattered across my vanity. Garnet's words echo in my ears.

We're going to get you out.

I force my mind to work, push down my terror, and try to fit the pieces together. I'm trapped in my bedroom in the palace of the Lake. How does Garnet, the Duchess of the Lake's own son, have an arcana? Is he working with Lucien, the Electress's lady-in-waiting and my secret friend and savior? But why wouldn't Lucien tell me?

Lucien didn't tell you that childbirth kills surrogates,

either. He doesn't tell you any more than he thinks you need to know.

Panic grips me as I picture Ash, trapped and bleeding in the dungeons. Ash, a companion to royal daughters, who endangered his very life by loving me. Ash, the only other person in this palace who understands what it feels like to be treated like a piece of property.

I shake my head. How much time have I spent staring at the arcana—ten minutes? Twenty?

Something needs to happen. After the Duchess caught us in his room together, he was beaten and thrown in the dungeon, and no one has been sent to save him. If Ash stays there, he'll die.

The terror resurfaces, rising in my throat like bile. I squeeze my eyes shut and all I can see are the Regimentals bursting through the door to his bedroom. Ripping him from the bed. His blood spattering across the comforter as a Regimental slammed a pistol into Ash's face again and again while the Duchess looked on.

And Carnelian. The Duchess's wicked, horrible niece. *She* was there, too. She betrayed us.

I bite my lip and wince. I look at myself in the mirror—hair disheveled, eyes red and puffy. My lower lip is split at the corner and the beginning of a bruise darkens my cheekbone. I probe the tender spot, remembering the feel of the Duchess's hand as she struck me.

I shake my head again. So much has happened since the Auction. Secrecy, alliances, death. I was bought to bear the Duchess's child. I can still see the fury in her eyes as she saw Ash and me in the same room, in the same bed. *Whore*, she called me, after her guard of Regimentals dragged Ash away. I don't care about her insults. I only care about what happens now.

Lucien gave me a serum that I was supposed to take tonight. It would make me appear dead, and he could get me out of the Jewel, to somewhere safe where my body wouldn't be used for royal purposes. But I didn't take it. I gave it away—to Raven.

Somewhere, in the neighboring palace of the Stone, is my best friend, Raven. Her mistress is using her for a darker purpose. Not only is Raven pregnant with the Countess of the Stone's child, but she is being tortured in ways I can't imagine. She is the shell of the girl I once knew.

And I couldn't leave her there. I couldn't let her die like that.

So I gave her the serum.

Lucien will be upset when he finds out, but I had no choice. He'll have to understand.

With trembling fingers, I pick up the arcana and sit on the edge of my bed.

"Garnet?" I whisper to it. "Lucien?"

No one answers me.

"Garnet?" I say again. "If you can hear me . . . please. Talk to me."

Nothing.

How can I be rescued with Regimentals guarding the door? How can Ash be rescued?

My head throbs—it hurts to think. I curl up on my bed with the silver tuning fork clutched tight between my fingers, trying to will it to buzz, to make someone speak to me.

"Please," I whisper to it. "Don't let him die."

I, at least, might have something the Duchess wants. My body might be enough to keep me alive. But Ash doesn't have that.

I wonder what it would feel like, to die. The wild girl appears in my mind, the surrogate who tried to escape the royalty and went into hiding. The one I saw executed in front of the walls of Southgate, my holding facility. I remember her strangely peaceful expression as the end came. Her courage. Would I be able to be as strong as she was, if they put my head on the chopping block? *Tell Cobalt I love him*, she'd said. That, at least, I can understand. Ash's name would be one of the last words on my lips. I wonder who Cobalt was to her. She must have loved him very much.

I hear a noise and jump up so quickly the room seems to tilt. My only thought is that I have to hide the arcana somewhere, now. It's my one connection to the people who want to help me. But there are no pockets on my nightdress, and I don't want to risk hiding it in the room in case the Duchess decides to move me.

Then I remember the Exetor's Ball, when Lucien first gave it to me. When Garnet ruined my hairstyle and Lucien came to my rescue, hiding the silver tuning fork in my thick, dark curls.

Has Garnet been working with Lucien since then? Did he muss my hair on purpose?

But there's no time to wonder about that now. I bolt to my vanity, throwing open the drawer where Annabelle, my own personal lady-in-waiting and my closest friend in the Duchess's palace, keeps my hair ribbons and pins. I twist my hair back into a thick, messy knot at the nape of my neck and secure the arcana inside it with pins.

I fling myself back onto my bed as the door opens.

"Get up," the Duchess orders. She is flanked by two Regimentals. She looks exactly the same as she did when last I saw her in Ash's bedroom, wearing the same golden dressing gown, her glossy black hair hanging loose around her shoulders. I don't know why this surprises me.

The Duchess's face is cold and impassive as she approaches me. I am reminded of the first time I met her, expecting her to circle me with sharp, critical eyes, then slap me across the face again.

Instead, she stops less than a foot away, and her expression turns from cold to blazing.

"How long?" she demands.

"What?"

The Duchess's eyes narrow. "Do not play stupid with me, Violet. How long have you been sleeping with the companion?"

It's jarring to hear her use my name. "I—I wasn't sleeping with him." This is partly true, since at the moment we were discovered, we were not actually sleeping together.

"Do not lie to me."

"I'm not lying."

The Duchess's nostrils flare. "Fine." She turns to the Regimentals. "Tie her up. And bring the other one in."

The Regimentals descend on me before I have a chance to react, yanking my arms behind my back and binding me with a coarse rope. I cry out and struggle, but the bonds are too tight. The rope chafes against my skin, the polished wood of the bedpost pressing against my back as they tie me to it. Then a small, willowy figure is marched into the room.

Annabelle's eyes are filled with fear. Like me, her hands are bound behind her back. She won't be able to use her slate—Annabelle was born mute and can only talk through writing. Her copper-colored hair is out of its usual bun, and her face is so pale that her freckles stand out clearly. My mouth goes dry.

"Leave us," the Duchess orders, and the Regimentals close the door behind them.

"She—she doesn't know anything," I protest weakly.

"I find that hard to believe," the Duchess says.

"She doesn't!" I cry, louder now, fighting against my bindings, because I can't let anything happen to Annabelle. "I swear on my father's grave, she didn't know!"

The Duchess studies me, a cruel smile playing on her lips. "No," she says. "I still don't believe you." Her hand whips across Annabelle's face with a sickening smack.

"Please!" I scream, as Annabelle stumbles back, almost losing her balance. "Don't hurt her!"

"Oh, I have no *wish* to hurt her, Violet. This is *your* fault. Her pain ends when you tell me the truth."

My wrists are raw, the rope cutting into my skin as I struggle against it. Suddenly, the Duchess is inches away from me, my face clutched in her iron grasp, her fingernails biting into the bruise on my cheek. "How long have you been sleeping with him?"

I try to answer her, but I can't open my mouth. The Duchess releases me.

"How long?" she says again.

"One time," I gasp. "It was just one time."

"When?"

"The night before," I say, panting. "Before the second time that the doctor tried . . ."

The Duchess glares at me, seething with rage. "Have you been intentionally destroying these pregnancies?"

I can feel the blankness on my face. "I—no. How would I even *do* that?"

"Oh, I don't know, Violet. You're clearly such a resourceful girl. I'm sure you could find a way."

"No," I say.

The Duchess's hand slams into Annabelle's face again.

"Please," I beg. "I'm telling you the truth."

One of Annabelle's shoulders is hunched up as if to try to cradle her swollen cheek. Our eyes meet and all I see is fear. Confusion. Her eyebrows knit together and I know she's trying to ask me something but I can't figure out exactly what.

"Here is my dilemma, Violet," the Duchess says, pacing back and forth in front of me. "You are a very valuable asset. As much as I might *want* to kill you for what you've done, it wouldn't be a very good business practice. Obviously, your life in this palace will be different from now on. No more balls, no more cello, no more . . . well, anything, I suppose. If I have to, I'll keep you tied to the medical bed for the duration of your stay. I've sent an emergency petition to the Exetor for the companion's execution, so he should be dead in an hour or so. That will serve as some punishment. But is it enough, I ask myself?"

I try to swallow the whimper that climbs up my throat, but the Duchess hears it and smiles.

"Such a waste, really—he is so very handsome. And quite skilled, from what I've heard. The Lady of the Stream *raved* about him at Garnet's engagement party. Pity I didn't get the chance to sample his talents myself."

A cold, slippery feeling squirms around inside me. The Duchess's smile widens. "Please, tell me," she continues, "what exactly did you think would happen with him? That you two would ride off into the sunset together? Do you know how many women he's slept with? It's disgusting. I would have thought you'd have better taste. If you're going to get all love-struck in this palace, why not choose Garnet? His manners might be atrocious, but he's good-looking enough. And he comes from an excellent bloodline."

At this, I can't help choking out a raspy, bitter laugh. "His bloodline? Do you honestly think that matters to anyone in this city besides the royalty? You people wouldn't even *need* surrogates if you didn't care so much about stupid bloodlines!"

The Duchess waits patiently for me to finish. "I would think you would choose your words more carefully," she says. This time when she hits Annabelle, the skin breaks open below her right eye. Tears stream down Annabelle's cheek.

"I need you to understand," the Duchess says. "You are mine. The doctor will not stop until my baby is growing inside you. I will no longer have any consideration for your pain, or discomfort, or frame of mind. You will be like a piece of furniture to me. Is that clear?"

"I'll do whatever you want," I say. "But please don't hit her anymore."

The Duchess becomes very still. Her expression softens, and she sighs. "All right," she says.

She walks to where Annabelle is bent over. In one fluid motion, she yanks Annabelle upright, holding her head back by her hair.

"You know, Violet," the Duchess says. "I cared about you. I truly did." She seems sincerely sad as she holds my gaze. "Why did you have to do this to me?"

I don't see the knife in her hand—just a flash of silver as it whispers across Annabelle's throat. Annabelle's eyes widen, more in surprise than in pain, as a crimson gash opens on her neck.

"NO!" I scream. Annabelle looks at me, her face so lovely and frail, and I can see the question now, clear enough on her face that she wouldn't need her slate to express it.

Why?

Blood spills down her chest, staining her nightdress a brilliant scarlet. Then her body crumples to the floor.

A wild, guttural wail fills the room, and it takes a second before I realize it's coming from me. I thrash against my bonds, ignoring the pain in my back and wrists, hardly feeling it at all, because if I can just get to Annabelle I can make this right; if I can hold her in my arms I can bring her back. There must be a way to bring her back, because she can't be dead, she can't be . . .

Annabelle's eyes are open, vacant, staring at me as blood pours from the wound on her neck, seeping toward me across the carpet.

"You needed to be punished for what you did," the Duchess says, wiping the blood from her knife on the sleeve of her dressing gown. "And so did she."

As casually as if it were nothing, she steps over Annabelle's body and opens the door. I catch a glimpse of my tea parlor and the two Regimentals guarding me before the door closes and I am left alone with the corpse of the girl who was my first friend in this palace.

~ Two ~

I SINK TO MY KNEES.

My shoulders protest as the bindings force my arms up into an awkward position, but I don't care. My legs can't support me right now.

Annabelle's body has run out of blood to spill. I stare at her beautiful, warm, trusting face, and all I can see is the girl who stayed with me that first night, even when she wasn't supposed to, the girl who held me in her arms on a pile of ruined dresses after Dahlia's funeral, who nearly always beat me at Halma, and brushed my hair out every night, and knew my name before anyone else did.

I loved her. And now I had killed her.

"I'm sorry," I whisper, and the tears that had held off up

to this moment begin to run in a myriad of tiny rivers down my cheeks. "I'm so sorry, Annabelle."

The certainty of her death swallows me up, a yawning, endless cavern of grief. The tears turn to sobs that rip through my chest, and I cry until my throat is raw and my lungs ache, to the point where there is nothing left inside me but an emptiness where Annabelle used to be.

TIME PASSES.

At some point, I notice that my arm sockets are aching, a dull burn that distracts me from my grief. But I can't seem to find the energy to move.

I think I hear something outside the door—a tiny pop, then two thumps. Maybe the Duchess has come back. I wonder who she'll kill in front of me next.

The door opens and a Regimental comes in. He's alone, which immediately strikes me as odd, and he closes the door behind him. He stares for one horror-struck moment at the body of my friend, then hurries to my side.

"Are you all right?" he asks. I've never heard any of the Duchess's Regimentals speak before, but this one sounds awfully familiar. It doesn't even occur to me to answer him.

He takes something out of his belt, and then my arms are free—I fall to the floor, not caring enough to try to stop myself. He catches me.

"Violet," he whispers. "Are you hurt?"

How does a Regimental know my name? He shakes me a little and his face comes into focus.

"Garnet?" I try to speak, but my throat is so dry.

"Come on," he says. "We've got to get out of here. We

don't have much time."

He pulls me roughly to my feet. I stumble forward a few steps and fall to my knees in front of Annabelle's body. Her blood is still wet on the carpet—I can feel it soaking through my nightdress. I tuck a lock of her hair behind her ear.

"I'm so sorry," I whisper. Very gently, I close her eyes with my fingertips.

"Violet," Garnet says, "we have to go."

I kiss the side of her head, the spot just above her ear. Her hair smells like lilies.

"Good-bye, Annabelle," I whisper.

Then I force myself to stand. Garnet is right. We have to go. Ash is alive. I can still save him.

Garnet opens the door and I see the two Regimentals sprawled out on the floor. I briefly wonder whether they're unconscious or dead, before I realize I don't care.

We hurry through the drawing room and out of my chambers. The hall of flowers is deserted, but Garnet turns right, heading toward one of the lesser-used staircases at the back of the palace.

"Did Lucien send you?" I whisper.

"Lucien doesn't know yet," he replies. "I couldn't get in touch with him."

"Where are we going?"

"Stop asking questions!" he hisses. We reach the staircase and hurry down it. A floorboard creaks beneath my feet.

The ground floor is eerily quiet. The doors to the ballroom are open, long, slanting shafts of moonlight reaching toward us across the parquet floor. I remember the first time I crept through these halls at night, to visit Ash in his bedroom.

"Where's the dungeon?" I whisper. Garnet doesn't acknowledge me. I grab his arm. "Garnet, where is the dungeon? We need to get Ash."

"Will you shut up?" he says. "We've got to get *you* out of here."

A familiar smell assaults my nose, and without thinking, I open the door to the Duke's smoking room and pull Garnet inside.

"What are you doing?" he says through clenched teeth.

"We're not leaving him here," I say.

"He's not part of the deal."

"We leave him here and he dies."

"So?"

"I just watched Annabelle be murdered and bleed to death." A tightness crawls across my chest. "She was one of the kindest, sweetest people I have ever known and she died because of me. What if she was in that dungeon? Would you leave her there to be executed? I've seen you two together. You were nice to her. She liked you. Does her life not matter to you?"

Garnet shifts uncomfortably. "Look, this isn't part of my job description, okay?" he says. "I'm not here to reunite some tragic love."

"That's not the point. This is about someone's *life*. So why *are* you here?"

"I owe Lucien. I promised to help you."

"Then *help me*," I say.

"I don't get it," he says. "He's just a companion. There are hundreds of them."

"And Annabelle was *just* a servant. And I'm *just* a surrogate," I snap. "You sound *just* like your mother."

Garnet freezes.

"Look at this," I say, grabbing a handful of bloody nightdress in my fist. "This is her blood. Your mother did this. When does it stop? How many more innocent people have to die because of her?"

He pauses. "Fine," he says. "I'll help you. But don't expect me to take the fall if we get caught."

"Why would I ever expect that," I mutter. We slip out of the room and back down the hall, past the library. There is a broad door to the left of it, with a sturdy handle.

"Hold this," Garnet says, handing me what appears to be a large black marble, about the size of an egg. Its surface is unnaturally smooth.

"What is this?" I ask.

"It'll knock out the guards," he says. "Don't ask me how; Lucien made it. It's how I got you out without those Regimentals seeing me."

Garnet takes out a ring of keys and slips a large iron one into the lock. The door opens with a muffled groan. He turns to me and takes the marble back.

"I'd say ladies first," he says, "but in this situation I think we should dispense with common courtesies."

The hall reminds me of the secret passage to Ash's room—its walls and floor are stone, cold under my bare feet, and pale glowglobes illuminate the way. A long set of stairs cuts down in front of me and I take them slower than I should, listening for any sound other than Garnet's boots and the padding of my feet. By the time we reach the bottom, I'm shivering in the chilly, stale air. Another door, wooden with iron slats in the top, stands ajar ahead of us.

Garnet is frowning.

"What?" I whisper.

But when I push the door open, all thought of stealth and secrecy is lost.

"Oh!" I cry.

Ash is lying in a crumpled heap on the floor of a cell a few yards in front of me. I rush forward and fall to my knees, gripping the cold steel bars.

"Ash," I say. Blood has congealed on his face and in his hair. His cheekbone is badly bruised and there is a gash on his forehead. He's only in his cotton pajama pants, his chest and feet bare. He must be freezing. Or, he would be if he was conscious.

"Ash," I say louder. "Ash, wake up." I reach my arms through the bars but he's too far away to touch. "Garnet, where are the keys?"

He appears at my side. "I don't know," he says. "The keys for the cells aren't on this ring."

A wave of despair rises up and threatens to crush me, but I grit my teeth and hold it back. I don't have time to lose hope. "There has to be something we can do. They've got to be here somewhere. Ash!" I pull at the bars, a useless effort. "Wake up, please!"

"Looking for something?"

My insides turn to stone as Carnelian emerges from the

shadows behind the wooden door. In one hand she holds a small golden key.

"Carnelian, what did you *do*?" Garnet asks, his eyes wide, but not focused on her. I follow his gaze to the bodies of two Regimentals, piled behind the door next to an empty cell.

Carnelian holds up her other hand and shows him a syringe. "You know, it's funny the things you can do when no one cares about you. The places you can go. The people you can manipulate. The doctor showed me some things once, when I pretended to have an interest in medicine." She looks at the needle fondly. "They're not dead," she says, "only paralyzed. And unconscious. They underestimated me, too. I could see it in their eyes. Poor little Carnelian. Poor, ugly, stupid Carnelian."

"Mother will kill you for this," Garnet says.

"She'll kill you, too," Carnelian replies. "What are you doing here with *her*?"

"Open the cell," I say.

Her eyes flash. "You weren't supposed to be with him. He was supposed to be mine. Why did you have to take him from me?"

"I didn't *take* anything from you," I snap. "He's not a puppy or a piece of jewelry. He's a human being."

"I know who he is," she says. "I know him better than you."

"I highly doubt that."

"He told me things he's never told anyone before! He said so himself. And I . . . I . . ." Red spots bloom on her cheeks. "I trusted him with my secrets. He was going to stay with me forever."

"Carnelian, he was never going to stay. He would have left anyway, once you got engaged."

"I was figuring out a plan," she says. "I was going to find a way."

"Well, none of that matters now because if you don't open this door, he's going to be executed." My gaze flickers to the key in her hand. "Is that what you want?"

"I don't want him to be with *you*."

"So you'd rather he be dead?"

A soft moan from Ash's cell effectively silences the room.

"Ash," I gasp, turning to press my face against the bars. Ash's eyelids flutter, once, twice, then open. He sees me and a smile breaks across his battered face.

"Violet?" he croaks. "Where are we?" He tilts his head back, taking in his surroundings. "Ah, right."

"It's okay, I'm here to save you." I don't sound as confident as I'd like.

"That's nice," he breathes. His eyes lose focus for a second, then they come back to me. "What happened to your face?"

"I'm fine," I say as Ash gingerly pushes himself up off the ground. He winces and puts a hand to his swollen cheek.

"So," he says, crawling over to the door of his cell. "How do I get on the other side of these bars?"

I glance behind me, and Ash seems to notice for the first time that we have company. His brow furrows as he takes in Garnet, then Carnelian. She has lowered the syringe.

"Carnelian has the key," I say. Then, against every impulse I have, I get up and back away. I can't make

Carnelian open the door. But Ash can.

She walks forward slowly, her eyes locked on Ash's face. When she reaches his cell, she sinks to her knees exactly where I was a few seconds before.

"I'm so sorry," she whispers, wrapping her hand around his where it clutches the metal bar. "I thought if I could get her out of the way, we could be together."

Ash manages another smile. "I know."

"I thought . . . I had a plan . . ."

"I know," Ash says again. "But it wouldn't have worked."

Carnelian nods. "Because no matter what, you can't stay with me."

"No," he says softly. "I can't."

"Can I ask you one thing?" The key hovers by the lock.

"Of course."

"Was there anything between us that was . . . real?"

Ash brings his face so close to hers I want to scream. He whispers something I can't hear, and Carnelian's whole face brightens. After a moment, she pulls away, turns the key in the lock, and opens the door. I'm at Ash's side in an instant, helping him to his feet. Carnelian glares at me.

"I won't tell for his sake," she says. "Not yours."

I don't get to retort before Garnet jumps in.

"Yes, well, while this has all been bizarrely entertaining, it really is time to go."

"Are you okay?" I whisper to Ash. His chest is cold against my thin silk nightgown, but his arms feel strong when they wrap around me.

"Let's get out of here," he whispers back.

"Cheer up, cousin," Garnet says. Carnelian is staring at Ash and me with a half-furious, half-broken expression. "Think about Mother's face when she finds out they're both gone."

The corner of Carnelian's mouth twitches.

Garnet nods. "Thanks for the help," he says with a wave of his hand. He turns to us. "Now let's *go*."

~ Three ~

WE RUN UP THE STAIRS AND OUT OF THE DUNGEON AS quickly and quietly as we can.

The halls are empty. Ash keeps one arm wrapped around his ribs, clutching his left side. His free hand grips mine.

"Are you all right?" he asks, with a nod to my nightgown. Annabelle's blood has nearly dried. It stains my knees and shins. A lump swells in my throat.

"That's not mine," I whisper.

Ash's eyes widen. "Who—"

I shake my head hard. I can't talk about that right now.

We pass the dining room and emerge into the glass promenade that connects to the east wing, where Ash's quarters are. It's like this night is replaying itself in backward fashion. But Ash is with me now. I squeeze his hand to remind myself.

"What's his story?" he breathes in my ear, his eyes trained on Garnet.

I shrug.

"His story is he's trying to get the two of you out of here without ending up dead," Garnet replies. "So shut up and keep close."

"Where are we going?" I ask.

"We need transportation," Garnet says.

"Right. So what's the plan?"

"Seriously, Violet?" he says, stopping for a moment. "Does it look like I'm following an instruction manual? I'm making this up as I go. If you have a better idea—"

"No, no," I say quickly. "Whatever you think is best."

"He knows your name," Ash murmurs as we continue down the hallway.

"Lucien," I say. Ash mutters something I can't hear.

Past Ash's former living quarters, left turn, right turn, left again, we move deeper into the east wing than I've ever been.

"How do you know the servants' wing so well?" Ash asks Garnet.

Garnet raises an eyebrow and shoots me a leering grin. "I get around."

I cringe, thinking of all the unsuspecting kitchen maids that Garnet might have preyed on, but Ash is unfazed.

"No you don't," he says.

Garnet snorts. "How would you know?"

"I would," Ash replies. "And I do."

Garnet's mouth turns into a sneer as we reach a door at the end of a hall. He unbuttons his Regimental coat and tosses it to me. "You'll need this," he says. I slip it on. The sleeves fall well past my fingers and I'm inexplicably reminded of my mother's bathrobe, how huge it was when I used to wear it around my house in the Marsh, back when the scariest thing I could imagine was leaving my home for Southgate Holding Facility.

Garnet opens the door and I'm hit with a blast of frigid air. My teeth are chattering before we step outside. I move to offer Ash the coat, since he doesn't even have a shirt on, but he holds it tight around me. Icy grass crunches under my bare feet, and my toes are numb in seconds. The night has turned cloudy, no moon or stars to light our way, but Garnet is sure of his direction. A black shape—a low, boxy structure—appears in the darkness. When we reach it, I hear Garnet fumble with the key ring.

A lock clicks, and we move from the freezing night air to a chilled, quiet place.

The door closes behind me and a light flicks on. A row of gleaming motorcars stretches out in a cavernous space. I see the white one the Duchess and I took to Dahlia's funeral at the Exetor's palace, and the black one I took to all the balls, but there is a bright red one, a silver one, and pale blue and lemon yellow as well.

Garnet heads straight to the red motorcar and opens the trunk.

"Get in," he says.

I never imagined I'd be willing, if not eager, to climb into the trunk of a car.

"Don't you think someone will notice if a car is missing?" Ash mutters as he climbs in beside me. I scoot back to make room for him.

Garnet grins. "This is mine. It won't be the first time I've taken her out for a late-night joyride."

Then he slams the trunk shut.

Panic tackles me with a ferocity that leaves me breathless. The darkness is too close, too confining. My palms slam against the top of the trunk until Ash's cold hands find my face.

"It's okay, Violet," he whispers. "Breathe."

My lungs expand and the weight of everything overwhelms me. A torrent of tears pours out of me as I bury my face in his chest. The car starts, a low vibration running through my body. I hear the muffled sounds of a garage door opening and closing, and then I'm slammed against Ash as Garnet backs out of the driveway. The car circles in a dizzying movement, and my back is thrown against the other side of the trunk, Ash's body crushing mine.

"You know," Ash gasps, "I think he's enjoying this."

And then, like with the tears, I burst into hysterical laughter, my stomach contracting so hard it hurts, and Ash laughs, too, only his laughter dissolves into a spasm of coughing.

"Are you okay?" I ask, kissing every part of him.

"I'm fine—ow," he says as my lips land on his bruised cheek. "What exactly happened? The last thing I remember is the Duchess coming into my room."

I tell him about the arcana with Garnet's voice on the other end, and the Duchess tying me up, and Annabelle . . .

"I left her there," I say. "All alone."

"You had to," Ash murmurs. "Violet, you *had* to."

We're quiet for a moment. The guilt and pain and grief that I'd managed to suppress during our flight from the palace swells up inside me. I see her face in the dark, smell the lily scent of her hair.

"It's my fault," I whisper. "If I hadn't . . . if we . . ."

"No." The word is loud and authoritative in our cramped quarters. "The Duchess killed Annabelle, Violet. Not you. Not me."

I rest my head against his shoulder and make myself a silent promise. To not forget her, ever. To keep her alive the only way I can.

"Do you know where we're going?" he asks.

"No." Now that we're on the road, the ride is very smooth. I wriggle out of the jacket and throw it over Ash.

"Violet, I'm not—"

"We'll both use it," I insist, snuggling as close as I can into his side. His skin is freezing.

Ash strokes my hair. The vibrations of the car engine are a soothing, numbing sound.

"You saved my life," he whispers, his breath warm against my temple.

"I wasn't going to just leave you there."

He laughs softly. "I appreciate that."

"You would have done it for me."

We ride like this for what seems like hours before the

car stops abruptly, and the trunk is thrown open. The moon must have come out again, because Garnet is silhouetted against its silvery light.

"Did you two have a nice ride?" he asks with a grin.

Ash climbs out of the trunk and helps me, throwing the coat around my shoulders. "Where are we?"

I look around. It's some sort of dark alleyway, bordered by two plain, rectangular buildings.

"The morgue," Garnet replies.

I shiver.

He leads us to an iron door, painted white to match the building's exterior.

"It's not locked?" I ask.

"This is the morgue for servants and surrogates," Garnet explains.

"Right," I mutter.

The morgue's interior is chilly and sterile. Garnet takes a small flashlight from his belt, illuminating several long hallways that are a dreary green and smell like antiseptic. My feet stick to the waxed floor.

"Where are we going?" I whisper.

He shines the beam of the flashlight to the left and then to the right. "Good question. Lucien didn't happen to tell you where exactly you were going to meet him?"

"I was supposed to be dead," I say.

"Right."

"We could always follow the arrows." Ash is standing by the corner where two halls intersect, staring intently at the wall. "Garnet, bring the light."

Garnet shines the flashlight on the wall where there is a directional sign.

SURROGATES ➤
LADIES-IN-WAITING ▲
SERVANTS ▲

We take the right hall, through a set of swinging double doors into another hallway. Ash tries the handle of a door across from us.

"Locked," he says.

"This one isn't," Garnet says, opening the door. He flicks on the light and gleaming silver compartments come into view, lining the walls, row upon row of square doors. Everything is sharp and pristine.

"Are those for the . . ." I can't bring myself to say the word *bodies*.

"Yes," Ash says.

"Are they all . . . full?" The thought of so many dead surrogates makes me colder than I already am. Annabelle's blood pricks at the skin on my knees.

"I hope not," he replies.

"Do you think Raven is here already?" I ask. When I gave her the serum at the Duchess's luncheon this afternoon, Raven was practically catatonic. But she roused when she heard my voice. I have to hope she understood me.

Ash swallows. "There's only one way to find out."

"Who's Raven?" Garnet asks.

"My best friend," I reply. My legs start to shake as I

approach one of the compartments. "The Countess of the Stone's surrogate. I gave her Lucien's serum."

"You *what*?" Garnet shakes his head. "You know, if Lucien wasn't so intent on saving your life, I think he might kill you."

I ignore him, my fingers trembling as I turn the handle and pull open the door.

Empty.

I release the breath I was holding.

"One down," Ash says, coming up beside me. "A few dozen more to go."

Methodically, Ash and I begin to open all the doors. Garnet watches us with a bemused expression. We've opened seven empty chambers before Ash says, "Violet."

I move to his side and follow his gaze to the black bag filling the long rectangular space. Together, we pull out the metal sheet it's resting on. Ash reaches to unzip the bag.

"No," I say. "I'll do it."

Very gently, I pull down the zipper, revealing a pale face, stony in death. My breath catches in my throat.

"That's not Raven," Ash says.

I shake my head, tears filling my eyes.

"Did you know her?"

"No," I say. "But I met her once."

It's the girl from Dahlia's funeral, the one who was looking for her sister. I put my hand on her icy forehead. She looks so young.

I am overwhelmed by the unfairness of this whole situation. What makes me special? Why am *I* worth saving and not this girl, or the lioness, or Dahlia? I feel a surge of anger toward Lucien for forcing me to acknowledge this terrible truth but not giving me a way to *do* anything about it.

You saved Raven, a voice whispers in the back of my mind.

Not yet, I think. *And it's not enough.*

I zip the bag up and return the girl whose name I will never know back to her metal tomb.

"Let's keep looking," I say to Ash.

We find four more girls, none of whom I recognize.

"What if she didn't take it?" I say. Panic begins to creep up the back of my throat.

"She did," Ash reassures me, but his words are meaningless and I can tell he knows it. There is no way to know whether Raven understood me or not.

"They probably haven't found her yet," Garnet says. He's leaning against the wall casually, hands in his pockets, as if he'd hung out in morgues on a daily basis.

"Why are you still here?" Ash asks.

Garnet shrugs. "I want to see what happens when Lucien finds out *you're* here." Then he smirks. "Besides, this is the most fun I've had in a long time. Being royal is so boring. Any chance I get to stick it to my mother, I take. Stealing her surrogate right out from under her nose? From her own house? Too good to pass up."

"Why do you hate her so much?" I ask.

"Um, gee, Violet, you lived with her for two months," Garnet says. "How do *you* feel about her?"

He does have a point.

"Now multiply that by your entire life." Garnet scratches the back of his neck. "It's a miracle that I'm so well-adjusted."

The echoing *boom* of a heavy door closing freezes us all in place.

"The light!" Ash hisses. Garnet's hand darts to the wall and we're engulfed in darkness. For several seconds, there's nothing but silence. Then the unmistakable sounds of feet and voices float down the hall.

"We have to hide," Garnet says.

"Where?" I ask. "I can't see anything."

There's a click off to my left, and Garnet's flashlight flickers on. The beam of light falls on Ash. He's crouched by the one of the compartments, the lowest one in the far left-hand corner. The door is open and his eyes meet mine.

"No," I whisper.

"Do you have a better idea?" Garnet says, grabbing my arm and pulling me toward Ash, keeping the flashlight trained down. I crouch by the black square hole where so many dead surrogates have been stored, my stomach churning with something stronger than disgust and sharper than fear. The wrongness of hiding in here makes my limbs numb and clumsy.

"We don't have a choice," Ash says. I open the door next to his compartment and force my feet to move, my body to bend and shift and slide until I am lying facedown on the cold metal slab. The voices are so close I can almost make out individual words, along with a faint squeaking sound. The flashlight goes out. Garnet's door closes, then Ash's.

I take a deep breath and shut myself inside.

Four

THE DARKNESS INSIDE THIS METAL TOMB IS FAR, FAR
worse than the blackness of Garnet's car trunk.

I press my forehead against the cold steel and try to pretend I'm somewhere else, or that Ash is with me, or that this
is all a dream and I'm about to wake up back in the Marsh.

The light in the room switches on.

Pale yellow leaks into my hiding place. There is no handle
on the inside of the door, so I've left it cracked the tiniest bit.
The voices of two men are muffled.

". . . didn't want anyone noticing, I suppose."

"Don't see why anyone would care. How many surrogates has she gone through over the years? Twenty?"

"Not your place to count, lad. We do as we're told."

The first voice is definitely older and has a rough, grizzled quality. "They say House of the Stone, pickup at midnight, and that's what we do."

House of the Stone! They have Raven! I nearly cry with relief.

There's the strange squeaking noise again, then a door creaks open. I hear the wrinkling of plastic being manipulated.

"She's not very heavy, is she?" the second voice says.

"Ain't none of them is heavy, lad. You'll see."

Plastic scrapes and shifts over metal. The door closes.

"Now," the first voice says gruffly, "it's back to bed and let's hope there's no more calls tonight."

Their shoes make tiny sticking sounds as they leave. The light switches off.

I keep still for as long as I can, hardly daring to breathe, waiting to see whether they come back. Finally, I can't take it anymore. My fingernails scrape the door, pushing it open. I wriggle out of the compartment as fast as I can and tumble onto the polished floor as Ash and Garnet open their own doors. I scramble to my feet and push up the arms of the oversize Regimental coat, running my palms along the wall until I find the light switch.

The light is painfully bright after so much darkness. Ash's face is drained of color, and he climbs to his feet slowly. Garnet stays on the floor, leaning against the cabinets and smoothing back his blond hair, looking more rattled than I've ever seen him.

"She's here," I say to Ash.

"I know," he replies.

A smile breaks across my face, and I begin opening doors with a single-minded ferocity, pushing Garnet out of the way until I find one that was empty before.

I yank on the metal sheeting and Raven's body slides out, hidden underneath a thick layer of black plastic. Ash and Garnet join me as I pull the zipper down and open the bag.

Raven's face is as cold and lifeless as all the other girls' in this place, and for one paralyzing moment, I fear she's actually dead. Her beautiful caramel skin is waxy, her once-glossy black hair lank and tangled. She is naked. I quickly shrug out of the Regimental coat and throw it over her body, but not before seeing how painfully, sickeningly thin she is—every rib is visible, and her hip bones jut out in sharp points on either side of the tiny bump of her belly.

I press my hand against her cheek. Her skin is like ice.

"Raven," I say, my voice trembling. I watch for a flutter of her eyelashes, or a parting of her lips, but there's nothing. My best friend is deathly still.

"Raven, it's me," I say. "It's Violet." It hurts to swallow. "Please wake up. I've saved you. Please come back to me."

The silence that follows is crushing. Pieces of me break under the weight of it.

"Maybe she's really—" Garnet begins, but I whirl around and slam my hands against his chest, sending him stumbling backward.

"She is *not* dead!" I hiss. I turn back to Raven and shake her. Her head lolls on the metal slab. "Wake *up*, Raven! Come on, you took the serum, I *know* you did, so please, WAKE UP!"

I slap her hard across the face.

But nothing happens.

I feel Ash's hand on my shoulder. "I'm so sorry."

I shrug his hand away. I don't want anyone's pity right now. "She—"

Suddenly, Raven's eyes fly open. Her body arches, her eyeballs bugging out of her head, then she jerks onto her side and vomits on the floor. Ash and Garnet jump back as Raven's body convulses, coughing and retching, but I collapse on top of her, my forehead falling onto her shoulder, one hand smoothing her hair, blissfully grateful to feel her breathing and moving and alive. She rolls onto her back, panting. Her eyes wheel in her head until they find me.

"Violet?" she croaks. Tears stream down my cheeks, but I don't bother to wipe them away.

"I'm here," I say. "You're safe now."

Her gaze slips to the ceiling. "I saw my mother," she says. "She was brushing my hair. Then they took all her skin away."

"What?" I say. "Your mother is alive and in the Marsh."

"They took her skin away," she says again. "They showed me her bones."

Her eyes become unfocused and her body relaxes. She goes very still.

"Raven?" I whisper. I brush my fingertips across her cheek. She's breathing, but it's like a light has been switched off inside her.

"What did they do to her?" Ash asks in a hushed voice.

"I—I don't know." I run my hands through Raven's hair and feel a tiny scar, maybe half an inch long, on her scalp.

Then I feel another. And another.

"Well," Garnet says, clapping his hands together, "this has been a great night, really one for the record books, and as much as I'd love to stay and watch Lucien freak out about all this, I think it's time for me to be getting back."

"Of course it is," Ash mutters.

"Hey, I saved your life, what else do you want from me?" Garnet snaps.

"Absolutely nothing," Ash says.

"Right," Garnet says. "Good luck with all the escaping and whatnot."

"Thank you," I say.

"Sure." Garnet's hand is on the doorknob when Raven sits up. The move is so unexpected and abrupt that I'm barely able to keep the jacket from falling off her shoulders.

"You're a coward," she says, her dark eyes on Garnet. There is a haziness in her gaze, as if she were focusing on two things at once.

We all stare at her in shocked silence.

"Raven?" I say tentatively.

"He's a coward," she says. "He breaks all the wrong rules. The easy ones. He's afraid." Then her face goes slack, her eyes returning to normal. "I'm tired. It's not time for the doctor yet."

She lies back down on the slab and starts muttering something to herself. I can't understand what she's saying, but I hear her name once or twice.

Garnet watches her for a second, then shakes his head. "Whatever. She's your problem."

With a halfhearted wave, he walks out the door. I put

my hand on Raven's forehead, but she's gone back to that empty place, staring at the ceiling.

"What now?" Ash says.

"Now we wait for Lucien," I reply. "Lucien will come."

HOURS PASS.

Or, at least, it feels like hours. There's no way to tell time in this room. We turned the lights off to be safe. Ash and I sit on the floor against the wall, huddled together to keep warm. Raven hasn't moved or spoken since Garnet left.

I wonder what will happen when the Duchess discovers I'm gone. That Ash is gone. I wonder whether Garnet will be able to keep Carnelian from telling. I wonder whether *Garnet* will tell. He has no loyalty to us and he doesn't seem particularly trustworthy—I can't imagine why Lucien chose him to help. Carnelian, at least, can be counted on not to do anything to endanger Ash's life.

I remember their exchange in the dungeon. "What did you tell her?" I say. It's been so long since either of us has spoken, my voice sounds creaky and louder than it should. Ash's cheek is resting against the top of my head.

"Mmm?" he breathes against my hair.

"When Carnelian asked you if anything was real, what did you say?"

I don't expect him to hesitate. He lifts his head and turns his face away from me. "That's private, Violet."

"You're going to keep secrets from me?"

"How many secrets have you kept from me?" he says.

I chew on my lip. "That's not the same. I had to. I made a promise to Lucien."

"And what of the promises I've made?"

"But you were hired to make her promises. That isn't the same as what we have."

"I know." Ash's profile is black against the darkness as he stares up at the ceiling. "But must I betray her confidence because you don't like her?"

I don't know what to say to that. I guess I always assumed Ash hated Carnelian as much as I do.

He sighs. "It isn't about keeping secrets from you. Carnelian is . . . extremely sad. And that sadness has been twisted into bitterness and anger. I don't wish to be another in a long line of people who have let her down, even if she would never know the difference."

I thread my fingers through his. "You don't have to be so noble."

"Not at all. I . . . I understand her a bit."

"Well, someday, you'll have to explain her to me."

I hear footsteps outside. Ash and I scramble to our feet, but we don't have a chance to hide again before the door opens and the light switches on.

Lucien enters the room. He wears his usual white dress with the high lace collar, his chestnut hair in a perfect top-knot on the crown of his head, indicating his status as a lady-in-waiting. And it means more for him than it does for a female lady-in-waiting—male ladies-in-waiting are eunuchs, castrated so as to be considered "safe" to work alongside royal women.

A large satchel hangs from one shoulder. His eyes move from me, to Ash, to Raven, and back to me. He shows no surprise at seeing two more people than he expected—he must have talked to Garnet.

He closes the door and puts the satchel down. With measured steps, he walks up to Ash, grabs him by the throat, and slams his head against the wall.

"Lucien!" I cry.

"Is it true?" he snarls. Ash looks dazed. I grab the arm that isn't holding Ash's throat and pull.

"Stop it!"

Lucien turns on me. "Do you know what they're saying?" he hisses. "They're saying that this piece of trash raped you."

"What?" I gasp.

Ash comes back to his senses. In one lightning-fast movement, he grips Lucien's wrist and twists it. Lucien cries out in pain as Ash bends his arm back in a way that makes Lucien bow forward.

"What did you say?" Ash growls. I've never seen him use physical force like this before.

"Release me," Lucien barks.

"Ash!" I cry.

"He believes it. Do you see, Violet? He *believes* it." He bends Lucien's arm back a little more.

"And why shouldn't I?" Lucien says. "I know what you do, what you really do. All you companions, with your charming smiles and your filthy minds. I should never have let you get near her."

Ash yanks Lucien's arm again. "You don't know anything about me."

"I know you sleep with more women in a year than most men do their entire lives."

"And you think I *enjoy* it? Or are you just jealous that I can?"

At that, Lucien lets out a strangled yell and rips his arm from Ash's grasp. But Ash is too quick. In a second, he has Lucien pinned against the wall, his forearm cutting across Lucien's throat.

"Ash, you're hurting him," I say. He turns his head to meet my gaze. "Please, stop. Let him go."

Reluctantly, Ash relaxes his arm and backs away. Lucien leans against the wall, massaging his shoulder.

"Ash would never touch me against my will, Lucien," I say.

"Well, I'd like to think you're not stupid enough to do it on your own."

"When will you stop?" Ash interrupts, taking a step forward. His face is flushed, making the bruise stand out sharply on his cheekbone. I immediately put myself between them as a physical barrier. "You're not her father. You don't get to lecture her about what she does."

"I think I know a little bit more about what's best for her than a companion," Lucien retorts.

"In case you hadn't noticed, I'm not a companion any-more," Ash says coldly.

"Enough," I say, pulling Lucien away from Ash. "You two can fight all you want once we're out of this awful place, but there are more important things to discuss right now. What's the plan?"

Lucien shakes me off, retrieves the satchel, and tosses it to me. "There are clothes for all of you in there. Get dressed, quickly. We were going to take the train, but that's not possible anymore."

I unzip the bag and find three pairs of brown woolen pants, three sweaters, and three pairs of shoes. There is also water, a flashlight, bandages, and antiseptic ointment. I use some of the water to wash Annabelle's blood off my legs, and tend to the wound on Ash's forehead and cheek. His eye is still swollen and I smear antiseptic around it.

"You, too," he says, dabbing some ointment on my cut lip. It stings a little.

Once we're dressed, I turn to Raven. She's still staring at the ceiling.

"Should we—" Ash begins.

"No, I'll do it," I say. I look at him, then Lucien. "Turn around, please." Raven might not be fully aware, but I know she would not want two strange men seeing her naked. I maneuver her into the pants—she is so light, so thin—but the sweater proves more difficult.

"Oh, Raven, can you sit up?" I mutter without any real hope. So I'm shocked when she does.

"Violet?" she says. Her eyes are bright, like they used to be.

"Put this on," I say, holding out the sweater.

"I've never been in this room before," she says, looking around as I put the shoes on her feet and help her off the metal slab. "It's very shiny."

"This is the friend you asked about, I assume," Lucien says. "The Countess of the Stone's surrogate?"

"This is Raven," I say.

"I'm Raven," she repeats.

"And you gave her the serum intended for you."

My spine straightens. "I did."

He raises his eyes to the ceiling. "Of all the surrogates in that Auction," he mutters. "Leave the coat here; I'll be back for it. I'll need to clean that up, too." He glances at the puddle of Raven's vomit and shakes his head. "This would have been so much easier if you'd listened to me."

Ash stuffs our nightclothes in the satchel and throws the strap over his chest. Lucien leads us out of the room and down the hall to another door marked DANGER: RESTRICTED. It isn't locked, which I find strange, and Lucien opens it easily.

Immediately, I am assaulted by a wave of intense heat and the scent of something burning. The room is empty except for a cast-iron behemoth with a large door set in its center.

"This is what's happening," Lucien says. "Your absences have been discovered. For reasons I can only assume stem from self-preservation, the Duchess has not revealed that you, Violet, are missing. She has accused him"—he jerks his head in Ash's direction—"of rape. A companion sleeping with any unsterilized female is a criminal act, but add to it that the female in question is a surrogate . . . well, the royalty are out for blood. All trains have been stopped in and out of the Jewel. Every available Regimental is combing the streets searching for him. In a few hours, his photograph will be posted in every circle of this city."

I feel hollowed out. "So what do we do?"

Lucien turns the handle on the cast-iron door and opens it. A wall of brilliant yellow flame burns inside, making the room even hotter. "This incinerator leads directly to the sewer system. You can at least make it to the Bank through the tunnels—the sewers for the lower circles aren't connected to these. There's a map in that bag. I've outlined your path in red. I'll have an associate waiting for you in the Bank, and we'll go from there."

"How will I know who your associate is?"

"Ask them to show you the key."

"What key?"

"You'll know it when you see it." He pauses. "You didn't, by some small miracle, happen to bring the arcana with you?"

"I did!" I exclaim, putting a hand to my messy bun. "It's in my hair."

Lucien smiles, a real, warm smile. "Good girl. I can track you using that."

"But . . ." I glance at the leaping flames. "How are we supposed to get down there?"

His smile fades. "You'll have to use the Auguries to put out the fire."

"What?" I stare at him, hoping that he's joking. "How?"

"I don't know. But you can do it."

"Lucien, that's not what the Auguries do. I mean, I wouldn't even know where to start."

"Listen to me." Lucien puts both hands on my shoulders. "It *can* be done. It's been done before."

My mouth falls open. "What? By *who*?"

"That doesn't matter right now. You have to do this. Otherwise . . ." He looks from me, to Raven, and finally, reluctantly, to Ash. "Otherwise, you're all dead."

~ Five ~

I WALK TO THE INCINERATOR, THE WAVES OF HEAT CARESS-
ing my face. Beads of sweat begin to form on my hairline
and dew in my armpits. I feel a soft pressure on my wrist.

"Wait," Ash says. He looks from me to Raven and back
again. "These Auguries . . . are these the things that made
Raven get sick?"

I nod, remembering how Raven vomited blood and
effectively ended the Duchess's luncheon.

"Will they make you sick?" he asks.

I hesitate. "Probably." *There's no point in lying.* "Yes."

Ash looks like he's about to protest, but I hold up a hand
to silence him. I need to think.

I consider which of the three Auguries to use—Color, Shape, or Growth. Not Color, certainly—I don't see how changing the incinerator's color is going to help. Shape? Am I meant to change the incinerator's shape somehow? No, it's the flames that are the real problem. I think about Dr. Blythe, my doctor at the palace, and the oak tree in the Duchess's garden. He'd taken me out to it to test my Auguries. He insisted I make the oak tree grow and I never thought I'd be able to; it was so massive and so old. But I did.

I take another step forward, the heat stinging my cheeks. I can't touch the flames, but maybe touching the incinerator will be good enough. Its surface is hot, but not unbearable, the iron rough under my palm.

Once to see it as it is. Twice to see it in your mind. Thrice to bend it to your will.

But I have no image to bend this fire to. I envision a black space, empty and cold, but nothing happens. I don't even feel the beginnings of an Augury.

"I can't . . ." My throat tightens. "I don't know what to do."

An icy hand wraps around mine. Raven stands beside me, her face looking almost alive again.

"It has to die, Violet," she says. Keeping our hands clasped, she places her other palm on the incinerator. "It's not Growth. It's Death."

And then I see it, as clearly as if it were real. The flames growing weaker, smaller, like a mammoth pillow is pressing down on them, smothering them. I feel their resistant flickers, struggling for life, but the invisible pillow is stronger, and they grow frailer and thinner until they are nothing but pathetic wisps of smoke.

Blood droplets trickle down my nose. My head throbs strangely, but not necessarily in a painful way. The place where my skin touches Raven's is hot.

"Did we do that together?" I ask.

Raven retches, blood spattering the incinerator and streaming down her chin.

"Ash, give me my nightgown!" I cry. I keep one arm firmly around her waist, practically holding her up as she doubles over, coughing up more blood. One hand I keep on the incinerator. I have a terrible feeling that if I let go, the fire will come back.

"I'm sorry, I'm sorry," I say to her, over and over.

I turn to see Ash staring at the fireless incinerator with an expression of utter disbelief.

"Ash," I say again, and he starts.

"How did you . . ."

"The nightgown, please."

"You're bleeding," he says, hurrying forward with the satchel.

"I'm fine. It's stopping already, it stops on its own," I say, wiping it away with the sleeve of my sweater. "That wasn't that bad. Help Raven."

"It gets *worse* than this?" He's looking at me like he's never seen me before.

Raven's coughing has stopped. Ash wipes her face with the nightgown.

"So much blood," she mutters. "Always so much blood."

"You have to get going," Lucien interrupts. "Now."

He tries to sound commanding, but his eyes are wide and his voice a bit too shaky.

"I've seen you before," Raven says to him. "But I can't remember if you're real . . ." She presses the heels of her hands against her eyes. "Why is there always so much blood?"

Now that the fire is out, I can see a rectangular tunnel that slopes downward into blackness. "Ash, take Raven and go," I say. "I'll be right behind you."

"I'm not going anywhere without you," he says.

"Please," I say. "I can't let go of this or I think the fire will come back. You need to get down there safely. Make sure nothing happens to her." I glance at Raven's stomach, the tiny bump hidden by the sweater.

Ash's fingertips brush down the side of my face. Then he climbs into the incinerator and helps Raven in after.

"Ash will take care of you," I say to Raven. She looks at him and then at me but says nothing.

They slide down the tunnel, which has cooled considerably since the flames are gone, and out of sight.

I turn to Lucien. I can feel the deadened fire, like a heartbeat waiting to start.

"When will I see you again?" I whisper.

"Soon," he says. "I promise."

"I don't know how to thank you," I say.

He smiles. "Stay alive."

I laugh, but it comes out like a hiccup. "All right."

He kisses my forehead. "Go."

I climb inside the incinerator, careful to keep my palm pressed hard against it. My shoes slip and skid on the smooth surface and I grip the edge with my other hand. I take my last look at Lúcien.

Then I descend into darkness.

THE TUNNEL IS STEEP.

I can't see where I'm going, but I'm sliding very fast. Warm air blows strands of hair around my face. I manage to sit upright and keep one hand pressed against the smooth surface, even though it burns my skin, the metal racing beneath it so quickly. I'm tempted to call Ash's name, but I'm afraid if I open my mouth I might throw up.

At some point, I pick up more speed. My heart kicks into a sprint.

I see a flicker of light ahead.

Then I'm falling.

For a weightless second, I'm suspended in the air, disoriented. As soon as my fingers leave the wall of the incinerator, flames erupt inside it, a brilliant burst of heat and light.

Then I crash to the ground, all the breath knocked out of me. My back arches, every cell in my body craving oxygen, then my lungs expand and I choke in my eagerness to breathe.

"Violet?" Ash's arms wrap around my shoulders, cradling my back against his chest. He holds the flashlight in one hand—in the light of its beam, I see Raven's feet.

My coughing subsides. "I'm okay," I gasp.

He helps me up and we stare at the space above us, a gaping hole filled with flames.

"Lucien said there's a map in there," I say, pointing at the bag. Ash rummages through it, takes out a folded piece of paper, and hands it to me. I study the blue lines that criss-cross and interweave, creating a myriad of tunnels.

"I've seen this before," I say. It's the blueprint Lucien was looking at in the locked room in the Duchess's library. That was the day he told me he could help me get out of the Jewel. "The whole time he must have known . . . he must have suspected . . ."

"What?" Ash says.

"That we might need a different escape plan. But how did he know about the incinerator? And that it empties out into these tunnels?"

"At the moment, I don't think that matters."

"I don't like this place," Raven says.

"Neither do I." There's a red line on the blueprint creating a trail through the tunnels. I turn the paper until I find our location. "We need to go . . . that way," I say, pointing to the left.

Ash shines the flashlight down the tunnel and we move. But we haven't gone more than a few steps when there's a sickening crack under my foot.

"What was that?" I whisper. Ash grabs my elbow. The beam of his flashlight falls on a strange-looking cage protruding from the ground. Its bars are curved, blackened and burned, and it has no visible door.

"Why would someone throw a cage down here?" I whisper.

"Violet," Ash says slowly, "I don't think that's a cage."

As I stare at it, the image clicks into place. It's a set of ribs.

Raven tugs my arm and I jump.

"Everyone is dead," she says.

"Not us," I say. "We're alive."

Raven looks at me as if the thought had never occurred to her. What did the Countess do to her? Who is this shell of the friend I used to know? I don't want to think about why there were so many scars on her skull. I have to get her to safety. That's all that matters.

Then I remember that she's pregnant. Is there any safe place for Raven anymore?

She slips her hand into mine, and I push those thoughts away. Right here, right now, she is alive. And she needs me, like I needed her at Southgate. I remember the day when she helped me learn the first Augury, how she refused to leave my side until I was able to turn that stupid block from blue to yellow. I won't leave her side now.

Ash stays right by my elbow, and the three of us make our way down the tunnel. I gnaw on my lower lip, wincing every time I hear the crack of bone beneath my feet. I wonder if this is where they incinerate the surrogates' bodies, after their cold stay in those awful metal compartments. I could be walking on the surrogate of the Lady of the Glass. I could be walking on Dahlia.

It seems to take forever, but finally we make it to a point where several other tunnels branch off. The air is dank and smells like spoiled food, but I'm grateful to be on a solid surface again.

"Which way?" Ash asks.

My hands are shaking as I study the map. "Left," I say, keeping my eyes trained on what's ahead. I clutch Raven's hand firmly in my grasp.

We start down a tunnel whose floor is covered with an

inch of what I can only imagine is the filthiest water in the Jewel. The beam of the flashlight reflects off its murky surface. No one speaks. Occasionally, I hear the tiny squeaking and scuttling of rats. Ash shines the light at intervals on the map to check we're going the right way, but unfortunately, there aren't any markers on it besides Lucien's red line, so I find myself wondering whether it's *this* left or *that* left, or which fork is which. Twice we take a wrong turn, find ourselves at a dead end, and have to double back.

"Do you think it's this way?" I ask after studying the map for the sixth time and deciding on a different tunnel.

I can't see Ash's expression in the darkness. "I don't know."

"Do you smell that?" Raven says.

"The sewer?"

"No," Raven replies, with an almost normal Raven-like air of impatience. "The *light*."

I look toward where I think Ash's face is with an incredulous expression.

"The light?" I ask hesitantly.

"Violet, don't tell me you can't smell it," she says. "It's so *clean*. Come on."

I have no idea what she's talking about. Who can smell light? But she tugs on my hand and starts to lead us down a different tunnel with more enthusiasm than she's shown since she woke up. I barely have time to glance at the map before she's taking a left and we're at another dead end.

"Oh, Raven." I sigh. "We've gone the wrong way."

"Don't be ridiculous," Raven says, and again, I'm startled by how much she sounds like her old self. "Now we go up."

Ash's flashlight trails the wall, where a series of metal rungs form a ladder up into the darkness and out of sight. High above our heads, a tiny light twinkles, like a lonely star.

Without waiting for further discussion, Raven starts to climb.

"Wait!" I say, grabbing her ankles. "Are you sure?"

"Of course I'm sure," she says. "You want to get out of here, don't you?"

"Yes, but . . . how do you know?"

"I know. I just do."

Ash shines the beam of the flashlight up so I can see his face. His mouth is set, his eyes determined. He nods once.

I stuff the map into the satchel and follow Raven up the ladder. Ash brings up the rear, still holding the flashlight.

The metal rungs are endless. My arms begin to ache, the muscles in my thighs burn, and my stomach growls with hunger, but I force myself to keep moving, trying not to think about the long drop below me, getting progressively longer the higher we climb.

No one speaks. Slowly, the tiny star above us gets brighter. And bigger. It looks like a flower, petals of light emanating from one circular beam in its center.

Raven stops, and I bang my head on the bottom of her shoe.

"This is it," she says.

"What?" I ask, rubbing the top of my head.

"The end," she says. Carefully, I lean over to one side, gripping the rungs tightly, and see a circle of metal with slits cut into it. Raven pokes her fingers through one of the petal-like holes.

"How do we open it?" she asks.

I try to control my breathing, because the thought of climbing all the way back down this ladder to the sewers below is unacceptable.

"There has to be a way," I say.

Raven's fingers are still wriggling through the petal when the whole metal circle shifts to the left.

"Oh!" she cries, and her foot slips off its rung. I grab her shoe with one hand, my heart hammering in my throat.

The metal thing is lifted up and a brilliant circle of sunlight floods the tunnel. For a moment, I am completely blinded by it—my eyes water, my retinas are seared, and all I can see is white. Then a shadowy figure comes into view, looking down on us. I blink, and a face comes into focus.

"You made it," Garnet says with a smile. "Welcome to the Bank."

~ Six ~

"WHAT ARE YOU DOING HERE?" I ASK AS GARNET GRABS
Raven's arm and helps her out of the sewer.

"I'm taking you to the safe house," Garnet says. He's
dressed in his Regimental uniform—he must have gotten
a new jacket. I scramble out of the hole and Ash climbs up
after me.

We're in another alley, but this one isn't nearly as creepy
as the one by the morgue. It's sandwiched between two
buildings made of pale reddish stone. The air is cold, but
the sun shines brightly in a clear blue sky. About fifty feet
away, the alley ends in a bustling street. I see an electric
stagecoach trundle past.

"I thought you were done with us," Ash says.

Garnet shrugs. "Figured I could still be helpful." His eyes dart to Raven. "Don't think this makes you right," he snaps, as if worried she might call him a coward again.

Raven frowns. "Who are you?"

"He's helping us," I say, wishing desperately that I could fix whatever is wrong with Raven's brain. This isn't her at all. Raven should remember him.

"Get in there," Garnet says, pointing to a wide alcove in one of the buildings, stuffed with a few empty metal trash cans. "You're all going to have to change again."

There is a canvas bag, larger than the satchel, wedged next to the cans. I unzip it and pull out two dresses made of plain brown cloth. I hand one to Raven, whose eyes have gone blank. She clutches the dress and stares at the wall with a vacant expression. I change into my own dress before helping her into hers.

"Is it time for the doctor?" she whispers. She looks terrified.

"No. No more doctors," I say, smoothing her hair back from her face. "Here, put this on."

Ash trades his sweater for a collared shirt and tweed jacket, with a matching short-brimmed hat. It doesn't quite hide the welt on his cheek, but at least his eye isn't as swollen. A dark bruise has blossomed beneath it, purplish black.

"Take these," Garnet says, handing him a stack of newspapers. Ash hoists the stack onto his shoulder, and the papers hide his face. He could be any other newsboy.

"We can't move together. I volunteered to help search the Bank for him"—Garnet jerks his head in Ash's direction—

"so I could come and meet you. My mother practically died of shock."

"Do they know how I escaped?" Ash asks.

"Whatever Carnelian gave those guards, it completely wiped their memories. They don't even remember locking you in the cell." Garnet smirks. "You know, she's actually pretty clever. If her blood was pure, she'd make one very impressive Duchess of the Lake."

"Great," I say, eager to get off the topic of Carnelian and onto the more pressing matter at hand. "But where are we *going*?"

"To a place not far from here. I only have an address, I don't know who's meeting you or what's happening after."

"Isn't the whole point of this to get to the Farm?"

That's what Lucien said. Get me to safety. There is safety in the Farm, the fourth and largest circle of the Lone City. But it feels like the Farm might as well be on a different planet right now.

"I don't know what the point is, Violet. You think Lucien tells me everything? I've got an address, you can either come with me or figure out something on your own. And you should know by now, Lucien likes to keep things mysterious," Garnet says.

"Yeah, I know," I grumble.

"So I'll go first. Then the companion will follow me."

"His name is Ash," I say.

Garnet ignores me. "Then you two follow him. Oh, put your hats on," he says. I riffle through the bag and pull out two white caps with a lace fringe on them.

Garnet starts down the alley, when Ash grabs his arm.

"Wait," he says. "What quarter are we in?"

"East," Garnet says. "Near the southern border."

Ash swears under his breath.

"What?" I ask.

"We're close to my companion house," he replies. "Someone might recognize me."

The companion house is like Southgate—it's the place where Ash was trained how to escort the young ladies of the Jewel.

"No one's going to recognize you," Garnet says. "Your face is a mess. But at least you know where you are. The address is Forty-Six Twenty-Two Plentham Street. In case we get separated. You take them there."

We skirt the wall, creeping down the alley until we get close to the street. Garnet holds up a hand signaling us to stop.

"Wait five seconds," Garnet says to Ash, "then follow me. You two wait five seconds more and follow him. Got it?"

I nod as Garnet walks out of the alley, turns right, and disappears down the street. I count to five in my head. I only get to three before Ash's arm wraps around my waist, his lips pressing, gentle but firm, against mine. It takes me by surprise, but it comforts me.

Before I can say anything, he's gone.

I forget to start counting.

"That boy kissed you," Raven says.

"Yes," I say. "Come on. Stay close to me, all right?"

She smiles playfully. "Where else am I going to go?"

I take a deep breath, and we walk out onto the streets of the Bank.

AFTER LIVING IN THE HEART OF THE JEWEL FOR NEARLY three months, the Bank shouldn't be overwhelming. It's the second circle of the city, where the merchant class lives, and the wealthiest after the Jewel.

But I haven't been around so many people at once, and I'm awestruck by the crowds. I forget for a moment that I'm supposed to be following Ash and Garnet, forget to keep my head down and try to go unnoticed, because there are people everywhere—coming out of slender brownstones, strolling arm in arm down the bustling sidewalks. Many of the women are accompanied by young girls in brown dresses, who follow a few steps behind their mistresses with arms full of brown-wrapped parcels, or carrying hat-boxes, or leading sleek, well-groomed dogs on leashes. One woman, wearing a hat made out of real roses and holding a tiny monkey in her arms, pushes past me and says to her friend, "I *do* hope they find him soon. I finally managed to secure an invitation to the Royal Theater this weekend and if the Jewel is still sealed off I won't be able to go!"

I scan the streets for Ash and find him a few feet ahead of us, the stack of newspapers bobbing up and down as he walks. There are Regimentals everywhere, splashes of bright red among the crowds. I can't tell which one is Garnet, so I keep my eyes locked on Ash. My nerves are taut, all the exhaustion I felt climbing out of the sewers erased by a new flood of adrenaline. We're so exposed. I walk quickly, my arms tense at my sides, waiting to feel a hand on my shoulder or a shout of "There she is!"

They're not looking for you, I remind myself. But that reminder doesn't make me feel better.

The bobbing stack of papers crosses the street and turns left down another road. Raven nearly gets hit by an electric stagecoach as we follow after it; I grab her hand and pull her safely out of the way as a driver shouts at us to watch where we're going.

The street Ash took is lined with shops—glass-paned storefronts selling everything from the latest fashions in women's dresses to gilt-framed paintings of bowls of fruit and girls doing ballet. Diamond rings glint at us, nestled in blue velvet cushions. Puppies bark and play in a pet-store window. A red satin chaise lounge takes up an entire window display under a sign proclaiming, SALE!

And in every window, on every door and lamppost, a sign with Ash's face is plastered, bold print proclaiming, WANTED. FUGITIVE.

I feel like I've fallen down the incinerator shaft again—the air in my lungs is too thin and my head starts spinning. In the photograph, he's maybe a year or two younger than he is now, his hair parted on the side instead of tousled, but it's so very *him*.

This plan suddenly seems reckless, foolish. What happens if they catch him?

For one heart-stopping moment, I wonder whether Lucien organized it this way intentionally. Get Ash out of the way. Still save me.

Then I remember Lucien's warning about the key. I

didn't even think to ask Garnet. What if this is a setup? What if Garnet isn't working for Lucien after all?

"All right there, ladies?"

A Regimental blocks our path. He's about Garnet's age, and very tall, with a mop of dark curly hair. His eyes skim over my body in a way that makes me wish I were wearing about ten more layers.

I have no idea what to say, so I curtsy. That always worked in the Jewel.

This seems to please the Regimental. "I saw you girls nearly get run over by that coach. You ought to be more careful." His eyes flicker to the bruise on my cheek. "You don't want to get more of those." He reaches out, like he's actually going to touch my face, and I shrink away. He laughs. "I won't hurt you. I'm here for your protection." His chest swells a little as he says it. "You heard about that companion, right?"

I nod once, a short, tight movement.

"Dangerous fellow. But don't worry, we'll find him soon enough." He winks at me. "Has anyone ever told you, you have absolutely stunning eyes?"

I finally find my voice. "We need to be getting home," I say. "Our mistress will be wondering where we are."

"I'll gladly escort you to—"

"No, thank you," I say, ducking around him and pulling Raven with me. Raven mutters something under her breath, but I keep walking and don't look back. We weave our way through the crowds, and I'm so focused on getting away from the Regimental that it's a few moments before I realize I've lost Ash. I slow my pace, frantically searching for the stack of papers. The crowd swells around me as the street empties out into a large square. Other streets pour into it from all directions.

The square is host to an open-air market; stalls are set up all around. Many boast large wicker baskets filled with all sorts of vegetables—bunches of carrots, strings of onions, heads of broccoli, potatoes, kale, beets, winter squash. The scent of fresh bread hovers around a baker's stall. A potbellied man shouts out prices for large glass jugs of cider.

"I can't find him," I whisper. "Raven, do you see him?"

We can't stay in one place—I fear the Regimental might follow us, and the best way to find Ash is to keep moving. I try searching for Garnet instead, but there are so many Regimentals and they all look the same. Raven and I move slowly among the stalls. I hear snatches of conversation, most of which are about Ash. There is an overtone of shock and outrage, but I sense that the people of the Bank are loving this story. Such juicy gossip, a companion and a surrogate. I wonder whether any of them know him, personally. Whether he has friends in this market or—I shudder—former clients.

"C'mon," I mutter to myself. "Where are you?"

Suddenly, Raven stops walking. Her face has gone pale, her eyes taking on that strange, double-focused look, like she's seeing something I can't see.

"What is it?" I ask.

"She knows him," she says.

"What?"

Without another word, Raven bolts.

"Raven!" I cry, grabbing for her arm too late. I run after

her, squeezing my way through the crowd, and trip over a basket of cabbage. Next thing I know I'm sprawled on the ground with scraped palms, leafy green balls tumbling all around me.

"Are you all right, miss?" the stall owner asks, but I scramble to my feet, pushing through the crowd, because I can't have lost them both, I can't be without Raven and Ash.

Then I see him. Time freezes for a moment and the world slows as Ash appears in the far corner of the market. Raven is only a few feet away from him. How she knew where he was, I have no idea—as I watch, her head turns to the left. I follow her gaze and see a woman speaking to a Regimental and pointing in Ash's direction.

I feel a strange whooshing sensation, as if a great tunnel of wind had dropped down through my torso. Raven's words echo in my head.

She knows him.

Raven reaches Ash at the very moment I hear the whistle blow.

"There he is!" someone shouts.

The market erupts in chaos.

Regimentals are everywhere. People pushing and shoving, stalls are toppled over, more whistles blow . . . I get knocked down again and by the time I get to my feet, I can't see Raven or Ash anywhere. I can't find Garnet among the sea of red uniforms.

I am all alone.

I push my way to the edge of the square, fighting against the swarm of people who can't seem to decide which way they want to go.

"Did you see him?"

"Is he *here*?"

"Have they caught him?"

"Right here, in Landing's Market, *imagine*!"

I finally make it past the last of the stalls and onto one of the smaller streets, so wrapped up in panic that I run smack into a petite blond girl.

"Oh!" I cry as we both tumble to the ground.

"I'm so sorry, I—" The girl blinks and looks at me. "Violet?" she gasps.

It's Lily.

~ Seven ~

As soon as we're on our feet, Lily throws her arms around me.

The last time I saw her was on the train from Southgate to the Auction. I remember her singing that Marsh-song in her plaintive, sweet voice. She was so excited to start her life as a surrogate.

"What are you doing here?" she asks. "Why are you dressed like a servant? What happened to your *face*?"

Lily is wearing a simple gray coat and a pretty purple hat with a yellow ribbon on it. She looks cared for. She looks healthy. I want to hold on to her and never let go. I want to make sure she's real.

But I can't stay here.

"Help me," I gasp.

"Of course," Lily says. "Are you lost? Do you need help finding your mistress? Oh, Violet, I thought I'd never see you again! You live in the Jewel, don't you? You must, I knew of course that someone in the royalty would have bought you. Did your mistress take you shopping? Have you seen Raven at all? Is she in the Jewel, too? Oh, have you heard about that companion!"

I'd forgotten just how much Lily can talk—a strange sensation bubbles up in my chest, a mixture of happiness and exasperation.

"Lily," I interrupt, before she can keep going, "I need a place to hide."

Her eyebrows knit together. "From what?"

A few Regimentals run past us at that moment, one of them yelling, "Search the alleys!"

I shrink back against the wall. "From them," I say.

Lily looks from the retreating Regimentals to me and back again. I see something click in her expression. The next moment, her hand slips into mine.

"Come with me," she says.

We hurry down narrow streets that blur together, pink and gray and red stone, glinting glass windows, trees with neatly trimmed branches, bare and leafless now that winter is here. The houses get smaller, plainer, the farther away from the market we go. Finally, Lily stops in front of a pale-yellow house, sandwiched between a red one and a gray one. It's only two floors, but it has a cheery blue door with a wreath of hellebore hanging on it.

"Quickly," she says, hurrying up the steps and taking out a key. We slip through the door into a combination of front hall and living area—a smattering of mismatched couches and armchairs surround a low wooden coffee table to my left. Directly in front of me is a set of stairs.

"This way," Lily says, as we run up to the second floor. It's a single hallway, lined with a worn red carpet. All the doors are closed. Lily reaches one hand up, a gesture that makes no sense until I see the dangling rope, then a hatch opens and a ladder descends from the ceiling.

"Up, up, up!" she says. I climb into semidarkness, expecting Lily to follow me. Instead, I turn to find her folding up the ladder.

"I'll be back tonight," she says. Then she closes the hatch before I have a chance to thank her, or ask any questions, or wonder if there might be something to eat up here.

I am sealed off, in an attic, in a strange house, in the Bank.

I am utterly on my own.

EXHAUSTION OVERCOMES ME, AND I FALL ASLEEP DESPITE the ache in my stomach and the fear that clogs my lungs.

I don't remember the last time I slept. Over twenty-four hours, at least. I suppose I needed it. But it doesn't make me feel better.

When I wake, I am completely disoriented. For a second I think I'm in the dungeons, in the palace of the Lake, but then I feel the lumpiness of the ancient, sagging couch I collapsed on, and my eyes adjust, and I remember.

The attic has a musty smell. There is a small, half-moon window that looks out over the street—I can tell from the dimness of the light that evening has fallen. There are several rolled-up rugs piled against one wall. I find some moth-eaten sheets draped over the back of the couch. A broken lamp, a few boxes containing books and some old photographs, an empty birdcage, and stacks of yellowing newspapers are scattered about the narrow space. The ceiling slants downward, so I have to crouch a bit as I make my way to the window.

The sound of voices freezes me in place. A man's first, then a woman's. I clap my hands over my mouth, a physical reinforcement to ensure I don't make a sound.

I can't hear what they're saying. I think they're on the ground floor. The voices become more muffled, finally vanishing into some part of the house too far away for me to hear.

The couch springs creak as I sit down. My whole body is trembling. My head throbs and I realize I'm clenching my jaw so hard my teeth are grinding together.

My solitude comes crashing down on me. Where are Raven and Ash? Have they been caught? My empty stomach contracts at the thought of Ash once again thrown into a cell. Ash, with his head on the chopping block. Raven, sent back to the House of the Stone. Or worse—side by side on a matching block with Ash.

I squeeze my eyes shut and will the images to disappear. I don't know anything and thinking the worst will not help. I press the heels of my hands against my eyes and a flurry of sparks appears in the darkness behind my lids.

The base of my skull begins to buzz.

I have a wild, fleeting thought that I've snapped from the stress before I remember the arcana. I gasp and struggle with the knot I made in my hair, so many lifetimes ago, when Annabelle was still alive, and I lived in the Duchess's palace.

I finally tug it free, barely feeling the sharp sting when a few hairs come out with it. It rises in the air, hovering inches away from my face.

"Lucien?" I whisper.

His voice comes across immediately. "Where are you?"

"I . . . I'm . . ." I don't know how to answer him. I have no idea where I am. "I'm in the Bank."

"What happened? Why didn't you make it to the safe house with the others?"

"I got—oh, Lucien, are Raven and Ash okay? Are they there?"

"Yes, but what happened to *you*?" Lucien's voice is clipped, impatient.

Raven and Ash are all right. They're safe. My legs melt into the couch.

"We got separated," I say. "And then I ran into a friend, another surrogate. Someone I knew from Southgate. I'm hiding in her attic." I want to hold the arcana, cradle it in my hands but I don't know whether touching it will end the communication or harm it in some way.

"What do you mean? Who is she?"

"I literally ran into her. I knocked her down in the street. I didn't even know she lived around here. But she's a good person, Lucien. She helped me. We can trust her."

"Violet, we don't know who we can trust."

"Well, she was my friend and right now she's all I've got."

"She doesn't have a key. You must *always* ask about the key."

"Garnet doesn't have a key."

"Did you ask him if he does?"

". . . no."

There's a long pause.

"What is your friend's last name?"

"Deering," I say. "Her name is Lily Deering."

"Lily Deering," he repeats. "I'll find out where you are." He sounds disgruntled.

"We did everything we were supposed to," I insist. "Someone recognized him."

"I'm glad you're safe." I can sense Lucien holding back what he'd really like to say, and again, I worry that he'd be happier if Ash had been arrested in that market. If that was what he intended all along. "We'll speak again soon."

"Wait!" After everything I've been through, I'm tired of all the mystery. I deserve some answers. "I've followed your orders. I've done what you asked, but you haven't given me a single, solid reason why. Why is this worth it? Why am *I* worth it?"

There is another long pause.

"Are you happy with the way this city is run, Violet?"

"You mean, the royalty? You know I how I feel about them."

Lucien sighs. "You are not seeing the larger picture. This is not just about surrogates. This is about an entire population enslaved to serve the needs of the few. And it gets worse with every passing year. You have a power that you cannot even begin to comprehend. I am trying to help you realize that and do some good with it."

"And yet, you don't tell me what you want, or what that power is, or how I'm supposed to help. Let me *help*, Lucien."

"Do you honestly think that all the Auguries are good for is making healthy royal children?"

I suppose I hadn't really thought about it. I don't like using the Auguries at all, so I never considered there could be another purpose for them. But I was able to put that fire out. Well, with Raven's help.

Lucien takes my silence as an answer. "Exactly. You have more power than you think, but I am not the one who can show you how to use it."

"And once I know how to use it, then what?"

"Help me. Help me tear down these walls that confine us, that separate us. Help me save not only the surrogates but everyone who is under the royalty's thumb. The ladies-in-waiting. The servants. The factory workers who die of black lung, the farmhands who feed the royals but barely have enough to eat themselves. The children dying from lack of basic necessities in the Marsh. I am not the only one who thinks the royalty's time is coming to end. We have all been bound to them in some way. We have all suffered for them." He says that last part so softly, I barely hear him. "We deserve to be free."

I think about Annabelle, so sweet and frail. I see the bloody gash across her neck and have to shut my eyes for a moment, swallowing back a sob. What was her crime? Nothing. Being my friend. Annabelle did not deserve to die. And no one will be punished for her death. The Duchess will go on as if it had never happened.

I think about Hazel—how much longer will my little sister be able to stay in school? How long until she has to join Ochre, working to keep my family alive?

How much longer before she is forced to take the blood test for surrogacy? The thought sets my stomach in knots. I picture Hazel ripped from my family, arriving at Southgate, alone, afraid. I see her nose bleeding as she learns the Auguries, see her standing on that silver X on the platform at the Auction House. Hazel cannot be a surrogate.

But I don't see how I can help them. I hate that I'm stuck in this attic, alone and powerless. Lucien seems to sense my hesitancy.

"I don't expect you to understand everything right now. Keep the arcana close. Someone will come for you."

I open my mouth to argue but find I'm too tired. "Okay," I agree.

"Get some sleep, honey. You've had a long day." There is another pause. "And remember. Don't trust anyone until they show you the key."

The arcana drops into my open hands, leaving me with even more questions than I started with. I sigh and secure it back into my hair.

I'm in that strange state between waking and dreaming when Lily comes to see me.

It's very late. There's hardly any light in the attic, just

a tiny sliver of moonlight on the floor by the window. I'm lying on the couch, my thoughts tangled up in dark tunnels and dying fires and Annabelle and wanted posters, when the hatch creaks open.

I sit up so quickly it makes me dizzy. A flickering light illuminates Lily's face as it pops up through the hole in the floor. She climbs into the attic, carrying a tray laden with two small jars, a glass of water, a fat white candle, and—my stomach groans—a covered plate that brings the faintest scent of cooking.

"Hi," she whispers, setting the tray down on the floor. I practically fall off the couch toward the food. Lily's brought me several slices of pot roast smothered in thick brown gravy, and cold boiled potatoes. I want to ignore the utensils and shove the food hand over fist into my mouth.

"When was the last time you ate?" she asks.

"I don't know," I say through a mouthful of potato.

Lily lets me eat in silence until the plate is clean. I let out an involuntary sigh and lean back against the couch.

"Thank you," I murmur, taking a huge gulp of water.

Lily moves the tray aside. "I brought these for your face," she says, unscrewing the tops of the jars of cream. One she spreads on my cheek—it sends a pleasant, cooling sensation through the bruise. Ice ointment. I remember when Cora, the Duchess's lady-in-waiting, used it, after the Duchess hit me for the first time. The second one smells sharply antiseptic, and Lily dabs it on the cut on my lip. It stings a little.

"There," she says. "That bruise should be gone by tomorrow."

She replaces the caps on the jars and covers the empty plate. Then she sits up on her knees and looks at me with wide blue eyes.

"So," she says, in a tone of voice I know so well, one that I heard countless times, whenever a new issue of *The Daily Jewel* arrived, or the lot numbers were given out, or any particularly juicy bit of gossip reached her ears. "What *happened*?"

I'm so full and exhausted, and I can't bear to lie anymore. I tell her everything—almost. I don't mention Lucien by name, only insinuate that someone inside the Jewel helped me escape, and I don't tell her where I'm going (not that I know myself). I tell her about Raven, and how I helped her instead of my taking the serum. Lily practically cries when I tell her I was bought by the Duchess—"A Founding House? Oh, Violet!"

And then I tell her about Ash.

"Shhhh!" I hiss as she lets out a yelp.

"*You're* the surrogate?" Lily whispers. "But . . . but they're saying he *raped* you, Violet."

"That's a lie," I say vehemently.

"But did you . . . I mean, you didn't have . . ."

I nod.

Lily gasps and her hands fly to her chest. "It's like . . . it's like . . . the most forbidden romance *ever*. It's better than the Exetor and the Electress!"

I smile at the simplicity of it. "I'll tell you about it later," I say. After all that food, it's a fight to keep my eyes open. "Where are we?"

"Thirty-Four Baker Street. It's not the nicest part of the

Bank, but it's prettier than the Marsh, isn't it? Some people call this area the Cheap Streets," Lily says with an indignant sniff. "But I think it's very pleasant."

"Who do you live with?" I ask. "Are they nice?"

"Oh, they're lovely," she gushes. "Reed and Caliper Haberdash. Caliper's a wonderful mistress—she's quite old, almost thirty, and she and Reed have been saving up for ages to buy a surrogate. She can't have babies of her own." Lily's face darkens. "Not like the way the royalty can't—there's something wrong with her body. She's very sad about that." Then she perks up. "I sold for nine thousand seven hundred diamantes. Can you imagine? How much were you?"

I shift uncomfortably. "I don't remember." I don't want to talk about the price of my body. It doesn't matter much whether I sold for six million or six hundred diamantes. There's something more important that she needs to know.

"Lily," I say, "you can't get pregnant."

She looks offended for a moment, then laughs. "Of course I can! What a silly thing to say. That's what we're here for, isn't it?"

"No, I mean—" I grab her wrist and hold it tight. "Don't let them get you pregnant."

"Violet, you're hurting me," she says, wrenching her arm out of my grasp.

"Lily," I begin again, alarmed that I didn't think of this before, furious that my appetite and exhaustion over-shadowed everything else. "If you get pregnant, you'll die. That's why surrogates never get to come home—childbirth kills us."

She stares at me for a minute. "No," she says, shaking

her head. "That's not possible. Caliper wouldn't do that. She cares about me. She's already told me she wants me to stay with them after the baby is born."

"She's lying," I snap.

Lily goes very still, and I can tell I've hurt her feelings.

"Caliper wouldn't lie to me," she says. "Not about something like that."

"I—I'm sorry, but it's true. I've seen the morgue where the dead surrogates go. I was told by someone who *knows*."

Something settles in Lily's expression, some strange mixture of acceptance and determination.

"It doesn't matter," she says. "I went to the doctor yesterday."

"But you don't know yet, right?" I say.

She tucks a lock of hair behind my ear. "You look exhausted. Sleep. I'll come back tomorrow, when everyone's left."

"Tell me."

She bites her lip and nods.

Lily is pregnant. Lily is dead.

"No," I gasp. "No, no, no—"

"Shhhh," she whispers. "It's okay, Violet. It's all right."

"No!" I shout, then lower my voice before I wake anyone up. "No, it is definitely *not* all right. Nothing is all right about this. You can't . . . you can't . . ."

Lily takes both my hands in hers and holds them tight. "Listen to me. I *want* this. I'm happy."

"You'll die," I snap.

"You don't know that for certain. But . . ." She gestures

toward the ladder, to the house below. "I love it here. I love them. And they want this baby. And, contrary to what you and Raven might feel, I have *always* wanted to have a baby."

"It's not your baby," I say.

Lily sighs. "No," she says. "It's not. But these people have become my family. You *know*. How it used to be for me. What my parents were like." She squeezes my hand. "Weren't you just telling me how important it is to be able to choose? How you chose to be with the companion, even when it was dangerous? How you helped Raven, at personal risk? Am I not allowed the same choice? Can I not have the same freedom you have? To choose what I want. Choice is freedom, Violet."

I shake my head. "You're twisting it all up. You don't get to choose to *die*."

But Lily smiles, as if we were back at Southgate getting ready for bed. "You should get some sleep. You've had a long day."

I want to keep fighting, but the food in my stomach is pulling my eyelids down against my will. I climb back up onto the couch and rest my head against the threadbare cushion. "You won't tell anyone I'm here, right?"

Lily kisses my temple, the way I kissed Annabelle's before I left her for the last time. The loss of her, which has been overshadowed by the incinerator and the sewers and the marketplace, rears up, raw and aching. It tunnels through my chest and squeezes my lungs into my throat.

"No," Lily murmurs. "I won't tell. It's so nice to see you again."

The tears are close, brimming behind my lids. "Good night, Lily," I croak.

She picks up the tray and leaves, the soft thud of the door in the floor telling me I'm alone.

I think I keep crying even after I fall asleep.

~ Eight ~

I SPEND A GOOD PORTION OF THE NEXT DAY TRYING NOT to pace back and forth across the attic.

It's hard to keep still. I can hear muffled voices, and at one point, the soft strains of a violin.

So these people allow Lily to play music. That's nice. But no matter how nice they are or how well they treat my friend, they have sentenced her to death.

Sometime in the late afternoon, the voices stop. The house becomes silent. I get up and look out the half-moon window. I see a couple, a tall man in a long coat and a woman with a white hat walking away from 34 Baker Street. The rest of the street is quiet, except for a harried young man walking about six dogs. They yelp and bark, tangling their leashes together. I watch them until they disappear around a corner.

I go back to the couch and fiddle with the arcana, making sure it's still secure in my hair. I think back to my conversation with Lucien last night. What did he mean about a key? And who exactly is going to be showing me this power I'm supposed to have? I rub my eyes with the heels of my hands. I'm sick of Lucien's doublespeak, of knowing only fragments of what's to come. I have trusted him. It's time for him to trust me.

The doorbell rings and I sit up. My heart pounds in my ears. I think I hear the door open, and Lily's voice. Then nothing but silence. It seems to go on and on.

The door to my attic opens and I freeze, gripping the couch cushions.

"197?" The voice is not Lily's. It's a man's. I cringe at the use of my Lot number.

I walk to the opening in the floor and look down. The man standing at the foot of the ladder has graying hair and wears gold-rimmed spectacles. He peers up at me curiously.

"Who are you?" I ask.

"I have been sent for you," he says.

Lucien's voice enters my head. *Remember the key.* "Show me the key," I demand, glad that I sound confident, since I have no idea what to expect.

I feel even less confident when he opens his tweed coat and begins to unbutton his shirt. He opens the shirt collar wide. At the place where his collarbone meets his shoulder, there is a tattoo of a small black skeleton key.

"I work for the Society of the Black Key," he says.

"What's the Black Key?"

"He is not a what. The Black Key is our leader."

Of course Lucien would use a code name.

"Come with me, 197," the man says. "We don't have much time."

I climb down the ladder as he buttons up his coat.

"Don't call me that again," I say as we walk down the stairs to the front door. "I have a name. It's Violet Lasting." I'm done with being called anything but who I am. "What's your name?"

The man purses his lips. "You may call me the Cobbler."

"How long have you—oh!"

Lily's body lies crumpled at the foot of the stairs. "What have you done?!" I run to her, tilt her head back, and nearly cry with relief when I feel her breath on my cheek.

"She is fine," the Cobbler says. "She will be awake in a few minutes. We have to go."

"What did you do to her?" I demand. "She was helping me."

The Cobbler shrugs. "A necessary precaution."

I stand up, my blood boiling.

"This is not the time to be crying over a simple dose of sleep serum," the Cobbler says. "There is work to be done." He picks up a large brown parcel from where it sits by the door. "Carry this. Walk two steps behind me and keep your head down."

"Wait." I am so tired of being told what to do, and I don't even know this man, and he certainly doesn't know me. So I'm going to do one thing before I leave with him. I bend down and adjust Lily's body so that she's in a more comfortable position. I take her hand and squeeze it. "Thank you," I say to her. Then I stand, take the parcel, and look the Cobbler straight in the eye. "All right. Let's go."

We walk out the door, and I make sure to follow his instructions and stay a few paces behind him. The air is colder than it was yesterday and I clench my teeth together to keep them from chattering. I wish I had thought to borrow a coat from Lily.

We make our way back through Landing's Market, which is quieter today than it was yesterday. There are still some remnants of the search for Ash scattered about: a broken basket, a trampled cabbage. Half-torn signs hang from lampposts, with Ash's face and the words WANTED. FUGITIVE. Two little girls are playing while their mother haggles over the price of potatoes. As we pass, I hear one girl say to the other, "I was the surrogate yesterday! Let me play the royalty this time."

My throat goes dry. Are these the sort of games children play in the Bank?

I'm so distracted, I almost lose sight of the Cobbler as he turns onto a different street. I hurry to catch up.

This street is wide and airy, much nicer than Lily's, so I begin to understand why her area might be called the Cheap Streets. Though it's ridiculous to think anything in the Bank is cheap. The houses have space between them, separated by hedges or high brick walls, but not like the ones that surround the palaces in the Jewel. These are clean and pretty and friendly, not topped with vicious spikes. Many of the houses are three or four storied, with wide porches and balconies, and some even have miniature turrets, like they're trying to impersonate a royal home.

The people on the streets are fancier, too—the men wear bowler hats and long overcoats and carry silver-topped canes. The women are in colorful dresses made of velvet or silk, with fur stoles around their necks and sleek leather gloves. Servant girls dressed in brown trail behind them. One carries a birdcage with a brilliant green parrot inside. Her mistress sees the Cobbler and stops.

"I was on my way to your store," she says. "I need a new pair of shoes to match the gown I bought for the Magistrate's Gala."

"Of course, Mrs. Firestone," the Cobbler says. "I am making a delivery. Then I will be happy to attend to you."

"Come to the house," Mrs. Firestone says. "This is a special order. And don't send your apprentice like last time. That boy was all thumbs."

The Cobbler's shoulders tense, but he nods. "As you wish."

The woman breezes past us, her servant hurrying along in her wake.

"She seems lovely," I mutter.

The Cobbler fixes me with a cold stare. "She is better than most."

"Is that why you're working for—" I stop myself from saying Lucien's name just in time. "Him?"

"Now is not the time for questions," the Cobbler says. I grip the box so hard my knuckles whiten. I am tired of hearing that.

He walks away and I have no choice but to follow.

Eventually, we leave the wide boulevard of upscale houses

and turn onto smaller streets. We pass a theater with a gold marquee proclaiming, THE LONG WAY BACK: A NEW PLAY BY FORREST VALE. ONLY TWO PERFORMANCES LEFT! and a restaurant with large glass windows and linen-covered tables.

We reach a street made of rough cobblestone. The buildings here are big and boxy, with metal awnings and dirty windows with iron bars on them. A wagon sits under one of the awnings as two men haul large slabs of meat off it under the watchful gaze of a butcher in a stained white apron. He glances down at the clipboard in his hands.

"Four diamantes more per pound than last month," he says to himself. "What is the Exetor playing at with all these new taxes?"

Then he seems to realize he's speaking out loud and glances worriedly at the men, but they are too busy lifting a long cut of ribs onto the loading dock to notice.

The Cobbler stops in front of a small warehouse with chipped green paint and a sliding iron door. "This is where I leave you," he says, taking the package from my arms. "I do hope the Black Key was right about you."

"Why are you doing this?" I blurt out. "Why are you helping me, helping . . . him?"

The Cobbler looks away. "They took my son," he says. "Because he was large and strong. He liked making shoes, but they wanted him as a Regimental. He is theirs now." His eyes meet mine and I see years of anger in them, of loss, and of the desperate need for hope. "But their time is over."

I never thought about how the Regimentals came to be Regimentals. Did I think it was voluntary? Is anything in this city voluntary?

"I'm sorry," I say.

He huffs. "Don't be sorry. I don't need your pity. I need my son back." He yanks open the door. "Someone will come for you. Do not trust them until you see the key."

Without another word, he turns and walks back the way we came.

"Violet?" Raven's voice pulls me away from the Cobbler's retreating back. I step inside the warehouse and slide the door shut.

Raven throws herself into my arms, and I can feel the sharp points of her shoulder blades as I hold her. The small mound of her stomach presses softly against me.

"You're real, right?" she whispers in my ear.

"I'm real," I whisper back.

She pulls away. "He said you were real, that you were here and coming back to us, but I didn't believe him. They lied to me so many times; I don't want to be lied to anymore."

I look behind her to where Ash is standing, healthy and alive and smiling at me. I don't want to let go of Raven, so I hold out my hand to him. He takes it.

"You made it," he says with relief.

"You didn't trust Lucien?" I ask wryly.

"To save you? Absolutely. To bring you here? Not a chance."

"Who's Lucien?" Raven asks. Her face crinkles with concentration. "Was he . . . is he . . ." She glances at Ash.

"I'm Ash," he reminds her gently. I get the impression this isn't the first time she's asked.

"Lucien is a lady-in-waiting. You met him at—" I'm

about to say the morgue but think that might be the wrong word to use. "In the room with the fire," I finish.

Raven blinks. "Yes. I remember the fire. We put it out together." Then her face goes pale. "But it burned him. It burned him alive." She holds her head in her hands. "No, no, no . . ."

"Raven," I say, reaching for her again but she scuttles away from me and curls up against the far wall. She holds her knees and starts muttering the same thing I heard her say in the morgue, but I can understand the words now.

"I am Raven Stirling," she says. "I am sitting against a wall. I am real. I am stronger than this." She taps the knuckle of her right thumb against her forehead three times and repeats the mantra.

I move toward her, but Ash's arm wraps around my waist. "It's okay," he murmurs. "She does this sometimes. It's better to leave her be for a moment."

My body melts against his and I tear my eyes away from my friend to look him full in the face. I reach out and run my fingertips over the smooth skin where his bruises used to be.

"Garnet fixed me up," he says. He touches the corner of my lip with his thumb. "Looks like someone fixed you up, too."

I nod. "Where is Garnet now?"

Ash shrugs. "Back in the Jewel, I imagine. I'm surprised we saw him again at all."

"How did you escape? There were so many Regimentals . . ."

He glances at Raven. "She saved us. I don't know how.

It was like when we were in the sewers and she found the exit. She. . . knows sometimes. She senses things. Right as the whistle blew she pulled me into this alley, and there was a door in the ground. It led to this underground tunnel that connected to a bunch of different stores. There was a lot of junk in it. And she knew exactly where to go, and when to stop, and where to hide. We stayed down there until it got dark, then she found an exit that let us out about fifty yards from Landing's Market. And then I found our way here, to the address Garnet gave us. I guess it ended up being lucky that I knew the area." He smiles. "Garnet was pretty impressed we made it at all. Not that he was any help."

"What did that woman do to her?" I mutter. In my mind, I can see the Countess of the Stone's fleshy arms and cruel eyes.

"I don't know, but whatever it was . . ." Ash's jaw hardens. "She goes places sometimes. She thinks she's somewhere else. Bad things happen to her there. There's someone named Crow—I think he's her brother or something—he burns alive a lot. And you lose your eyes—that was the worst for me to hear. And I think her mother gets skinned." He shudders. "It's so real for her."

I don't know what Lucien's plans are, but I am going to make sure they involve making the Countess of the Stone pay for what she's done.

The iron door slides open. I freeze at the sight of the Regimental looming in the doorway, but relax when I see that it's Garnet.

"Oh, good, you're here," he says to me, closing the door behind him. "We've got a problem."

"Doesn't that make for a nice change," Ash says.

"What's going on?" I ask.

"Nothing," Garnet says. He hands me a canteen and I drink from it greedily before passing it to Ash. "All the trains are still canceled. Every inch of the Bank is being searched by Regimentals. I think this might be the first time in Lucien's life where he actually doesn't know what to do."

"So what, we have to stay here? Wait it out in this warehouse?"

Garnet shrugs. "I don't see another option."

"But it's not safe. If they're searching *every inch* of the Bank, they'll find us, eventually."

"I'm not Lucien," he says. "I don't have backup plans upon backup plans."

"What are you doing here then?" I snap. "If you don't really want to help, then go!"

I didn't mean to yell, to take my frustration out on Garnet. But I want to get wherever it is we're going and I want to get there now. His pale face flushes dark red.

"You don't think I want to help?" he says. "What do you think I've been doing this whole time? Getting you out. Getting your *boyfriend* out. Lying to my mother. Dealing with Carnelian. For the Exetor's sake, I let one of Lucien's followers tattoo me!" He opens his shirt to reveal a skeleton key tattoo, like the one the Cobbler had, on his chest, just above his heart.

I am stunned. "What if your mother sees it?"

Garnet looks embarrassed. "She won't. And even if she did, she'd think it was some stupid prank or that I did it on a dare. She wouldn't take it seriously."

"I was wrong about you," Raven says. I didn't real-ize she'd been listening. She looks at Garnet with a single-minded ferocity. "You aren't a coward." Her eyes become glassy. Double-focused, as I suppose I've come to think of it. "You've never had real friends. You just needed something to fight for."

For perhaps the first time in his life, Garnet seems uncomfortable taking a compliment. "Sure," he says. "What-ever you say."

Raven keeps staring. "If you admit you need people, you can lose them." Her gaze sharpens, returning to the present. "But needing people can save your life."

"We have to get to the Farm," I say. I've trusted Lucien this far, I may as well trust him when he says the Farm will be safe. "We're all part of this group . . ." I remember the Cobbler's words. "The Society of the Black Key. Even if we're not marked as such."

"Sorry, the what?" Ash says.

"I can explain it later, or maybe Lucien is the one to explain. At any rate, let's think. We can't stay here."

"Do you have any ideas?" Garnet asks. "I'm all ears."

"Actually," Ash says, stepping forward. "I think I do."

~ Nine ~

"I KNOW THIS CIRCLE," ASH CONTINUES. "BETTER THAN any of you. And I think there's one train that can get us out of here undetected."

"Where?" I ask. "All the trains are suspended."

"At Madame Curio's," he replies. "And that train always runs."

The name sounds vaguely familiar, and obviously means something to Garnet, because his mouth pops open. "Are you *insane*?"

"What's Madame Curio's?" I ask.

"It's my companion house," Ash explains. "She's . . . well, she *was* my Madame. I told you about her, remember? She recruited me."

And then it clicks. She was the one who found Ash when he took his sister, Cinder, to the free clinic. When Cinder was diagnosed with black lung—the reason why Ash became a companion at all. *I bet you drive all the girls crazy.* That's what Madame Curio had said to him.

"What, um, does she do there?"

Garnet snorts with disgust.

"She runs the house," Ash says. "She oversees the companions, our education and training, and she matches us with our clients."

But there's a pink flush creeping up his neck that makes me think it's something more than that.

"All the companion houses have a private train station," he continues, changing the subject. "Their trains won't be monitored in the same way as the public ones. If we can get on that train, maybe we can make it to the Farm."

"So, we're supposed to stroll into your former companion house and ask to use the train?" Garnet says. "I thought they educated you guys in that place. This is the stupidest idea I've ever heard of."

Ash throws him a sharp look. "There's more than one way to get onto the grounds."

"But, Ash," I say hesitantly, "are you saying there won't be any Regimentals on the train at all?"

"No, there probably will be," he says. "But it won't matter."

"And why not?" Garnet asks.

"Because," Ash says, "not everyone who works at a companion house is a companion. Many of them don't come willingly."

"What, you mean they're kidnapped?" I ask. "Why?"

"The boys are taken for sparring practice, fencing, sword fighting, manual labor, any job Madame sees fit." The idea of Ash sword fighting is strange. "The girls are taken for . . ." Ash clears his throat and the blush on his neck climbs up to his cheeks. "For . . . practice." He is looking determinedly at Garnet, avoiding my eyes.

Garnet raises an eyebrow.

"Wait, so—" I begin, but Ash cuts me off.

"There are secret compartments in the train. It's how they smuggle them in. And that's how we can get out."

A long silence follows. I can't help thinking about all those girls, kidnapped and brought to the companion house. Held against their will. Like I was.

"So how do we get you guys in?" Garnet asks.

"We'll have to wait until tonight," Ash says. "And we're going to need some new clothes . . ."

ASH GIVES GARNET A LIST OF ITEMS TO GET.

There's nothing to do but wait. I sit beside Raven—she hasn't moved from the wall. Ash sits on a wooden box by the front door, lost in thought.

"How are you feeling?" I ask her.

Raven looks at me with a deadened expression. "I'm not in that palace anymore. This is the best I've felt in a long time." She blinks. "Did I thank you?"

"For what?" I ask.

"For saving my life."

I smile. "Don't worry about it."

Her fingers thread through mine—hers are so thin and

frail I worry that if I squeeze too hard they'll break. "Thank you," she whispers. Her gaze travels down to her stomach. "Sometimes I forget," she says, putting a hand on it—the little bump is barely visible under her dress. "It used to hurt all the time."

"When did it happen?" I ask.

Raven closes her eyes. "I—I don't know. Emile, my lady-in-waiting, took me out for a walk in the garden one afternoon. I'd wanted to see whether you'd sent another flower, but you hadn't sent me anything. Then I went to the doctor . . ." A tear slides out from under her eyelid. "They made it grow so fast. It ate me up from the inside. My bones ached and shriveled and it grew and grew and wouldn't stop."

That would have been only three or four weeks ago.

"How?" I whisper.

She opens her eyes. "Did they ever use the stimulant gun on you?"

I nod. "Once."

The stimulant gun was created to incite the Auguries against the surrogate's will. I remember the all-consuming agony when the doctor used it on me, the blinding pain, the thick green vines covering the medical bed, crawling up to the ceiling. Dr. Blythe's words echo in my head, from the day I made the oak tree grow.

The stimulant gun heightens your abilities, but it weakens you physically. If overused, it can have some very nasty side effects.

Raven's smile is a tiny crack across her face. "The doctor used it all the time, especially after I got pregnant. Three or four times a day. The Countess didn't care how much blood I threw up, or how much I screamed. She just wanted results." Raven flinches at some memory. "She got what she wanted. He said . . . I was twelve weeks along? Fourteen? I don't remember. I didn't want to listen."

"So she was trying to make you have a baby fast," I say. "That's what the Duchess wanted from me, too."

"The Countess liked experimenting," Raven says coldly. "To see what she *could* do. She wanted to pull the strings, to have complete power over my mind, my memories, the Auguries, everything."

"Is that what . . ." I swallow. "Is that what those scars are from?"

Raven probes her skull with one hand. "She liked cutting into me. She liked making me see things that weren't real." Something glitters in Raven's eyes, a fragment of her old mischief. "She didn't know about the whispers, though. They tried something new one day. The doctor thought it would be an 'interesting experiment.' They cut me somewhere different and they thought nothing happened. But that was when the whispers started."

I hesitate, watching her, wondering if it would hurt or help to press for more information. "What do they say?"

"All kinds of things. I can hear when someone is afraid or when they're pretending to like someone, but they really hate them. I know when someone is lying or if they're secretly in love. The whispers tell me. They come and go. The Countess has very dark thoughts. About her mother. About her husband. About the surrogates." Raven rubs her eyes.

"It's like the Countess unwittingly gave you an extra sense or something."

"I knew that blond boy would come back," she continues. "He likes us. He feels connected to us. And . . ." She looks at Ash, her brows crinkling. "Ash," she says finally. "He's Ash, right?"

I nod.

"He hates himself," she says.

A lump forms in my throat. I don't know anything about Ash's life in the companion house. He's never shared that with me.

"I don't want to be this person, Violet." Raven's face softens and she leans her head back. "Emile was kind to me. He used to sneak me extra food sometimes. And he took me out to the garden often, letting me send you messages. But he also told me things. He told me the Countess buys a surrogate every year. She doesn't care about having an heir. She cares more about seeing what we're capable of. How much we can *take*." Her face falls into a mournful expression. "He probably thinks I'm dead now."

"I'm sure he'll be all right," I say.

"You don't understand," she says. "All I had in that place was him and you. I held on to the hope that you were safe, that the Duchess wasn't torturing you, even when they put me in the cage or stabbed me with Frederic's weapons or used the muzzle. But it was so hard when they started cutting into my brain. She took my memories and used them against me and I couldn't tell what was true and what wasn't. Emile helped me. He reminded me. He'd say your name sometimes when I started to forget." A tear slowly runs down her cheek. "He couldn't say my name but he could say yours."

"She'll pay for this," I say. "Raven, I promise."

"How, Violet? How are we supposed to do that? Look at me." She gestures weakly to herself. "I am broken now. And I'll never be the same. I am damaged beyond repair."

I sit up on my knees and look her straight in the eye. "Listen to me," I say. "You were there for me in Southgate when I was scared and when I was weak. You gave me courage. If you think I'm not going to do the exact same for you, then you'd better think again. You were with me every single day I was in that palace. *You* were my strength. Now let me be yours." I put my hand on her shoulder. "I'm going to help you get better. I'm going to protect you."

Raven's hand slides once more over her stomach. "Can you protect me from this?"

I look down. The lump in my throat is so big it's hard to breathe.

She rests her cheek on my fingers. "I'm so tired, Violet. Can I go to sleep now?"

"Of course," I say. My voice is rough and low.

"You won't leave, right?" she asks, panic rising in her tone.

"No," I say. "I'm going to be right here."

I stretch out my legs as she settles down so she can use my thigh as a pillow. Within minutes, her breathing has slowed, her body relaxing. I brush her hair away from her face. She looks like my Raven from before.

She still is, I tell myself.

"Is she all right?" Ash asks softly, from his seat by the door.

"I don't know," I reply.

Gradually, the light fades, night usurping day. The warehouse grows dark and cold. I fold my arms across my chest and try to stop shivering. Ash comes over and puts an arm around me. I lean into him, grateful for his presence as much as his warmth.

"You've saved a lot of people recently," he says.

"Not yet," I remind him.

"I think you might be selling yourself a bit short."

I don't say anything because I'm not feeling particularly proud or saviorlike at the moment.

"Will your plan work?" I ask. "Can we get out through the companion house train?"

"I don't know, Violet. But I don't know what else to do. Like you said, we can't stay here."

I nod and we sit in silence. I should probably sleep but my mind is racing. So many things I don't want to think about—Raven in a cage, Lily being pregnant, Annabelle lying lifeless on the floor of my bedroom . . .

"What was it like?" I ask Ash after a while. "At the companion house. You've never talked about it."

His body stiffens and I know he wishes I hadn't asked. But after a moment, he says, "It was very pleasant. They took extremely good care of us."

I smile. "You're lying." I shift under his arm. "You're using your companion tone. The excessive politeness. You only use it when you're lying."

There is another long moment before he whispers, "It was awful."

I sit up so I can look him in the face. The dim light creates shadows around his eyes. He won't meet my gaze, but I don't look away. The seconds tick past.

"You don't want to know," he says finally. "Trust me."

"If I didn't want to know, I wouldn't have asked. You're talking about boys being kidnapped and girls being used for sex and I feel like there's this whole part of your life I don't understand. What happens in that place?"

Ash's whole body seems to harden again. "You want to know what life in a companion house is like?" he says, and his voice is sharper than I've ever heard it. "Fine. After I was bribed away from my family at the age of fourteen, I was trained for a year, educated in art, history, mathematics, music, dueling . . . It was nice, at first. Then on my fifteenth birthday, I was called to Madame Curio's room, where she taught me some things I hadn't learned yet. That was the first time I had sex."

An unpleasant prickle crawls up my spine.

"Then my lessons changed. They brought girls to me. Madame said I had to please them. I didn't want to—the girls were so scared. I was scared. But you don't go against Madame. My teachers watched. They judged and instructed me. It was humiliating. Then they sent me off to charm daughters during the day and sleep with their mothers at night. I've slept with women old enough to be my grandmother. All because Madame Curio saw me outside the clinic and thought I was handsome."

Ash stands abruptly. He starts pacing back and forth,

his mouth twisted, his hands clenched.

"Do you understand how much I *hate* how I look, hate my face?" he says bitterly. "Do you know how many times I've put a razor to my eye and thought about using it? But I always had Cinder to keep me sane. Cinder needed me. If I ruined my face, I would lose my position, and with it, the money for her medicine. I've seen it happen many times. Do you know what the suicide rate is for companions? No one does, because it's not talked about. Because who cares, right? But I have known six boys who have taken their own lives—and those are only the ones I've known personally. The ones who don't kill themselves cut their bodies, but not in places you could see—usually behind the knees or between the toes. Or they dope themselves with opiates, until their addiction is noticeable and then they're Marked and tossed out onto the streets. Some develop violent predilections for sex, abusing the House Girls or consorting with common prostitutes. And for every friend you make, you lose three, and it doesn't matter how, and it doesn't matter why, because there are always new boys being brought in, and you're just one in a hundred, as disposable as the latest fashion trend." He looks at me with a viciousness I've never seen before. "So *that's* how it was in the companion house."

I am speechless. I want to arrange my face into some kind of calm or understanding expression, but I can't make my muscles work. I assumed the companion house would be similar to Southgate. But drugs? Violent sex? Suicide? "That's not who you are, though," I say.

"That IS who I am!" Ash shouts. Raven wakes up with a start. "You *don't* want to know about this, Violet."

"Please don't fight," Raven says, holding her head in her hands.

"We're not," I reassure her. "Ash and I were . . . talking."

Raven's presence has calmed Ash down.

"I'm so sorry," he says to her. "I didn't mean to wake you."

"You don't want to go back to that place," Raven says, rubbing her eyes. "You're frightened."

There is a stunned silence. Raven turns to me, her eyes focused on something far away.

"He loves you, do you see that? He loves you and he hates himself and he'll never, never be good enough, not for you or his family or anyone. He was stolen, taken away and twisted, and everything that was pure inside him was left to rot and decay. He's ashamed." She returns to the present and looks at Ash. "We all have things we are ashamed of."

Ash's lips are parted, his eyes wide. "How did you—"

The door to the warehouse slides open and we all jump.

"Got it," Garnet says, dropping a large canvas sack onto the floor and shutting the door. "Everything you asked for is in there." He takes in the room, me and Raven on the floor, Ash standing over us with a shocked expression. "Am I interrupting something?"

"No," I say, getting to my feet.

"Then get changed and get going," Garnet says. "I told Lucien and he's pretty—"

The arcana starts to buzz. I rip it out of my bun as Lucien starts speaking.

"I don't like this plan," he says.

"I don't like it, either, Lucien, but it's not like there are a variety of other choices. You want me safe and in the Farm? This is our best bet."

"I still don't like it."

I throw my hands up. "Well, you do plenty of things I don't like," I say. "But I trust you. You have to trust me."

"I do. It's *him* I don't trust."

"If you're referring to Ash, you can trust him, too."

"Violet, once you're on the grounds of the companion house, I can't help you. You'll be totally on your own."

I glance at Raven, then Ash. "No," I say. "I won't."

"You know what I mean."

I sigh. "I do. And I don't want to argue with you, Lucien. I'm trying to do what you wanted me to. I'm trying to survive."

There is a pause. "I know, honey," he says wearily.

"What's happening in the Jewel?" I ask. "Is there anything we should know about?"

I can almost hear Lucien smile. "Well," he says. "The Duchess is enjoying an unusual upswing in popularity. It seems your rape"—I wince at the word—"and the companion's evasion of capture have painted a very sympathetic picture. Everyone wants an audience with her."

"What happened to . . ." My throat tightens as I picture my bedroom, the last time I saw it. "To Annabelle?"

"I don't know," Lucien says. "She was most likely cremated at the morgue. Nothing has been said about it in the servant circles. Except to show sympathy for Cora, of course."

I frown. "Why Cora?"

"Didn't you know?" Lucien says. "Cora was Anna-belle's mother."

"What?" I gasp. I'd never considered who Annabelle's family might be. I feel ashamed that I never thought to ask. I try to think whether I'd ever seen Cora act in any way motherly toward Annabelle. But in all my memories, she was always ordering her around like any other servant.

I wonder how she can stand to live there, to serve the woman who killed her daughter.

"I have to go," Lucien says suddenly.

The arcana goes silent and falls. I hold out my hand in time to catch it.

Raven is staring at the space where it once hovered, awestruck.

"Was that . . . real?" she says.

"Yes," I say firmly. "But now we have to change our clothes."

Ash has already riffled through the sack and is holding some fabric in his hands.

"Violet," he begins, but I shake my head.

"It's fine," I say.

"It's not," he says. "I shouldn't have—I didn't mean to yell."

"I know." The companion house sounds about a hun-dred times worse than Southgate. I wouldn't want to go back to it either. But this isn't the time for arguments or apologies.

Ash nods and holds out the canvas bag.

~ Ten ~

RAVEN AND I GO TO THE BACK OF THE WAREHOUSE FOR some privacy.

I open the canvas sack—a swirl of bright colors, frothy foams of lace, and the sheen of satin are all jumbled together. I dump out the contents of the bag and sort through it. There doesn't seem to be enough fabric. Though I suppose that's the point.

"All right," I say to Raven with forced cheerfulness, holding up two pairs of stockings. "Which color do you want—red or pink?"

She shrugs, and I hand her the red stockings. She pulls off the brown servant's dress and I see a welt the size of my fist at the base of her spine, bluish-red veins radiating out of it.

"Oh, Raven," I gasp. Raven puts a hand to the welt, covering it, like she's embarrassed.

"The needles were worse," she mumbles as she yanks the stockings up and touches her scalp with her fingers.

The dresses are more like undergarments. Flimsy lace skirts and corsets that leave our arms and shoulders bare. Raven is so thin the corset is loose on her, but mine is extremely tight, revealing much more flesh than I'm comfortable with. I wish I had a scarf or something.

There's some makeup in the bag, lipstick in a garish shade of red, blush for our cheeks, and black liner for our eyes. We put it on each other, though neither of us have much training or skill in this particular area.

"All right," I say, shoving our old clothes into the sack. "Let's go."

The looks on Ash's and Garnet's faces when we emerge from the back of the warehouse are both flattering and uncomfortable. At least with Ash, I know it's nothing he hasn't seen; Garnet is an entirely different story. And he stares at Raven like he's never seen her before. With the makeup on, she doesn't look as drawn, and you can definitely see hints of her old beauty. Her skin is noticeably healthier, the caramel tint a nice contrast with the ivory satin corset.

Raven notices him staring. "What?" she says aggressively.

He looks away quickly. "You better get going," he says to Ash.

Ash has also changed into an outfit similar to the one he wore the first day I met him—beige pants and a white collared shirt, with a long overcoat. I wonder if that's the standard companion uniform.

"You're going to want to keep close to me," Ash says. "It's pretty cold."

"I suppose we don't get coats," I say.

Ash flashes me a half smile. "Covering up would be a bit beside the point."

I'm not worried about myself, but Raven is so exposed...

Even as I think it, she shoots me a look. "I'll be fine," she says.

"I hope this works," Garnet says.

"You and me both," Ash replies.

Garnet looks at each of us, opens his mouth, closes it, then runs his hand through his hair. "Yeah, well . . . good luck."

He turns and leaves the warehouse.

"Ready?" Ash says.

"Wait," I say. "Your face is everywhere in this circle. What if . . ." I've never performed an Augury on a person before, but I don't have the luxury of doubt right now. I reach up and wrap my hand around a fistful of his hair.

"What are—" Ash starts to ask, but I'm already focusing on the Augury.

Once to see it as it is. Twice to see it in your mind. Thrice to bend it to your will.

Shoots of blond spread out from my fingertips, changing Ash's hair from brown to gold. My head throbs.

"There," I say, rubbing my left temple. "Maybe that will

help a bit. We don't need you getting recognized again."

Ash musses his hair and pulls his hand back to look at it, as if maybe the color had come off. "Wow," he says.

We leave the warehouse and keep to smaller, darkened streets, receiving only a few disapproving glances. Most of the neighborhood is deserted. It must be nearly midnight. The air is frigid—within seconds my teeth start chattering. Ash wraps his arm around my shoulders.

We walk for about twenty minutes before we come to what is unquestionably the shabbiest part of the Bank I've seen yet. All the buildings are old and decrepit, with sagging porches and boarded-up windows.

"All right," Ash says. "Just . . . both of you put your arms around me. And it wouldn't hurt to pretend we're all drunk."

I can't help thinking a glass of wine—or two, or twelve—wouldn't have been a bad idea. This whole street screams danger. Raven drapes her arm across Ash's shoulders and I slide my arm around his waist.

Only one block in, we come upon the first tavern. Then another. And another. Loud music—fiddles and a banjo and drums—pours out onto the street when the doors to one abruptly bang open, two men wrestling with each other, throwing punches, getting knocked to the ground. It reminds me too much of how my father died. I tighten my hold on Ash and we pick up our pace.

We pass a trio of men who are visibly intoxicated. They whistle at me and Raven. One of them approaches Ash and says, "You interested in sharing? I got some prime blue, if you want to make it a party."

"Piss off," Ash snaps. "Get your own slag."

"Ash," I hiss once the men have grumbled and shrugged and walked off. "Really."

Ash laughs once, a hollow sound. "Welcome to my world."

We turn down another street and I'm immediately assaulted by a wave of scent—a strong, flowery perfume that doesn't quite hide the smell of something slightly sour underneath.

"Hey, handsome," a young girl, no older than fourteen, calls from in front of a garishly painted pink-and-yellow house. She's wearing less clothing than Raven and I. "Want another date?"

"Piss off," I shout.

She shrugs and lights a cigarette.

"Very convincing," Ash whispers into my neck.

"This place is awful," I whisper back.

"It's called the Row," he says. "The East Quarter's number-one destination for sex and drugs."

"Is that what blue is?" I ask.

He nods. "A form of opiate. The liquid has a bluish tinge, hence the nickname."

We pass three brothels and a couple more taverns before we finally reach the end of the Row. The change is disturbingly sudden—one second, we're surrounded by seedy buildings, the next, we've emerged into a neat little park, lit with gas lamps. A clock tower across the square tells me it's after midnight. A couple sits on a bench nearby and a man is walking his dog a few yards away, but other than that, the streets are deserted.

"Almost there," Ash mutters. We cross the park quickly.

The man with the dog sees us and shakes his head, muttering to himself.

When we reach the opposite side, Ash grabs my arm.

"Stop," he says.

A wall stretches out along the entire length of the street, topped with tiny spikes. It reminds me of Southgate, how enclosed it was, like a fortress in the middle of the Marsh.

Two Regimentals are patrolling outside of it. My heart leaps to my throat.

"Kiss me," Ash murmurs. I press my mouth to his, for the first time not thinking about his lips or his body against mine, only aware of his heart hammering in time with my own. I listen for a shout or an alarm to be raised.

Finally, he pulls away. I turn and see the backs of the Regimentals as they round the corner. "Let's go. Quickly."

Raven and I hurry along behind him as he crosses the street, running his hand along the rough stone. He stops abruptly. "Here," he says.

I only see more wall. Ash grips something and pulls, and a piece of stone breaks away, revealing a large black combination lock.

"Do you know the combination?" I whisper.

Ash stares at the lock. Several seconds pass. I'm about to remind him that we're pressed for time, when he begins to turn it, first right, then left, then right again.

The lock clicks.

Ash yanks open a door, completely disguised within the wall.

"Get in," he hisses. I go first, pulling Raven in after me. Ash closes the hidden door behind us.

I turn and pull up short. The companion house isn't quite what I was expecting. Six short redbrick buildings are scattered around a large green lawn. Winding gravel roads weave through them, and there's a pond to my left that's beginning to freeze over, surrounded by little copses of trees. Gas lamps are set at intervals throughout the grounds.

It's actually very pretty.

"The station is on the other side," Ash whispers. "This way."

We follow him down one of the roads, gravel crunching under our feet, the heels of my shoes wobbling. Everything is still and shadowy.

Suddenly, the back door of one of the houses opens, freezing us in our tracks, as a figure steps out onto the path in front of us. There is the scratchy sound of a match being lit, then the end of a cigarette flames up like a tiny ember. The figure sees us and laughs.

"Been out to the Row again, Till?" he says. His voice is deep. "Madame's out but Billings is on patrol. You better get them inside quick."

"Rye?" Ash says, moving forward. The figure steps toward us into the dim light. He's a young man about Ash's age, but taller, with dark skin that reminds me of the lioness. Tight black curls frame a very handsome face with broad features. His eyes, like chips of flint, are wide with surprise.

"Ash?" he says. "What—how—what are you *doing* here? The whole city's looking for you! And what's with your hair?" He glances from me to Raven. "This is a pretty strange time to start experimenting with working girls."

"They're not working girls," Ash says. "We need to get to the train."

"The train's gone," the boy named Rye replies, frowning. "It's in the Smoke."

My heart sinks. *What do we do now?*

"Will you help us?" Ash says. "We need to hide. Until the train gets back."

Rye takes what I feel to be an inordinate amount of time before answering. He takes a long drag of his cigarette and exhales a thick stream of smoke. Then he flicks the cigarette into the darkness. "Sure, man, I'll help you out. You're going to have to tell me how you escaped from Landing's Market with about a thousand Regimentals crawling all over the place. Come on."

We follow Rye inside, to a hall that smells like dried flowers and wood smoke, then up a flight of stairs and down another hall. My body is tense, my nerves coiled up like watch springs. I don't know who this boy is, but I'll trust him if Ash does. But there are so many other boys living in this place. I felt much safer at the warehouse.

Rye opens a door, switches on a light, and ushers us inside.

We walk into a very large, very pleasant bedroom. Two beds are pushed against opposite walls. The décor is all white with gold accents. A striped couch and matching armchair are clustered together by the one large window. But the most dominant features of the room are the enormous gilt-framed mirrors that hang over two vanities, if a vanity is something one could find in a boy's dormitory.

One bed is pristine, its owner's vanity boasting a neat

array of jars and bottles and combs. The other bed is unmade, with various articles of clothing strewn over the blankets, and its vanity is a mess, open jars and spilled face creams and a scattering of little orange pills.

"Home, sweet home," Ash mutters as he looks around.

"Is this *your* room?" I ask. Raven hovers by the door, as if uncertain about this place.

"Rye and I are—were roommates," Ash says. His expression abruptly changes, and I follow his gaze to the neater vanity. He walks to it as if in a dream and picks up a silver-framed photo. Clutching it in both hands, he sinks onto the bed.

"Is that . . ." I sit beside him and stare at the photograph. "Is that your family?"

Ash nods. The photo is black-and-white, taken in front of a very shabby-looking house. A broad, imposing man with Ash's nose has his arms around two stocky boys, both of whom are grinning at the camera with Garnet-worthy expressions of mischief. A woman stands beside them, and she looks so very much like Ash it's startling. She has both her hands on a little girl's shoulders. The girl has a wild tumble of curly hair and the biggest smile I've ever seen. Though they look nothing alike, she makes me think of Hazel.

"Is that Cinder?" I ask. Ash nods again. "She's lovely," I say. "Where are you?"

He clears his throat. "I took the picture. One of our neighbors had bought a photographic camera. He showed me how to use it."

He turns the frame over and removes the back. Very carefully, he takes out the picture, folds it in half, and puts it in his pocket, leaving the empty frame on the vanity.

"So," Rye says, bursting our bubble of privacy. "Care to explain exactly what in the Exetor's name you're doing here? And who these girls are?"

Raven shoots him a glare. He has flopped onto his bed and is unscrewing the cap on a little vial. The liquid inside is tinged blue.

Ash sighs. "Since when did you start using?"

Rye shrugs and removes a thin tube of glass from the vial. He tilts his head back and shakes a drop from the tube into each eye.

"You don't even want to know what I had to do for my last client," he says, blinking and wiping the excess liquid from where it's spilled down his cheeks. "I need this." He laughs, a heady, relaxed sound. "Better hope you never get assigned to the House of the Downs. That woman has some *very* strange appetites."

I remember the Lady of the Downs from Garnet's engagement party. She seemed like any other royal woman. I don't want to think about what she does behind closed doors.

"She went through about six companions before her daughter finally got engaged," Rye continues. "Bale was the last one. I think he's still recovering—he hasn't had a client since he got back. Neither have I, for that matter. Not that I'm complaining." He laughs again. "I guess that's not a problem for you anymore, is it? No more clients." He leans back against his pillow and sighs. "Remember the Lady of the Stream? We both had her, right? She was something else."

"He doesn't do that anymore," I say.

Rye chuckles. "What are you, his girlfriend?"

"We need to get on the train," Ash says. "And we can't hide in this room waiting for it to come back."

"You can't go anywhere now, brother, all the buildings are locked," Rye says. "Might as well stay here for the night."

"This place is rotten," Raven says. "I don't like it here."

"We'll leave soon," I say.

She moves to stand in front of one of the mirrors, staring at her reflection. "I let them take your eyes away," she says to me. "Pluck them out like little jewels and offer them to me as gifts. They made me choose and I chose wrong, always, every time." Raven strikes her fist against her temple twice before I grab her wrist to stop her.

"I am Raven Stirling," she mutters. "I am looking in a mirror. I am real. I am stronger than this."

"Okay, Ash, you've got to explain," Rye says, staring at me and Raven with a mingled look of incredulity and suspicion. "What. Happened. All we hear is that you raped some *surrogate* and—"

"He didn't rape anyone," I snap.

Rye's eyes widen. "No," he says to Ash. "You're not saying . . . *she's* the surrogate?" All the hazy laughter in him vanishes as he jumps off the bed, his expression deadly serious. "They need to get out. Now. I'll help you, but I'm not risking my life for some surrogate. Are you crazy? Do you know what—"

"I love her," Ash says. He makes a gesture with his palms open, like he's offering his words in surrender. "I fell in love with her, Rye."

Rye runs a hand through his black curls. He sits on the

edge of his bed and rests his chin on his hands. He looks from me to Ash and back again. I feel ridiculous in this stupid outfit. I wish I could unzip my skin and show him the place inside me where Ash lives, tangled up in blood and bone and muscle, impossible to separate or remove. I want him to see that we are the same.

"Prove it," Rye says, as if in response to my thought.

"We got caught together," Ash says. "That's what really happened. You know me. Do you honestly think I'd force myself on a surrogate? Do you think I'd even look at a surrogate? I was *very* good at my job. She . . ." He smiles my favorite, secret smile. "She took me by surprise. But once I allowed myself to love her, I couldn't take it back."

"So you risked execution for her?" Rye asks.

"I did."

"You risked *Cinder's* life for her, too, then," he says.

Ash's jaw tightens. "I know."

For some reason, this thought had never occurred to me. Cinder's life is wrapped up in Ash's profession.

I am dumbstruck. He knew. He knew and he loved me anyway. My stomach squirms with guilt.

Rye chews on his lower lip, mulling over Ash's words, then shakes his head. "Get some sleep. We'll figure it out in the morning."

He glances back at me with a wondering look, as if I were something out of a fairy story, like the water spirit from *The Wishing Well*—something that doesn't exist in real life. Then he pulls off his sweater in one fluid movement. His dark skin is smooth over a very muscular chest and heat flames in my cheeks. In my peripheral vision, I see Ash roll his eyes.

"Good night, Rye," he says.

Rye flashes a grin at me. "Unless you want me to find you some X," he says to Ash.

"*Good night*, Rye," Ash says again.

"What's X?" I ask as Raven and I head to the bathroom to wash the makeup off our faces. "Another drug?"

Ash's face flushes. "Black-market contraceptive."

I gasp. "What?" Contraception is outlawed in the Lone City. Everyone knows that.

Ash starts opening the drawers of his dresser, pulling out bedclothes, and keeping his face turned away from me. "There's a serum that can cause a man to be infertile for several hours. However, it's quite unpleasant to use, and if caught with it, the sentence is death."

"Why is it unpleasant to use?" I ask as he hands me an oversize cotton shirt.

He winces. "You have to inject it into a very sensitive area."

"Oh," I say, my eyes widening.

By the time we are washed and changed into the make-shift pajamas, Rye is snoring lightly.

"You two take the bed," Ash says. "I'll sleep on the couch."

I help Raven under the covers and turn to him.

"Cinder," I say, "I didn't even think . . . what will happen to her?"

He pauses, looking down. "I don't know."

"Isn't there . . . can't we do something? Help her some-how?"

He barks out a laugh. "Violet, we can't even help our-selves."

He's right. I struggle for something to say, words of comfort or inspiration, but there's nothing. Saying I'm sorry isn't enough. And saying I wish this hadn't happened is a lie.

Ash misreads my expression. "We'll figure it out," he says, running his hands down my arms. "Rye will help us."

"And you're sure we can trust him?" I ask.

"I trust Lucien on your say-so," Ash snaps. "Can't you trust Rye on mine?"

"Of course," I say, trying to keep the hurt out of my voice.

He sighs. "Let's try to get some sleep for now. We all need it."

As I crawl under the covers, Raven leans her cheek against my shoulder. My head sinks into the pillow, and it's been so long since I've slept in an actual bed that I'm asleep in moments.

~ Eleven ~

I WAKE UP SOMETIME IN THE EARLY HOURS OF THE MORN-
ing, to the sound of murmured voices.

". . . was an accident," Ash is saying. "She wasn't even
supposed to be in that wing of the palace."

"So when did you know?" Rye asks.

"I'm not sure," Ash says. "It's hard to explain. But once
I saw her, I couldn't . . . *unsee* her. If that makes sense.
We don't look at them, you know? The surrogates. But
suddenly, she was a person, this smart, beautiful girl who
was treated so badly. You should hear her play the cello,
Rye—it's like being transported to another world. She made
me feel human again. She made me want things I thought
weren't meant for me."

"It must make a nice change, being with someone your own age who isn't a House Girl," Rye snorts.

"Don't be glib," Ash says. "It doesn't suit you."

"You haven't seen me in months," Rye retorts. "You don't know what suits me now."

"Dosing yourself with blue? Is that who you are?"

There's a heavy sigh and the creaking of a mattress. "I couldn't hold out anymore. Emory's dead. Miles is so strung out he's about to be Marked and tossed out on the streets. Jig is dead. Trac is starting to cut where it shows. Birch is about to age out. You're a fugitive. Who do I have left?"

There's a long silence.

"Emory's dead?" Ash says.

"Yeah."

"But he was always so—"

"I know." Rye's voice is hard.

"I didn't mean to leave you like this," Ash says.

"Don't start acting like you're responsible for everyone's problems. I make my own choices. So do you."

"None of us chose to be companions, Rye."

"Sure we did."

"Being lied to or bribed or coerced doesn't qualify as making a choice. If you knew what being a companion actually entailed, would you do it?"

"I had to," Rye says. "You know better than anyone. My family needed the money."

"Exactly. They didn't give us any other option."

"I don't see the point in thinking like that."

"Neither did I. Violet changed that for me. Surrogates

don't have an option, either. And yet, I treated them like furniture, like accessories. I didn't see them as people. I was as bad as the royalty I hated so much." He sighs. "I don't want to be like them anymore. I won't."

"So where are you going, exactly?" Rye asks, after a pause. "Do you honestly think there's any place in any circle of the entire Lone City where the royalty can't find you? And not any member of the royalty, but a Founding House? You should've fallen in love with a third-tier surrogate."

I can practically hear Ash's eyes roll. "We have some . . . help. From someone who can be trusted, even if I don't like him."

Rye chuckles. "Jealous of another man?"

"Hardly," Ash says, but there's something off in his tone that makes me think he's lying. That's strange. Why would Ash be jealous of Lucien?

"You know," Rye says, "it's weird that your escape is all over the papers, but a surrogate escaped and there hasn't been a word about it. No gossip, no whispers, no nothing. You're the hot topic, but your girlfriend . . . I mean, wouldn't *that* really be a big story?"

"I've thought about that," Ash says. "The Duchess is an incredibly smart, ambitious woman. If she hasn't revealed Violet's absence to the Jewel, she must have a reason."

At that moment, Raven sits bolt upright, making everyone in the room jump.

"Someone's coming," she hisses.

Ash is on his feet in an instant.

"Get in the bathroom," he says. Raven and I untangle ourselves from the covers and run, leaving Ash to remake the bed as fast as he can. Rye watches all of this with a confused expression.

"What's happening?" he asks.

"If Raven says someone's coming, someone's coming," Ash says. He finishes with the bed and hurries to join us in the bathroom. "We're not here," he warns Rye and slams the door shut.

Raven is curled up in the bathtub, hugging her knees. I perch on the edge of the tub. Ash stays pressed against the bathroom door. He puts his finger to his lips and I nod as he turns off the light.

We hear the door to the bedroom open and the sounds of Rye scrambling out of bed.

"Good morning, Madame."

"Good morning, Mr. Whitfield." The voice is like a honey-covered blade—sharp and sweet all at once. Ash sinks to the floor, holding his head in his hands. I can't help myself—I shift to kneel by the door beside him and press my eye against the keyhole.

For a moment, I see nothing but Rye's messy vanity and the striped sofa by the window. Then a woman sweeps into view and reclines on the sofa, directly in my line of sight.

It's impossible to tell how old she is—she wears a lot of makeup, and though she wears it well, I have the distinct impression her face has been altered, her skin tightened to remove wrinkles. Her eyes are slightly feline. Her body is wrapped in satin, and pearls drip from her neck and ears. She is large, but not disgustingly fleshy like the Countess of the Stone—Madame Curio is all curves, large breasts and wide hips. She has the air of someone who has seen a lot of life.

"Have you fully recovered from the Lady of the Downs's service, Mr. Whitfield?" she asks. "I know she requires quite a bit of endurance."

"It was a pleasure, Madame. I am quite well, thank you."

I can't see Rye, but if I didn't know better, I'd absolutely believe him. Madame Curio smiles.

"I'm glad to hear it. I have a new client for you. You've been particularly requested in fact."

"I am honored, Madame. Who might the young lady be?"

Madame Curio's smile widens. "Carnelian Silver, of the House of the Lake."

My heart skips a beat. Madame Curio traces a finger down her cheek, eyeing Rye thoughtfully. "The Duchess asked for you personally. A Founding House. It's very impressive. Let us hope you don't ruin this opportunity like your former roommate did."

"Of course not, Madame."

"I won't have it said that my house breeds surrogate rapists and fugitives from the law."

"No, Madame. I am eager to meet Miss Silver. I'm certain our time together will be most enjoyable."

Madame Curio purses her lips. "Come here."

It's like my eye is glued to the keyhole. I want to look away, but I can't. I feel Ash tense beside me.

Rye comes into view, still shirtless. The muscles in his back ripple when he moves. Madame Curio sits up and runs a hand over his chest.

"Very nice," she says. Her hand travels farther down.

"Hmm," she murmurs after a couple seconds. "You will come to my room this evening at six. Let's make sure you're up for the assignment."

"Yes, Madame."

"And you'll report to Dr. Lane this afternoon for the usual tests."

"Of course, Madame."

Madame Curio stands in a movement so fluid, it reminds me of the Duchess. She moves like royalty.

"Good boy," she says, patting his cheek. Then she walks out of my line of sight. I hear the door open and close. Rye stands still for a moment, then marches over to the bathroom. I scoot back as he throws the door open.

"So," he says. "I guess I'm your replacement."

"She knows," Ash says, looking up with a pained expression. "She knows you're connected to me, somehow. She's doing this to find me. To find Violet."

"It's not like I can tell her anything," Rye points out. "I don't know where you're going."

"But you've seen us," Ash says. "Together. And Raven."

Raven's head snaps up. "You can't tell her," she says. "She can't know I'm alive."

"Can everyone back off for a second?" Rye says. "I didn't ask for this. I didn't need you to come running into my life and messing it up."

Ash gets to his feet. "You're right. Tell her, don't tell her, it's up to you. But she's asked for you for a reason. I don't know how or when, but at some point, she will interrogate you about me."

A smile curls on Rye's lips. "Always top of the class,

weren't you? The Jewel's most-wanted." He shakes his head. "Come on, let's get you guys someplace safer than this room. Everyone should be down at breakfast by now."

Raven climbs out of the tub and walks with deliberate steps toward Rye. She grabs his wrist and fixes him with a sharp, piercing gaze.

"You're scared," she says. "That's good. You should be."

She drifts into the bedroom. Rye raises an eyebrow.

"I'm not scared," he says.

Ash and I exchange a look, but say nothing.

RYE CHECKS TO MAKE SURE THE COAST IS CLEAR, THEN the four of us hurry down the stairs and out the door we came in through last night.

The grounds are even prettier during the day. A dusting of frost makes the gravel roads twinkle like diamonds. We stocked up on sweaters and coats and scarves, so the cold isn't unpleasant, but Raven and I are both wearing a pair of Ash's shoes with extra socks stuffed into the toes so they'll fit. It makes walking a bit awkward.

We keep close to the walls of the dormitories, their windows following me like empty eyes. A larger building looms into view, one whole side covered with ivy. An impressive pair of oak doors are set at the top of a stone staircase.

And beyond it, on the very far side of the grounds near the wall that encircles them, a sleek black train sits at a long platform. It is even smaller than the one I took to the Auction, only one car attached to a steam engine. Billows of smoke rise from its chimney, as if it were getting ready to depart.

"It's here," Ash says.

"That's odd. Maybe there was a last-minute schedule change. Guess fate is on your side, for the moment," Rye says. "There's no way it's going to the Jewel—my train won't leave until tomorrow, after the doctor and Madame have finished with me. It has to be going to the lower circles." He claps a hand on Ash's shoulder. "You'd better get on it, while everyone is still at breakfast."

My stomach grumbles at the thought of food.

"Thank you, Rye," Ash says, shaking his hand. "Seriously. I don't know what we would have done without you."

"Probably gotten executed," Rye says, with a shrug and a grin. "So you owe me one."

"I do," Ash says, no hint of amusement in his voice. "Watch out for yourself in the palace of the Lake. Please. You don't need to worry about the client—she isn't interested in companions. But never, under any circumstances, tell Carnelian that you know me. She'll probably ask. You need to lie."

"Well, won't that make for a nice change," Rye says.

Ash's smile is taut. "I'm sorry."

"Stop saying that," Rye says. "This isn't your fault. Stop acting like you bear the weight of all companions. You don't."

"I know."

"And take care of yourself," he adds.

"I will."

"Thank you," I say to Rye. He gives me a nod.

"You know," he says, "I don't think I've ever heard a surrogate talk before."

I'm not entirely sure what to say to that. With a final glance at Ash, Rye takes off across the grounds.

The three of us turn and run toward the station. As we get closer, I see a painted wooden sign that reads MADAME CURIO'S COMPANION HOUSE. There's a little station house beside the sign, and Raven grabs my arm and pulls me beside it, Ash following. We've both learned quickly to trust her instincts. A few moments later, two Regimentals emerge from the train and saunter out onto the platform.

"All clear," one says to the other.

"He'd have to be a total fool to come back here anyway," the second Regimental says, as the two of them descend the steps to the platform and walk toward the grounds. The three of us press together against the rough wood of the house.

"I don't see why we have to be working double shifts to find some companion," the first grumbles. "It's not like he raped the Duchess herself."

"Don't let the Major hear you talk like that," the second one says. "You'll be shipped off to serve in the Marsh before you can say Founding House."

"Yeah, yeah," the first says. "Let's go see if the kitchen's open, I'm starving."

We wait until well after their footsteps have faded and quiet settles all around.

"Come on," Ash whispers. We hurry up the stairs and onto the platform. Ash opens the door to the train car and ushers us inside.

Unlike the Southgate train, the companion car has neat rows of wooden seats all facing the same direction. Curtains hang in the windows and the aisle is carpeted in green.

"Where are we supposed to hide?" I ask.

Ash stops at the third row.

"Here," he says. He bends downs and I hear a click. The entire row of seats lifts up, revealing a long rectangular hole. "You two get in this one. There's another compartment under the sixth row. I'll hide there. Hopefully whoever is leaving on this train is leaving soon."

"And hopefully they're going to the Farm," I add. I look down at the hole and shudder. It eerily resembles an open grave.

"I think I prefer the trunk of Garnet's car," I say.

"At least it's not the morgue," Ash says.

I step down into the hole—it's a little deeper than I expected. I reach my hand up for Raven. Her face is pale as she looks down at the empty space. Even her lips are white.

"Promise me, Violet," she says, "that if I get in there, I'm getting out again."

"I promise," I say.

She takes my hand and I help her inside. We both lie down—there's a surprising amount of room.

Ash looks at us with a pained expression. "Keep as quiet and still as you can. I'll come get you when we get to . . . wherever we're going."

There's nothing else to say or do except cling to the frail hope that this will work. He closes the seats over us, and Raven and I are plunged into darkness.

After a while, my eyes begin to adjust. Gray light creeps in through the wooden slats above us.

"Violet?" Raven whispers.

"Yes?"

"Do you think that this place we're going to in the Farm . . . do you think there's someone there who can fix me?"

The outline of her face is soft, almost blurred. I want to tell her she's not broken. I want to tell her there must be a way to undo what the Countess did. But I can't lie to her.

Her mouth pulls up into a sad smile. "That's what I thought." She wraps a piece of her hair around her finger. "Emile told me I was the strongest of all the surrogates he'd ever seen. I was the only one who survived being impregnated." Her other hand slides to her stomach.

"Emile, he was your lady-in-waiting?" I ask. She nods. "Well, he was right. You're the strongest person I know. And besides, Lucien's a genius—maybe he can figure out how to help."

"He must care about you very much."

"I remind him of someone he used to know," I say. "His sister. She was a surrogate. She died."

We're quiet for a while.

"Did his sister die giving birth?" Raven asks.

"I don't know, actually," I say. I think back to the Longest Night ball, when Lucien caught Ash and me together, when he told me the truth about the surrogates. His words echo in my mind.

I had a sister. Azalea. She was a surrogate. I tried to help her, tried to save her life, and for a while, I succeeded. Until one day, I failed.

He never told me exactly what happened.

"I'm going to die if I have this baby, aren't I?" Raven says quietly.

A knot of fear hardens in my throat.

"Yes," I say.

"Yes," Raven repeats. "I can tell. I can feel it."

I haven't let myself think about it, about the death sentence Raven carries inside her. I wrap my arms around my torso as if that would somehow keep me from falling apart.

At that moment, we hear a click and the door to the train car opens.

Raven and I freeze. Footsteps and voices fill the air above us.

"Far too early for this," a man says. His words are clipped and his voice has the subtle confidence of someone who is well educated.

"I've brought some coffee, sir," a younger voice replies.

"Excellent."

"And here's your paper."

Wood creaks as someone sits. The rustle of newspaper is accompanied by the sound and smell of coffee being poured.

"Ghastly business," the man says. "Madame Curio was devastated when she heard. I must admit, I was shocked as well. Ash Lockwood, a surrogate rapist? I trained that young man myself. He was an exceptional companion. One of the best."

"Maybe this is a misunderstanding, Mr. Billings," the boy says.

There's a loud whistle, and with a lurch, the train begins to move.

"Nonsense," Mr. Billings says. "We do not question the testimony of a Founding House."

"Yes, sir. Of course, sir." There's a pause. "Do you think

Mr. Lockwood's family will be amenable to the deal? I mean to say, are you sure he'll go back to them?"

I can hear Raven's heart thudding in time with my own.

"Well, for goodness' sake, Red, where else is he going to go? I can't imagine how he's evaded detection this long—with the exception of Landing's Market, of course, and what a disaster that was. No, he'll have to return home soon. And from what I've gathered of his father's character, Lockwood Senior will be happy to turn in a troublesome son to save a dying daughter."

Cinder.

I think of Ash, alone in a compartment somewhere nearby. He obviously knows this Mr. Billings. I wonder if he knows the boy, Red, too. From the little I know about Ash's father, Mr. Billings's assessment sounds accurate.

But Ash isn't going home.

And Cinder is dying.

Mr. Billings must be very involved in his paper, because there's nothing but silence for a long time. My muscles ache from the constant, unceasing tension. Raven and I are both too afraid to move, and my back and shoulders begin to cramp. The train chugs along at a steady speed, only slowing to a halt when we reach the massive iron doors separating the Bank and the Smoke. I can hear them groaning open. The heavy tread of Regimental boots entering the train carriage nearly stops my heart.

"Morning, sir," a deep-voiced Regimental says.

"Good morning," Mr. Billings says.

There's the scratching sound of a pen. "Going to the Smoke?"

"That's right."

"Just you and this young man, is that correct?"

"Yes. And this train was searched by your colleagues before it left the companion house."

Footsteps march up and down the aisle, passing the spot where Raven and I lie hunched together. Neither of us dares to breathe.

"Very good, sir," the Regimental says. The train door closes.

I exhale in a giant whoosh as the train rolls forward, picking up steam.

We've made it into the Smoke. Only one more circle to go.

~ Twelve ~

BY THE TIME THE TRAIN SLOWS DOWN, MY NERVES ARE fried.

Every muscle in my body is in agony, and there's a constant throbbing at the base of my skull, like an Augury headache.

"We're here, sir," Red says, his footsteps making the wood creak over our heads as he walks to the front of the car.

"Yes, I can see that. Take my briefcase, please. The coach should be waiting for us. I do wish we could have used the main terminal; it's so much closer, but the traffic will be a nightmare this time of day. I'm hoping we'll be back to the Bank before lunchtime—the Smoke always gives me such a terrible cough. You brought the lozenges?"

I don't hear Red's response. Back to the Bank? But what about the Farm?

The two men depart the train. Neither Raven nor I move.

"What do we do?" I whisper.

With a groan, the roof of our hiding place wrenches open. The light hurts my eyes, and I blink until they adjust and I can see Ash's figure looming above me.

His face is like stone, his eyes blazing. He reaches a hand out—I take it and he yanks me up and out of the compartment without a word. My legs give out, and I crumple to the floor, rubbing life back into my limbs and cringing at the invisible needles that stab my muscles as blood flows back into them. Raven collapses beside me.

"What do we do?" I say again. "This train isn't going to the Farm."

"Maybe we can hide in the station," Raven suggests. "Wait for another train."

"He's killing her." Ash's voice is as cold as his face. I've never seen him look like this. It scares me. "Do you know how much money I've sent to my family? There should be enough to buy Cinder medicine for at least the next few years."

"Do you think the royalty took it away?" I ask.

"No." Ash balls his hands into fists. "I think my father did exactly what I was afraid he would do. He took all the money for himself."

Ash has never spoken much about his father. During one of those stolen afternoons we spent in his parlor, he told me they weren't close, but the way he said it implied something much deeper. Resentment. Anger. Hatred, even. He said his father preferred his twin brothers, Rip and Panel. That they were loud and rough while Ash was quiet and reserved.

Still, would Mr. Lockwood sacrifice his son for more money?

"Ash Lockwood?"

The sound of Ash's name freezes us all in place. A small, soot-covered face is poking in through the open door of the train.

"It *is* you! The Black Key said to keep an eye on all trains coming into the Smoke, but, wow, I didn't think you'd actually show up." So Lucien's secret society has members in the Smoke as well. "Nice move, changing your hair. How'd you get by the Regimentals?"

The boy who has now entered the train compartment is about twelve. He wears pants that are an inch too short for him and a coat that is nearly worn through at the elbows. I'd guess his skin is a shade darker than Raven's but it's hard to tell with all the smudges of ash and soot. His shaggy black hair is so long it falls into his eyes.

But he said the Black Key.

"Show me your key," I say.

The boy rolls up the sleeve of his coat to reveal a black skeleton key on the inside of his elbow, drawn onto the boy's skin with charcoal. "You're 197, right?"

"My name is Violet," I say. "Are you here to help us?"

"I sure am. You can call me the Thief," he says with a toothy grin. "The Black Key says fake names are safer. My real name's stupid, anyway, so I don't mind. Are you really gonna help bring down the royalty? The Black Key says you have some sort of power. Can I see it?"

I can't help smiling at his enthusiasm. "Not right now," I say.

"Right. Guess there are more important things to take care of." The Thief pushes his hair out of his eyes. "I've got to get you to the main terminal. We think we found a train that can take you to the Farm. But you can't go out looking like that. Wait here."

Before I can ask him anything else, he's gone.

"Who's Cinder?" Raven asks.

I explain quickly about Ash's sister.

"I understand," she says, looking up at him. "You want your Reckoning Day. You want to say good-bye."

"Ash," I say gently. "You can't . . . we can't see her."

"I know," he snaps. Then he sinks down onto one of the train seats. "I was supposed to be saving her. I failed."

"You did the best you could," I say. "You did the *only* thing you could."

"And if it was Hazel dying?" he says. "Would you believe me if I said you did the best you could?"

My gut twists at the thought of Hazel dying. "I don't know," I lie.

"Don't worry, Violet," he says. "I get it. I can't say good-bye to my sister or confront my father for being the selfish bastard he is. You'd think I'd be used to being told what to do all the time by now."

"I'm not telling you what to do," I say. "But even if you were to make it to your house, see your sister . . . it's suicide, Ash. Would Cinder want you to die, too?"

"Don't," he says fiercely. "Don't talk to me about what she would want. Not right now, when she's so close." He looks out the window of the train. "The last time I was here, they were taking me to the Bank. I remember thinking this train was the cleanest thing I'd ever seen. It practically sparkled. Nothing in the Smoke ever sparkles, except maybe the coal dust in winter."

Ash's face contorts, and for a moment I think he's going to cry. But then the Thief is back.

"All right—" He stops when he sees Ash's face. "Everything . . . okay?"

"His sister lives here," Raven says. "She's dying."

"Oh," the Thief says with a sympathetic look. "Black lung?"

Ash nods.

"My best friend died of black lung last year. He wasn't even working in the factories yet. Got it from breathing the air around here. And the royalty sure aren't gonna dole out medicine for an orphan kid. It isn't fair, you know? They keep us penned in like animals. You're born a street urchin in the Smoke and that's how you'll stay, no questions asked."

"Not always," Ash says.

"Did they ask you if you wanted to be a companion?" the Thief says.

Ash's mouth twitches. "No."

"Yeah. They just take and take."

"What did they take from you?"

The Thief shrugs. "My parents."

"I'm sorry," Ash says.

"I don't remember them. Anyway, we've got to get going. Put this on your faces," he says, holding out his hands. Cupped in them is a mound of black soot.

The soot is soft like powder, but as I rub it on my cheeks my nose wrinkles in reaction to the smell—like creosote and asphalt mixed together, harsh and sharp.

"Do you two have hats?" he asks me and Raven. We both produce woolen caps, taken from Ash's room at Madame Curio's. "Good. Hide your hair."

"How did the Black Key find you anyway?" I ask as I shove my bun with the arcana inside up under the hat.

"I'm the best pickpocket in this quarter of the Smoke," the Thief says with pride. "I stole something he wanted. He was pretty impressed."

"Have you met him?" I ask. It seems awfully risky for Lucien to reveal himself to so many people.

"Oh no," the Thief says. "No one's met the Black Key. He always communicates through letters or codes or other people. The Seamstress recruited me. She gives me food sometimes, too. There's never enough at the orphanage." He looks us up and down. "All right, let's go."

"I like him," Raven mutters to me as we leave the train.

"Keep your heads down and your shoulders hunched," Ash says. "We should fit right in."

I train my eyes on the worn wooden planks beneath me. Then stairs, one, two, three, four, five, six, seven, eight . . . The air is dense, like I could chew on it. It's also slightly acrid, tinged with the same flavor and smell as the soot on our faces and clothes. I can see what the Thief meant about contracting black lung simply from breathing the air. We hit the pavement and I can't help looking up, because we're swarmed with bodies—scuffed boots and frayed pants and sunken faces. Some of the faces have a black sheen to them, like ours, with tired eyes; others are cleaner, fresher, their workday just starting. It makes me think of my father, the late nights he worked in the Smoke, coming home in the early hours of the morning.

I remember this circle from my train ride to the Auction— the chimneys belching smoke in various shades of gray-greens, dull reds, murky purples, the dimness of the light, the streets teeming with people. But it was a passing moment, one small part of an immense journey. Being down here, among the people instead of on an elevated train track, is entirely different. I can smell the grease, hear the muttered conversations. People bump into me constantly, and it's a fight to keep close to Ash and Raven, or to keep the Thief in sight. He's particularly deft at navigating the crowds, weaving through them so easily that sometimes I lose track of him altogether.

The street we're on is very wide, made of chunky cobblestones, with a rail track set in its center. It's lined with factories, tall buildings with barred windows and chimneys rising up into the cloudy sky. We seem to be moving with the flow of traffic—every now and then workers peel off and head inside one of the iron behemoths, often with a lot of pushing and shoving.

There's a loud clanging and half the crowd halts, Ash

and the Thief included. I bump into Ash as Raven runs into me. There is a wooden signpost with the number 27 painted on it in red. And under the sign is a poster with Ash's face on it.

WANTED. FUGITIVE.

I glance around nervously but no one is looking at us. We're covered in soot anyway.

Clang. Clang. Clang.

A trolley comes rolling up the tracks toward us.

"East Quarter woodworks and ironworks!" a conductor shouts.

The trolley is by far the cleanest thing in the Smoke. It's painted a cheerful red that contrasts sharply with its occupants. The conductor wears a smart uniform and a black cap. Over the front of the trolley, a sign written in bold letters proclaims, TROLLEY NO. 27. And underneath that, in elegant script, A MARSHALING SERVICE FOR THE WORKERS OF THE SMOKE.

The Thief leads the way as Raven, Ash, and I clamber on board, holding on to the rungs that hang from the ceiling. The trolley car is packed, every seat filled, bodies pressing all around us. I doubt I'd even need to hold on to the rungs to stay standing. One woman keeps coughing into her handkerchief—I can see spots of red on the white fabric where blood has seeped through. No one gives us a second glance. No one looks at us, period. There is an overwhelming air of defeat in this car. I can smell it, thick and sour.

Is this how Ash grew up? Is this future so much worse than his life as a companion? Then I think about the Marsh, about the vile stink when it rains, the emaciated children, the filth in the streets. If Ash saw that, maybe he'd think I was better off in the Duchess's palace. But it's not the outside of these circles that count. They have hidden hearts, all of them.

Except maybe the Jewel.

The trolley clangs its way down the cobblestone street until the factories take on a distinctly different look. A series of squat, brick buildings with short chimneys belching thick black smoke line the road. I can barely make out the sign painted over the door of the one closest to us—PADMORE'S IRONWORKS. And underneath in smaller lettering: A SUBSIDIARY OF THE HOUSE OF THE FLAME.

"Padmore's, Rankworth's, Jetting's!" the conductor calls as the trolley slows. Workers begin to push their way off the trolley while more wait outside to board.

About ten minutes later, we stop again. The air is a little clearer here, the buildings made of light gray stone, taller than the ironwork factories, and with less smoke swirling through the air—or maybe the smoke is of a lighter hue. A sign hanging over one entrance reads: JOINDER'S WOODWORKS. A HOUSE OF THE STONE COMPANY.

"This is us," the Thief mutters, as the conductor shouts out, "Joinder's, Plane's, Shelding's!"

He hops off the trolley as the rest of us shuffle off with other workers, following a group heading to Joinder's. Instead of filing into the factory, though, the Thief veers off to the side, down a narrow alley that empties out onto a broad thoroughfare. A pair of Regimentals strolls down the opposite sidewalk, occasionally harassing some of the workers. Ash pops up the collar of his coat to better hide his face.

"We should go back," he says. "Take the alleys behind the factories. They'll take us right by the main terminal."

The Thief snorts. "You haven't lived here in a while. Those alleys have been boarded up. We have to take the Boulevard of the Stone to the Gray streets."

Raven tenses beside me. Ash opens his mouth to protest, but the Thief interrupts him.

"This is my quarter," he says confidently. "I know every inch of it. You're going to have to trust me."

Ash closes his mouth and nods.

The Boulevard of the Stone sends my heart hammering in my throat. Wanted posters are everywhere. On every street sign, on every door and lamppost. The street is bustling with a mix of electric stagecoaches and horse-pulled wagons and buggies. Trees are planted at various intervals, giving it a cleaner, more affluent feel than the other parts of the Smoke I've seen. The buildings are spaced apart from one another—we pass a branch of the Royal Bank, two statues of lions guarding its entrance, and a post office with about twenty thin stone steps leading up to a huge set of copper doors. A magistrate's office dominates a large portion of the street, its columned facade hung with a giant flag boasting the Exetor's crest, a crowned flame crossed with two spears. Ash's face is in every window. There is an electric stage-coach parked outside of it. Painted on its doors is a blue circle crossed with two silver tridents.

The crest of the House of the Lake.

Panic grips me so completely it's hard to breathe.

"Ash," I gasp, nodding to the coach. "It's her."

"It's probably a House coach," Ash says. "Every royal House has them, for their foremen and factory inspectors. She'd never come here herself."

But he doesn't sound so sure and we both pick up our pace.

By the time the Thief turns down a smaller street, I'm sweating despite the cold air. We make a right, then a left, then another right. The streets turn from cobblestone to rough concrete. As we move farther away from the factories, houses begin to sprout up around us. They line the streets in rows, bunched together or leaning against one another like they're afraid of being separated from the pack. It looks like Lily's area in the Bank, but these houses aren't painted in reds or yellows or blues. They are completely uniform, gray shingled roofs and slanted chimneys and smudged windows. Each one has a small porch jutting out from its front door. Most of them sag, their paint chipped and peeling. A young woman is hanging laundry from a line stretched between two porch posts while a baby plays with a wooden rattle at her feet. A few houses down, a grizzled old man with a rounded back sits in a wicker chair, smoking a pipe. I feel his eyes on me and drop my gaze to the cracks in the cement sidewalk.

We round a corner and Ash stops short. He grabs my wrist and pulls me back, crouching behind a porch. Raven and the Thief follow suit.

"What is it?" I whisper.

"We're not supposed to stop here," the Thief says.

Ash leans his head against the weathered wood and closes his eyes.

"I don't believe it," he mutters.

"Ash, what?"

He opens his eyes. "Did you see it? The house?"

I peek around the corner. The row of houses look the same—small, shabby, uniform—until about halfway down the street. A three-story building looms up against the slate-colored sky. It looks as though it was once the same size as the other houses, but has since devoured those on either side of it, giving it a lumpy, swollen appearance. It has been painted a garish shade of green with blue shutters, a stunning contrast among so much gray. An electric stagecoach sits outside it, and two Regimentals guard the door.

"What a horrible color," Raven says.

"Who lives there?" I ask.

"I did," Ash says.

"Oh," I say. "It doesn't look quite like I remember from the photograph."

"It screams money," he says through gritted teeth.

I peek around the corner again as two men emerge from the house. One is a young boy with brilliant orange hair, the other an old man in a woolen coat wearing a bowler hat. Red and Mr. Billings. They get into the electric stagecoach and it pulls away from the house, leaving the Regimentals standing guard.

"They're gone," I say. "Those people from the companion house."

Ash turns to me, his eyes pleading. "Can't I . . . can't I look in the window? I don't have to talk to her. I only want to see her. Before she's gone forever."

I hold his gaze, knowing that it is absolutely foolish to attempt something like this.

"There are Regimentals outside," I say. "You wouldn't get two blocks before they arrested you."

"I can distract them," the Thief volunteers.

"I don't think that's the best idea," I say. "You don't need to risk your life for this."

"Risk my life?" The Thief chuckles. "Not only can I outrun those two, I can disappear like you wouldn't believe. I told you, it's my quarter. I know all the hiding spots. And I'm not afraid of Regimentals." He looks at Ash. "I understand. You have to say good-bye," he says, echoing Raven's words from earlier.

Ash's face is pale under all the soot.

I squeeze his hand. Cinder is so close. And he has asked so little of me.

"I'm coming with you," I say.

"No, Violet, you—"

"I wasn't asking for permission." We all have things we need to do, no matter how reckless or foolish. I helped Raven instead of taking the serum myself. I know what it is to risk your life for someone you love. I can't deny him this last chance. If it was Hazel dying and I was feet from where she was, I would do the exact same thing. But I won't let him face this alone. We've come too far for that.

There's a space under the porch stairs that should provide a good hiding place. I turn to Raven. "Stay here. And you," I add, looking at the Thief, "take care of her. No matter what else happens, you make sure she is safe."

"Don't do that," Raven says. "Don't talk about me like I'm not here. My mind may be twisted and turned against me but I am Raven Stirling. I can make my own decisions."

I have to smile. She's coming back. My Raven is coming back. The Countess couldn't destroy her completely.

"I know," I say. "But I can't bear for you to be in danger again. Please, Raven. For me. Stay safe."

She narrows her eyes a fraction. "You always did know how to lay on the guilt."

I laugh. "I'm glad I haven't lost my touch." I reach back to my bun and carefully extract the arcana. "Here. Keep this, just in case."

Raven's fingers wrap around the delicate silver tuning fork. "You're coming back," she says.

I nod. "Just in case," I say again. At least Lucien or Garnet or someone can find Raven if something happens to me and Ash. I'm not leaving her entirely alone.

"Ready?" the Thief asks. "You'll only have a few minutes."

Ash nods.

"Don't get caught," the Thief says with a grin. "That's my motto." He runs out onto the street.

"I saw him!" he shouts to the Regimentals. "That companion. He was out by Joinder's. This way!"

He jogs in the opposite direction of our hiding place. The Regimentals look momentarily stunned until one of them says, "After him!" They rush off, leaving the house unattended.

"Come on," I say. "We don't have much time."

Raven slips under the stairs as Ash and I hurry down the street. A lopsided porch encircles his house—the first floor boasts three large windows. We climb the steps as quietly as we can and crouch by the first window as the front door opens.

A woman walks out of the house, wearing a heavy coat and carrying a purse. I am struck by how much she looks like Ash. She's several years older than in the photograph I saw, but there is no doubt that Ash is her son. She frowns when she sees us.

"Excuse me, what are—oh!" Her hand flies to her mouth.

"Mother?" Ash says, rising to his feet.

They stare at each other for a moment. I remember my Reckoning Day, the day the caretakers at Southgate allowed us back home for one last visit with our families before we were sold. Ash never got that. He told me he hasn't seen his family in four years.

The moment breaks as Mrs. Lockwood rushes forward.

"Oh, Ash," she says, pulling him into her arms. "Oh, my boy . . . look at you, you're . . . you're all grown up. But . . . why are you here? Why would you come? They're looking for you, they—"

She glances around and sees that the Regimentals are gone. She also sees me.

"Who—?"

"I need to see Cinder," Ash says. "I don't have much time."

I have to give Ash's mother credit—she grasps the severity of the situation extremely fast.

"Of course," she says, opening the door and stepping inside. "But keep your voice down. Your father and brothers are out back."

The inside of the house looks similar to the outside, as if it were once a much smaller space that has been added to over time. There is a staircase to my right, and a large living area spreads out in front of me. The furniture is mismatched, some of it looking quite expensive while other pieces are clearly homemade. A chaise lounge sits against a wall beside a rough wooden stool. An ornately carved table dominates the center of the room, a tea tray with chipped cups resting on it. And in an armchair by the windows, a small figure in a white nightgown sits with a book propped up in her hands.

"Cinder?" Ash whispers.

The book falls to the floor. "Ash?" Cinder wheezes, before dissolving into a fit of coughing.

She is a ghost of the girl I saw in the photograph. All bones, her skin clings to her cheeks and arms, and there are large dark circles under her eyes. Her once-curly hair hangs lank around her shoulders. A blood-speckled handkerchief is clutched in one hand.

Ash collapses on his knees in front of her. "Hey, little turnip," he says.

"Why are you here?" she says. "They're looking for you."

"I wanted to see you."

Cinder's sigh turns into a cough. Her eyes droop. "Father will kill you."

"I wasn't supposed to get this far." Ash takes her hand gently. "I'm so sorry," he says. His head falls forward and his shoulders tremble.

It seems to take all of Cinder's energy to lean in and kiss his hair. Tears stream down Mrs. Lockwood's cheeks as she watches.

"This isn't your fault," Cinder says.

"I tried."

"I know."

"It wasn't enough," Ash whispers.

Cinder struggles to lift her hand enough to put it on his cheek. "It was," she says. "I know you think I don't know all the things you've done for me. But I do." Her hand falls limp into her lap. "Remember how we'd race to school? And you always let me win?"

"I didn't *let* you."

She wheezes out a laugh. "Right. And the year all the girls were getting porcelain dolls for the Longest Night and we couldn't afford one so you made me a doll out of straw and burlap and Mother's old dresses?"

The lump of sadness in my throat is so big, I can't swallow. Ash looks like he can't either.

"I think it was the ugliest doll in the whole city," he says with a heartbreaking attempt at humor.

"It was perfect. They all made fun of me, but I didn't care." Cinder leans back, like this conversation has exhausted her. "I'm sorry, Ash. I'm sorry I got sick and you had to go away. I'm sorry Father hit you and made you feel bad all the time. I'm sorry Rip and Panel and those other boys at school were mean. I'm sorry I couldn't do anything to keep you here with me."

"You don't have to be sorry for anything." A tear tumbles down Ash's cheek. "I don't want to leave you again."

Cinder's whole face goes from relaxed to alert. "You have to get out of here before Father finds you. Please. For me."

It takes an eternity for Ash to answer.

"Please," she says again. "He'll turn you in. I can't bear the thought of you dying, too."

The fact that she knows, that she understands exactly what is happening to her, and can speak of it so bravely, seems to break Ash in two. I have never seen him look so defeated.

"All right," he whispers.

She smiles at him. One of her front teeth is crooked. "I'm so glad I got to see you," she says.

Ash kisses her cheek.

"I love you, little turnip."

". . . shouldn't have taken the wretched job in the first place." A male voice carries from somewhere in the farther recesses of the house, and a door slams. "Should have stayed at Joinder's, with the House of the Stone. That damned boy ruined any chance for us. You think the Duchess is going to let me work anywhere except maybe cleaning furnaces for half a diamante a month? How are we supposed to survive on that?"

Mrs. Lockwood looks terrified. "Go," she hisses at her son.

"I wish Ash would come home, like the idiot he is," a second, younger male voice says. "And then this wouldn't be our problem anymore."

Before we can even move, three people enter the room and I recognize them immediately.

Ash's father is a large man with dark curly hair and heavily muscled arms and shoulders. His mouth twists down, giving him a perpetually mean expression. A brown glass bottle is clutched in one hand. Right behind Mr. Lockwood are two identical boys, who could be exact replicas of their father except they are shorter and their noses are snubbed, turning up at the ends. Rip and Panel. I don't know which one is which.

They stop short at the sight of Ash, who has risen to his feet and is staring his father down, eyes like green fire.

"Hello, Father," Ash says.

"You—how did you get in here, boy?" Mr. Lockwood turns on his wife. "This was *you*, wasn't it? Always spoiling him, never giving him a chance to become a real man. He belongs in jail!"

"Don't talk to her like that," Ash snaps.

"You're not part of this family anymore, Ash," one of the twins says. "Are you dumb enough to believe we'd protect you? When that Bank man came to see us, all certain that you'd come back here, I wanted to laugh in his face. But I guess you're as stupid as they think you are."

The other twin sniggers.

"I'm not twelve years old anymore, Panel," Ash says. "Your threats don't mean anything to me."

"They should," Panel retorts. "We turn you in and you're dead."

"And we get a fat pile of money," the other twin, Rip, adds.

"Boys, stop it, please," Mrs. Lockwood says.

"Then do it," Ash says. "Go ahead. Be the cowards I always knew you were."

"Oh, we're the cowards?" Rip says. "Who was always getting picked on at school? Who would always come running to Mother when things didn't go his way?"

"This isn't about us, you morons," Ash snarls. "This isn't about who's stronger or who can run faster or who Father likes best." He turns on his father. "You were supposed to be *saving* Cinder. What was the point, Father, of me going away? It wasn't so you could buy up the neighborhood and live like some Pauper Royal. You aren't royalty and you never will be. That money was for her!"

"That money was *mine*!" Mr. Lockwood shouts. "I raised you, you ungrateful bastard. I put food in your belly and clothes on your back. I had to live with all your weaknesses, all your failures. I'm your *father*—I earned that money, and I spent it how I saw fit."

"*I* EARNED THAT MONEY!" Ash is screaming now. His face is red and blotchy. "It was *my* body they took, *my* dignity! They used me and made me pretend to like it, they stole my life and you think *you* earned *anything*?"

"You got to prance around with royal daughters and you're actually *complaining*?" Mr. Lockwood says incredulously. "You got a gift, boy! And you squandered it, ruined it like you always do, and we're left to deal with the mess." He turns to his sons. "Go get the Regimentals and bring them back here. I don't know how he got rid of the ones outside but there must be a few close by."

At that moment, the door flies open as a Regimental storms into the room.

I gasp. Ash and his mother turn, as Cinder is seized by a coughing fit.

This is the end. The Smoke is as far as we're going to get.

Ash and I are caught.

~ Thirteen ~

"ARREST HIM!" MR. LOCKWOOD CRIES, POINTING AT HIS
son.

"Come on," the Regimental shouts at me.

Garnet.

Ash and I don't hesitate for a moment. We are out the
door and running before Mr. Lockwood has a chance to
realize what's happening. There is a horse-drawn wagon
parked in front of the house. Perched in the driver's seat is
the Thief, smiling at us like he's won first prize at the local
fair. A large piece of burlap covers the back of the wagon.
Garnet throws it up, revealing Raven, curled in the fetal
position, eyes wide.

"Quick," he hisses, and we crawl onto the bed of the

wagon beside her. The burlap is thrown down over us and the wagon lurches forward, leaving Garnet behind.

"Are you all right?" I whisper to Raven.

"I'm fine," she says. "The arcana started buzzing after you left—I guess Garnet was worried about us. I told him where you were. He must have been close, because he got here just as we heard shouting from inside the house. And then the boy showed up with this wagon, which I think he probably stole, and they showed each other those keys and then they told me to hide so I hid." She looks at Ash. "Did you see her?"

Ash is clenching his jaw so hard I think he might break his teeth.

"I should've hit him," he growls.

"I don't think that would have helped," I say.

"He's killing her and he doesn't even care." Ash slams a fist against the bottom of the wagon. "As if he earned anything. As if he has any right . . ."

"You got to say good-bye to her," I remind him.

He turns his face away from me. "Yes," he says. "But I wish I didn't have to leave her there."

Raven and I exchange a glance but say nothing.

The road is bumpy and the Thief drives fast, so the three of us are jostled around until I begin to get dizzy. After what feels like an hour, the wagon finally comes to a stop and the burlap is thrown back.

A young woman, in her mid-twenties I'd guess, stands before us. She wears a simple gray coat, and her dark eyes find mine.

"197?" she says. I don't bother correcting her because

this doesn't seem to be the time.

"Show me your key," I say.

She turns around and lifts up the bun at the base of her neck, revealing a small black skeleton key tattooed on her skin.

"The Seamstress will take care of you from here," the Thief says. "But you'd better get going. This quarter is going to be swarming with Regimentals in a few hours."

"Thank you," I say to him as I scramble down off the wagon.

"Sure thing. Maybe one day I can see that power the Black Key was talking about."

I smile, and out of the corner of my eye I see a tiny weed poking up from between the cobblestones. I bend down and yank it out of the ground.

Once to see it as it is. Twice to see it in your mind. Thrice to bend it to your will.

I feel the life inside the weed, pulling on the delicate strands, and my fingers grow hot as a dandelion shoots up from their grasp. The invisible needles boring into my brain are overshadowed by the adrenaline pounding through my body, as the bright yellow flower unfolds in my hand. I hold the dandelion out to the Thief, smirking a bit at the surprised look on his face.

He takes the weed slowly. "Wow," he breathes, holding it as though it were a precious gem.

"Come," the Seamstress says. "We need to hurry." She seems completely unfazed by the Augury as she leads us to another wagon, this one bigger, with two horses drawing it, and loaded with wooden barrels and crates. The Seamstress

climbs up and begins prying the tops off them. "Get in,"
she says, holding out a hand to help Raven up. Ash climbs
in beside her, and I bring up the rear.

One barrel contains rolls of fabric and balls of yarn.
"Raven," I say. "You get in this one." It seems like it would
be a little more comfortable. We push aside the fabric and
make a hole big enough for Raven to sit. The Seamstress
motions to a crate containing sheets of glass and packing
hay.

"I'll get in this one," Ash says. "You take that one."

He points to a barrel half filled with brilliantly colored
beads. I nod.

"This is it," I say, taking his hand. "No more running
after this."

He only half smiles and I know he is thinking of his
family.

"Get in," the Seamstress urges. Ash shudders as he
climbs into the crate and lies down on the glass.

The Seamstress has already closed the lid over Raven's
barrel and she moves to do the same with Ash's crate. I
stick one foot in the barrel of beads—they naturally move
around my leg until I reach the bottom. It's a bizarre sensation as I lower the rest of my body down, like sitting in a
sack of dried peas. I look up and see the Seamstress standing over me.

"This wagon is marked for delivery to the Farm," she
says. "You should be on a train in a few hours." I don't like
her use of the word *should*. "I do not know who will be
waiting for you or where they might take you. I have done
what I can."

She looks disappointed in herself. I wish I could stand up and face her instead of being curled up in a barrel of beads.

"Thank you," I say.

"This city has rotted for too long," she says. "They can't keep us from being who we are anymore. They can no longer be allowed to dictate our lives. Our hopes are with you and the Black Key."

I swallow hard, but don't get a chance to say anything before the cover slides over the top of my barrel and darkness engulfs me.

I don't know how long we sit on the wagon, waiting. The beads dig and pinch at my skin, and my head and back ache with fear and exhaustion.

Oh, Lucien, I think. *I hope this is worth it.*

I hate myself for thinking it. Of course this is worth it. Would I rather be back in the palace of the Lake, strapped to a medical bed until I give birth and die? I think about all the injustice I have suffered—losing my family to Southgate, losing my freedom to the Duchess. Annabelle's death, her blood on my hands. Lily, pregnant and sentenced to die in the Bank. I think about the Cobbler's son, taken to be a Regimental, the Thief's parents killed who knows how by the royalty. I don't even know these last two people but if I can do anything to make a single life even a little better, isn't that worth it?

I remember the utter hopelessness of the workers in the Smoke, how defeat hung as heavy as the clouds of soot in the air. I think about the sharp contrast of the Exetor's Ball, the unending bottles of champagne, the glittering dresses, the dancing, the music . . . They might as well be two different universes, not simply different parts of the same city. The royalty take and take and it never seems to be enough for them. They steal girls to make their babies, boys to protect them, or seduce them, or serve them. But we are not objects. We are not the latest fashion or the most expensive prize. We are *people*.

And I'm going to help make them see that.

FINALLY, THE WAGON PITCHES FORWARD. THE GROUND rumbles underneath me and I'm immediately on alert.

I can hear voices shouting all around, the grunts of men lifting heavy things, the crunch of gravel, and then the ear-splitting whistle of a train.

"Where to?" an official-sounding voice asks.

"The Farm. South Quarter. Bartlett Station." I don't recognize the voice of whoever is driving the wagon. I wonder whether they are in the Society, too. Or whether they simply don't know they are aiding fugitives.

"Papers?" There is a faint shuffling. I'm terrified to move, afraid that I might disturb the beads and give us away. "Very well, this all appears to be in order. Move along."

The wagon rolls forward. I can hear the hissing of steam engines, and more shouting, and I nearly let out a loud yelp as the barrel I'm in is lifted up. I clap one hand over my mouth and keep the other firmly pressed against the side of the barrel to steady myself. Thankfully, whoever is loading these barrels doesn't roll them. I bob around in the air, a rather disorienting sensation, until with a thump, the barrel is back on solid ground. I feel myself sliding backward until I hit something solid and finally come to rest.

There are more thumps and scrapings as the other barrels are loaded onto what I imagine is a cargo train.

There is another shrill whistle and the train begins to move.

My heart lifts. We are on our way to the Farm.

It's impossible to get comfortable in this barrel. Beads dig at me everywhere, and I long to stretch my legs. My stomach twists with hunger. When was the last time I ate? It must have been at Lily's. That feels like months ago. I begin to dream about the food I used to have in the Jewel. Soft-boiled eggs in little cups with toast. Smoked salmon and cream cheese on crackers. Lamb with mint jelly. Duck and figs over a salad of frisée.

The chugging of the train and the hum of the engine lulls me to sleep. I wake with a start to the clang of a door sliding open.

"Bartlett Station," a voice calls in the distance.

"Which ones, sir?" a young man, close by, says.

"Those three." Lucien's voice brings tears to my eyes. "Careful," he says, as my barrel slides across the train and I'm once again lifted into the air, landing with an unpleasant bump.

"That's the last one," the unfamiliar voice says.

"Very good. Here you are, that's for you."

"Thank you, sir."

I hear the clinking of metal on metal, then the crack of a whip and whatever mode of transportation I'm in starts to move. After a few minutes, I hear Garnet's voice.

"Should we let them out?"

"Not yet," Lucien replies. "Let's get to the woods first."

The road we're traveling on is bumpy and rutted, and I bounce around in my barrel, bruising my elbows, beads rattling around me. I hope these woods aren't too far away. All the fear from the past few days is slowly leaking out of me, replaced by the tiny hum of excitement. I'm in the Farm. Lucien is here. And Ash and Raven.

"You did very well," Lucien says after a while.

"I want to see this place, wherever it is," Garnet says.

"Yes, I believe you have earned that right." There is a pause. "Of course, Sil won't like it."

"I'm not afraid of her."

Lucien chuckles. "You should be."

We turn onto a smoother road, then onto another one that is rougher than the first. I'm just thinking that surely it must be safe enough now, that maybe I could risk calling out to Lucien and reminding him that we've been stuck in these barrels for who knows how long, when we finally come to a stop.

My heart kicks into a sprint as the top of my barrel is pried open and Garnet's face pops into the space above me.

"Hi, Violet," he says.

"Get me out of this thing," I say, reaching my hands up so he can pull me out.

As I step onto solid ground, my legs shake so badly they can't support my weight and I fall into him.

"Okay," Garnet says. "Let's get you down."

He practically carries me to the edge of the cart and helps me off it to where Lucien stands, a thick fur cloak wrapped around him.

I can't help it. I start to cry. Big, embarrassing sobs tear through my chest and escape my throat in ragged gasps, my stomach heaving.

"Oh, honey," he says as I fall into his arms. "I'm so proud of you." I want to argue with him, insist I didn't do anything except possibly make this whole thing more difficult, but I don't have the energy. I hear Garnet opening the other barrel and the crate.

Ash climbs down off the cart and I throw my arms around him.

"That was certainly not my favorite way to travel," he murmurs and I laugh.

Garnet helps Raven down. She looks around with a rapt expression on her face.

"The air here," she says. "It's so clean."

I hadn't noticed but now that she's mentioned it, I take a deep breath and look around.

It's nighttime—two lanterns hang from the driver's seat of the cart, giving a golden glow to the trees that surround us. That's all I can see. Trees. I turn slowly on the spot, my mouth gaping. Big trees and small trees, skinny trees with delicate branches, trunks as thick as the old oaks I'd seen in the Jewel, in the forest we had to drive through to get to the Royal Palace. I remember it being orderly and well manicured before it gave way to a garden of topiaries. But there is something even more beautiful about *this* forest and it takes me a moment to pinpoint what it is.

This place feels natural. It feels old. It has been allowed to grow as it pleases without the interference of man.

"You've made it this far," Lucien says, wrapping a thick cloak around my shoulders, "and I know it's been difficult, but you've got to help us the rest of the way."

"What do you mean?"

He points to a nearby tree with a pale gray trunk. A symbol has been carved into it, a *C* overlapping an *A*. "This is as far as I can get on my own."

"What's that?" I ask.

"A marking Azalea left for me," he murmurs. "The place we're going is nearly impossible to find without the help of someone who has the power of the Auguries."

"I don't understand," I say. I glance at Raven. She shrugs.

"I know," Lucien says. "But you will. Come on."

He leads me to front of the cart, where a shaggy horse is shaking its mane, its breath puffing out in white clouds. Lucien unhooks one of the lanterns and holds it out to me.

"Walk ahead of us," he says. Ash moves to walk with me, but Lucien holds up a hand. "No," he says. "She has to do this alone."

"Which way do I go?" I ask.

Lucien shrugs. "Follow your instincts."

My instincts? My instincts are telling me this is impossible, and I'm ready for someone else to take control. I thought once we got to the Farm it would be easy. Lucien is the one with all the plans and schemes. I just want to be safe. I want my friends to be safe, and I don't want to run anymore. I think about everything that's happened since that horrible night Ash and I were caught, the promises Lucien made, the close calls, Cinder dying, and Lily, too, eventually, and tears spring to my eyes and I snatch the lantern out of his hands and storm off into the trees.

I don't want anyone to see how terrified I am. I can't let them down.

But I'm so afraid that my instincts mean nothing.

I hear the *clop-clop* of the horse's hooves and the slow creak of the cart's wheels and I know they are following me. I clutch the cloak tight around my neck and hold up the lantern. The trees appear like ghostly apparitions as I move through them, their branches reaching out for me.

The farther into the forest I go, the denser the trees become. They curve and stretch in unnatural ways, their trunks bent at odd angles, their branches sometimes diving right into the earth. I worry the cart won't make it through them if they get any thicker. I worry I'm going in the wrong direction. There's no path to follow, nothing to guide me.

But then, right as I'm about to turn around and tell Lucien this whole thing isn't working, I feel it. A small, faint tug in my chest, like something has hooked around my rib cage and yanked on it.

"Violet, did you feel that?" Raven calls.

Not wanting to lose my concentration, I ignore Raven's question and make a sharp left. The pull gets stronger. It leads me through the trees and I'm suddenly sure of my way without knowing where I'm going, as if I'd been to this place before.

A light snow begins to fall. Delicate white flakes filter down through the soft light and the twisted trees. I look up at the sky and feel as if I were in a snow globe, a miniature world contained within a single glass ball. And when I look back at the trees, I see a light. A tiny twinkle in the distance.

I stumble forward, swerving around trunks and ducking

branches until I find myself standing on the edge of a huge clearing. At its center is a large, redbrick farmhouse, two stories high with a wide front porch. Behind it, in the distance, I can make out the shadowy shape of a barn.

A light shines through one of the windows on the first floor of the house.

"Well done," Lucien says as the cart comes into view. Garnet is sitting beside him, his eyes wide. Ash and Raven lean over the edge of the cart to get a better look.

"Like I said—it's nearly impossible to find." Lucien is smiling at me. "Believe me. I've spent hours on my own, wandering around these woods looking for it."

"But . . . what *is* it?" I ask.

"Your new home." His smile widens.

"Welcome to the White Rose."

～ Fourteen ～

THE DOOR TO THE FARMHOUSE OPENS. A SHORT FIGURE, silhouetted in the light, walks out onto the front porch.

"Lucien!" a gruff female voice calls. "Stop skulking out there like a damned burglar."

"That's Sil," Lucien says as he helps me up to sit beside him on the cart and sets the horse at a trot toward the farmhouse. There's a little path that leads us there, and I see a weathered sign sticking up from the grass. As we pass it, the lantern illuminates the faded lettering: THE WHITE ROSE. I glance back at Ash and Raven. Ash looks confused and a little suspicious, but Raven's face is joyous as she takes in our surroundings.

"Who is Sil, exactly?" I ask Lucien.

He hesitates. "I'm going to let her explain that herself."

As the farmhouse comes closer, I see a wild garden, dead now in winter, spreading out in front of the porch. Garlands of ivy wrap around the railings and climb up the redbrick facade.

Lucien stops the cart. The woman—Sil—doesn't come out to greet us. Instead she stands in the doorway, the light from inside the farmhouse obscuring her features.

"How many damned people did you bring?" she snaps.

"This is Violet," Lucien says, gesturing to me.

"I know who she is," Sil says. "Who are they?"

"They're my friends," I say.

"They're not welcome here."

"I'm not going anywhere without them."

Sil snorts. "You don't like to make things easy on yourself, do you?"

I don't say anything. I haven't come all this way to abandon Ash and Raven now. I won't.

"Sil—" Lucien begins, but she waves him off.

"Get inside, all of you," she says. "Before we freeze to death."

I'm not sure what to make of this woman, and from the looks on Raven's, Ash's, and Garnet's faces, they don't either. But we follow Lucien up the steps of the porch and into the house.

The first floor of the farmhouse is completely open—one large room that contains a living room, dining room, and kitchen. The floor is covered with handmade rugs in a variety of colors and patterns. Some are animal skins, others woven out of dyed wool. A loom sits by the wall to my left, the beginnings of something blue and purple at its base. Much of the furniture looks handmade, too—though not as high quality as the furniture my father used to make. An overstuffed sofa. A rocking chair, next to a fireplace that flickers with a dying fire. A dining room table. The kitchen hosts a large cast-iron stove, a massive sink, and a rack on the ceiling from which hang an assortment of pots and pans. A set of stairs in the far corner leads up to the second floor.

It's strikingly different from the opulence of the Duchess's palace, with its plush carpets, and chandeliers, and canopied beds. But I like this house better. It's cozy in here. It feels lived in and cared for. It feels like a home.

Something bubbles in a pot on the stove, filling the whole room with the scent of cooked meat and vegetables. My stomach growls.

"Well." Sil's voice brings me back to the present. "Let's have a look at you, then."

I turn and a pair of piercing blue-gray eyes, so pale they're practically silver, stares back at me. Sil is old, older than my mother, with skin the color of coffee mixed with cream. There are deep wrinkles around her eyes and mouth. Her hair is kinky and black, except for brilliant streaks of gray at her temples, and it frizzes out in a cloud around her face. She wears a pair of men's overalls, like what a gardener might wear, over a long-sleeved shirt. Her right hand, I notice, is severely scarred.

She's quite a bit shorter than me, but she studies me with a keen and critical eye. I'm reminded strangely of my first meeting with the Duchess, though I'm not nearly as afraid as I was then.

"So, you're the latest perfect score, are you?" she says, referencing the perfect 10 I received in the third Augury, Growth. Then she glances at Lucien. "She doesn't look as tough as Azalea."

"She is exactly what you asked for," Lucien says dryly.

I turn to him in shock. "What? What do you mean?"

"Didn't tell her, did you?" Sil says.

"Tell me what?" I demand.

"I said the only way this damned fool scheme was going to work was if we found a surrogate with a perfect Growth score," Sil says. "And that's you, isn't it?"

"But . . . I thought . . . Lucien?" I don't know what to say. Lucien never told me that. He said he chose me because I reminded him of his sister.

"Violet," he says, taking a step toward me. I instinctively take a step back. "What I told you was true. You remind me so much of her, of Azalea. And you also happened to have a perfect Growth score."

"You should have told me," I say.

"Would it have made a difference?" Lucien asks. "Would you have been any more or less willing to trust me?"

I don't want to answer that.

Sil laughs again. "Not the perfect father figure you were hoping for, is he? Azalea thought the same thing."

Pain flickers across Lucien's face.

"Don't say that," I snap.

"It took her dying for him to see—really see—that things need to change," Sil says.

"And what's your excuse for hiding out here for four decades?" Lucien retorts. "Was that some strategic planning move? You were as scared as I was. She changed you, too."

Sil's pale gray eyes narrow. "You have no idea what I went through to get here."

"You have no idea what *we* went through," I say. "And all the while Lucien's been telling me that I have some mysterious power and you're supposed to be the one to show me what it is, so can we get on with it, please, because I'm sick of the mysteries and the lies."

The hint of a smile twitches on Sil's lips. "Whatever you wish, Your Royal Grace." I grit my teeth. She turns to Garnet, Lucien, and Ash. "You three, take the horse to the barn and unload the rest of the supplies." She looks Raven up and down, something in her expression softening. "How many months?" she asks.

Raven glances at me.

"I don't know," she says, fiddling with her bulky sweater. "Three, maybe?"

Sil walks forward and rests her hand on Raven's stomach. Raven flinches.

"What did they do to you?" Sil murmurs.

"Everything," Raven replies.

She nods, then turns. "What are you still doing here?" she snaps at the men hovering in the doorway. "Out! No food until that wagon's unloaded."

Ash raises an eyebrow at me. I shrug. This is what we've come for. This woman might be unpleasant but I don't think she'll hurt me. We are safe here. I feel it. The three of them walk out into the night.

"Sit," Sil instructs, pointing to the dining table. Raven and I obey as she heads into the kitchen and comes back with two bowls of stew—beef and carrots and onions in a rich brown sauce. I can barely wait until she slams the spoon down next to me before digging in. Raven and I eat ravenously. The only sounds are the clinking of cutlery against ceramic and the occasional sigh of contentment. The bowls are empty in minutes. When we've finished, Sil looks at Raven.

"There are bedrooms upstairs," she says. "You look like you could use some sleep."

Raven hesitates.

"You're safe here, child," Sil says. "I promise you that."

"I'll be up soon," I say. Whatever Sil has to say, I have the feeling it needs to be said to me alone.

Raven rubs her eyes. "All right," she says with a sigh. Her footsteps are heavy as she walks up the stairs. I'm grateful we can all sleep in beds tonight.

Sil has gone back into the kitchen, returning with two steaming mugs of tea.

"Here," she says, shoving one into my hand and settling herself into the rocking chair.

I move to sit on the sofa near her and take a sniff of the liquid, which is dark and has an earthy tang.

"Go on, it's not poison," Sil says before taking a deep drink.

I raise the mug to my lips and sip—it tastes like bark and cinnamon.

"Which holding facility were you in?" she asks.

"Southgate," I say.

"Ah, a southerner." Sil takes another drink and rocks back in her chair. "I was in Northgate. What a nightmare, that place. Like a damned prison."

I nearly drop my mug. "*Northgate?* You were a surrogate?"

Sil chuckles. "I don't know how that man keeps all his secrets straight," she says, with a hint of grudging respect. "He said he wouldn't tell you a thing about me, but, oh, the way he talks about you, I was sure he'd let the cat out of the bag."

I'm still in shock. Sil can't be a surrogate. She's too old—she should be dead by now. Unless she escaped from Northgate? Or she had a protector in the Jewel?

I rub my eyes. There's too much in my head, and not enough space for it all.

Sil drains her mug and smacks her lips together. "Don't think too hard, you'll pop a blood vessel. I'll tell you my story from the beginning. But I'm going to need something stronger than tea."

She stomps back into the kitchen and returns with a full mug of something that carries a strong whiff of alcohol before settling into the rocking chair. The flames in the fireplace leap up, as if someone had added more wood or maybe put a bellows to them. I jump.

"It's cold," Sil says, as if that explained it. She takes a long drink.

"I was born," she begins, "in the North Quarter of the Marsh, oh, about sixty years ago. I was diagnosed when I was eleven. My mother had died of fever when I was six. My father worked in the Smoke—he died when his factory caught on fire and burned to the ground. My grandmother raised me and my three older brothers, until I was shipped off to Northgate." She scratches her chin. "We heard that some facilities let the surrogates see their families one last time. Is that true?"

"Yes," I say. "It's called Reckoning Day. The day before the Auction."

"Reckoning Day," she mutters. "In any case, that's not how things worked at Northgate. I did not get to see my family again. I was sixteen when the head caretaker informed me it was time for me to be sold. There were only twenty-two lots in my Auction—I suppose the royalty were not interested in having children that year. I was Lot 22. My scores were nearly perfect—in the case of the third Augury, they were." She levels me with a cold stare. "I was bought by the Duchess of the Lake."

I suck in a breath. But it couldn't be my Duchess—Sil is too old. She must have been bought by my Duchess's mother. My fingers go numb. I feel like my head has been stuffed with cotton, the world muted, my senses dulled. Sil smiles a cruel smile.

"Yes," she says. "I thought that would interest you. The House of the Lake can't seem to hold on to its surrogates, can it?"

She takes another drink. I get the sense that she is enjoying herself. "The Duchess was a frail woman. Always sickly. The Duke . . ." Sil pauses, and her eyes darken from silver to slate. "He ruled that house with an iron fist. Cold and spiteful and full of ambition. Usually it's the woman who deals with the surrogates, but not in the palace of the Lake. No, he had plans for me. He kept me much longer than is usual to keep a surrogate. All around me, girls were getting pregnant.

Or dying. Or both. Then the future Electress died."

I remember that from my old history classes. Originally, the Exetor's sister was named to succeed the throne. But she died from a fall off a horse when she was eight. And the Exetor, only two at the time, became the new heir.

"That's when the doctor started . . . well, I don't need to explain any of that to you, do I?" Sil says grimly.

I press my lips together in a tight line.

"I got pregnant. It wasn't until my second trimester that they discovered I was carrying twins. Don't know how the doctor missed that. And the Duke, damned evil bastard, wanted to get rid of one. His wife wouldn't let him. He told me I had to choose, to focus all of my Auguries on only one child, probably hoping the other would die as a result. And I did. I did exactly as I was told."

I put my tea on the floor and hold my head in my hands. The room is spinning. If what Sil is telling me is true, then she was the surrogate for *my* Duchess.

"One week before I was due to deliver, they took me away. There's a place where they kept us until we gave birth. All sterile, cold and white with bright lights. It was awful. There were three girls with me. One by one, they were taken away. And they never came back."

Sil stares into the fire. The lines around her eyes and mouth seem deeper, aged with the telling of this story. She and I both know what happened to those other girls. But it still didn't explain what happened to *her*.

"When it was my time, they took me to the delivery room. The doctor was there. He told me to push. A nurse held my hand. She was fat and her palms were sweaty. But mostly what I remember is the pain. Pain like nothing I'd ever known. Worse than learning the Auguries. And then the first baby was out." Sil's eyes sparkle like crystals, and she rubs her scarred hand against her jaw. "I remember thinking it strange how something could be so beautiful and so ugly at the same time. She was screaming at the top of her lungs. Her sister came out a minute later. She was smaller. Quiet. Then they took them away. They left me alone. Waiting for me to die." She takes a drink and mutters, "Bastards."

"But how?" I ask. This is the point, I feel, the purpose, where everything began. This is what Lucien brought me here to learn. "How did you survive?"

"Because I'm stronger than them!" Sil shouts, slamming her fist down on the arm of the rocking chair. "We have a power they can't possibly understand. They've twisted it, manipulated it to suit their bidding, but they can't pervert it completely. Oh, no. It is *ours* to comprehend." She rocks back and forth for a moment, her chair creaking. "What do you think the Auguries are, exactly?"

"I don't know. A genetic mutation, aren't they?"

"Don't recite that royal line of crap at me. Think. Think for yourself. What are they?"

I think about the images that sprang into my head when I connected with the old oak tree in the Duchess's garden, during my doctor's appointments. How I saw it in a field, its branches dancing in the wind, and then in winter, barren under the falling snow. The raw emotion that came from it.

"I—I don't know how to explain it," I say. "But

sometimes it's like . . . we're the same. When I use Growth, sometimes it feels like I know the plants or the trees. Like I'm tapping into their life, their history. And they know me."

"Everything in this world has a life inside it," Sil says. "Everything is connected. Human beings, we think we're so special because we can talk and think, as if having a mouth is the only way to speak, or having a brain is the only way to think." She pauses. There's no sound except the crackling of the fire. "Surrogates are the lucky few who can sense these lives. The power we possess isn't meant for parlor tricks. Why do you think they teach us Color and Shape first? They are unnatural—they are the ones that cause the headaches and the bleeding. They're not necessary. They are used to control and subdue. There is only one true Augury and it is not called Growth. It is called Life. And we do not own it or control it, but we have the ability to feel it, to acknowledge it. It calls to us as we call to it. They train us to conquer the Auguries, but this power will not and cannot be conquered. It can only be accepted as an equal."

"I don't understand," I say.

"I was lying on that medical bed, bleeding to death. I could feel the blood and life pouring out of me. And I asked for help." Sil rubs her hands together. "Something in that room answered me. It heard the call inside me and reacted. A brilliant heat flooded through my body, and the blood stopped seeping out of me, and my strength came back. And I . . ." She turns away and I get the feeling she's censored herself. "My surroundings sharpened and I felt a strange sense of comfort. It was as if a chorus of voices were saying, 'Hold on.' And I did. I held on."

"You heard voices?"

"No," Sil says. "You'll understand soon enough. If you can." She sniffs. "Let's hope you're stronger than you look."

"I've been through a lot," I snap, tired of her condescension.

"Oh, you have?" Sil retorts. "Ever give birth to two children, then discover you're not in a hospital but a morgue? Ever run until you can't run anymore, lost and alone, and find yourself cornered in a room with only a fire-breathing monster for company? Lucien knew about that incinerator because of *me*. Can you fathom what it took for me to extinguish that fire by myself?" She pushes up her sleeve and I see the scars extend up her arm, glistening in the firelight. "I barely made it out. And I didn't have anyone holding my hand. No one was looking out for me."

"I still don't see what you want me to do," I say. "Why am I here? What is my role?"

"For too long, the royalty have abused our power. Balance needs to be restored. We need someone strong enough to call on all of nature, all the elements. This island has been cut up and stitched back together by the royalty. It wants to be whole again. The royalty have an army, they have money, they have weapons. But that is *nothing* in the face of the brutal force of nature. This force needs help. It needs *you*. Think about it. Why have they built all those walls between each circle? To keep us separated and protect themselves from their own people. They are frightened, as all tyrants are, that one day their subjects will gather and rise up against them. Their walls are thick, impenetrable. But what if there was someone with the power to crack them, the power to open a space large enough to let a different army through?"

"You think I can break open pieces of the walls?" I've only ever seen the wall that surrounds the Marsh, and the Great Wall from a distance. They are made of thick black rock, cemented together. Like Sil said . . . impenetrable.

"Yes," she says gravely. "I believe you will be able to."

"Won't the royalty plug the hole back up?"

"And how long do you think that will take?" she asks. "Not overnight, to be sure. If they can no longer isolate each circle of the city . . . well, that would make for a very interesting turn of affairs, wouldn't it?"

"Why can't you do it?" I ask. "You have a perfect Growth score. What do you need me for?"

"I'm too old now. I thought Azalea could do it but her power was . . . limited. Let's hope you prove my theory correct."

Just then, the door opens, and Lucien, Garnet, and Ash come back in.

"Good," Sil says, before they have a chance to speak. "We're done for tonight. Food is on the stove. The bedrooms are upstairs. Tomorrow, we get to work."

She gets up and takes a scarf and coat hanging off pegs on the wall and throws them on.

"I hope she's everything you think she is," Sil says as she walks past Lucien and out the door. "Otherwise, we're all just a pack of idealistic morons, and we'll live like cockroaches under a rock for the rest of our damned lives."

Fifteen

Ash, Lucien, and Garnet help themselves to the stew.

"What did she say to you?" Garnet asks through a mouthful of carrot.

My head is heavy with the weight of that conversation.

"I'm not sure I understand yet," I say.

"You will," Lucien says. "Azalea did."

"I'm not Azalea," I snap. "I wish you would stop comparing me to her."

Lucien looks hurt for a second, then smooths out his expression. "I know you're not. But I know you can do this."

"I don't know what you want from me," I cry, throwing

out my hands. "I'm not that powerful, Lucien. Growth isn't that powerful."

But then I remember the afternoon at the palace, right before I met Ash, when the Duchess called me into the drawing room and asked me to perform Growth in front of the Lady of the Flame. How I made a plant grow so quickly and so intensely that it destroyed shelves of china and ripped paintings off the wall. Is it possible I could do that on a larger scale?

"You don't comprehend it yet," Lucien says. "That's all. If I could have taught you myself, I would have. But it takes a surrogate." He puts his spoon down. "Don't you want a chance to understand who you truly are? Don't you want to know what it's like not to be shackled to the very thing that took you from your family, that makes your nose bleed and your head ache?"

"Don't make this about me," I say. "You want your revolution and for some reason you think I'm the one to help."

"I do," Lucien says. "But don't you want this revolution, too?"

I dig my knuckles into my eyes. "I'm tired," I say. "I'm going to bed."

I trudge up the stairs to the second floor of the house, which consists of one long hallway with a faded green rug. I peek through the doors until I find Raven in a bedroom with two twin beds. She's fast asleep, moonlight piercing through the open curtains and illuminating her face. I sit beside her for a moment. Already she is doing so much better than when she woke up in the morgue. But still. I glance at her stomach.

The door creaks open and Ash enters the room. He

holds out his hand and I take it, allowing him to lead me away from Raven and into another bedroom. He closes the door behind him and I fall into his chest, his arms snaking around my waist. For the first time in a long time, we are completely alone together.

"We made it," he murmurs into my hair.

"We did," I whisper back. He smells like packing hay and soot.

"Do you really think it's safe here?"

"I do," I say, pulling back to look at him.

"That forest . . . I don't know how you found this place."

I shrug. "Lucien was right. As usual."

"Lucien isn't some supreme being," Ash says. "He's human. He's capable of making mistakes like the rest of us. Remember that."

"Do you think he made a mistake, saving me?" I ask, bristling a little.

"No," he says. "But he's putting a lot of pressure on you. I don't think that's entirely fair."

I stare at the wall, imagining Raven sleeping peacefully behind it in the next room.

"Raven's going to die," I say. "And I can't do anything to stop that. How will overthrowing the royalty help *her*? That was the whole point of this, to help. Save me so I can save more. And even if I can, so what? Can I help all the companions who are being abused? Can I help all the Cinders who are dying of black lung, or the Annabelles killed by their mistresses?" Tears well up and spill down my cheeks. "Maybe Lucien *shouldn't* have chosen me. What if I was the wrong choice?"

Ash tilts my chin up, his fingers brushing down my neck. "Listen to me," he says. "Raven was going to die in that place, alone, in pain, giving birth to a baby that isn't hers. Or not even making it to that point. You got her out. Maybe it's not the perfect solution, but at least she gets to be with friends instead of locked up in the palace of the Stone. And you got *me* out, when it seemed like I was going to die in the Duchess's dungeon. That's two lives you've already saved from the Jewel, not including your own, which you seem to put last on your list. You can't save everyone, Violet. It's not possible. So don't hold yourself up to some ridiculous standard. And don't ever let me hear you say you were the wrong choice again."

"I don't want to lose Raven."

"I know." Ash rests his forehead against mine. "I miss Cinder already. I know she's not gone yet but . . . she was my constant companion in that place. She kept me from falling apart." A tear leaks out from under his eyelid and I brush it away with my thumb. His jaw is rough with stubble.

It's been so long since I've felt anything good. I've existed in a haze of anxiety and fear and tension for days now. All of that melts away as I pull his mouth to mine.

Our kiss is gentle and slow. We don't have to rush anymore. We don't have to sneak around, to worry about Carnelian's lessons or being caught by the Duchess. We are in a safe place, and my heart aches with how much I have missed being close to him in this way. I slip my hands up under his sweater, my fingers tracing patterns on his lower back. His mouth moves down to my neck. His lips are soft and each kiss sets a flame burning deep in that secret place inside me that only he knows.

In one swift move, I pull his sweater up over his head. I'd almost forgotten the smoothness of his chest, the dip of his collarbone, the hard curves of his shoulders. I run my hands over his stomach and Ash lets out an involuntary sigh. He grabs two fistfuls of my own sweater and I raise my arms to help him slip it off me.

I shiver with need as his skin meets my skin. Everywhere he touches me is electric. I sink my fingers into his hair as his lips come back to mine.

I don't even realize I'm thinking it, but the mantra comes. *Once to see it as it is. Twice to see it in your mind. Thrice to bend it to your will.*

I don't need to open my eyes to know Ash's hair is shifting back to its original color. I want him to be him, as he is, exactly as he should be.

He chuckles against my cheek. "Did you change my hair back to brown?" His voice sets my skin on fire.

"How did you know?" I ask.

"It feels warm, when you do it. And kind of . . . tingles."

"It does?" I'm glad it feels nice to him. I barely notice the throbbing at the base of my skull.

"Mmm-hmm . . ." His fingers trace the line of my waist and I moan.

Suddenly there is a loud knocking on the door. "Violet?" Lucien's voice sends my heart plummeting to my stomach. I scramble to put my sweater back on.

"Great," Ash mumbles as he loops his own sweater over his head.

Once we're both fully clothed, I open the door.

"Hi," I say breathlessly. My face is burning, and I know I couldn't look guiltier if I tried.

Lucien's eyes flit from me to Ash. "If you even think about touching her that way, I will break you."

"Really, Lucien?" I say, exasperated.

"I think we've already established which of us can break the other," Ash retorts.

"Ash!" I say.

"I did not risk everything for her so you could satisfy your . . . urges," Lucien says. "She is here for more important things."

"You don't think I know that?"

"No," Lucien says, stepping forward into the room. "I think you have one goal on your mind."

"Stop it, both of you," I say.

"You're a genius, Lucien, everyone knows that, but sometimes," Ash says, shaking his head, "you can be breathtakingly stupid."

"Excuse me?" Lucien takes another step toward him. I grab his elbow to hold him back.

"You hate the companions because we have something you don't have," Ash says. "But can't you see something was taken from us, too?"

Lucien lets out a cold laugh that sends a chill down my spine. "You have absolutely no idea what you're talking about."

"Everything all right in here?" Garnet's voice makes us all jump. He leans in the doorway, a crooked smile on his lips. I wonder how long he was watching the fight.

"Everything is fine," Lucien says in a clipped tone. "Everyone needs to get some sleep. Especially you," he says, turning to me. "You have a big day tomorrow."

"I'm staying in Raven's room," I tell him. "Garnet can stay in here with Ash. But, Lucien . . ." I look up into his dark blue eyes. "I won't have any more of this nonsense about what I do or don't do with Ash. I didn't escape one prison to be thrown into another. You need to trust that I can make the right decisions for myself. Because I can and I will."

Lucien purses his lips and gives me a nod so brief it's almost nothing, just the slightest jerk of his head. Then he sweeps out the door without a glance in Ash's direction.

"Well," Garnet says, sauntering into the room and clapping Ash on the shoulder. "Exciting day, huh?" He leans in and mock whispers, "If you two want some privacy, I won't tell."

I roll my eyes.

"You do need to get some sleep," Ash says to me. "I don't know what she has in store for you, but that woman, Sil, is . . . intense."

I nod, and a yawn escapes my lips. Ash smiles. He kisses me softly above each eye before pulling my lips to his.

"Go," he murmurs. "I'll see you in the morning."

It aches to leave him but I'm so exhausted. Raven is still sleeping when I enter the room. I kick off my shoes, not even bothering to take off my clothes, and curl up in the empty bed. The blanket smells like heather—it reminds me of my bed at home, how on a particularly cold night or during thunderstorms, Hazel would crawl under the covers with me and we'd fall asleep curled up together.

"Good night, Hazel," I say, like I did so many times at Southgate late at night. "Good night, Ochre. Good night . . ."

But before I even get to my mother, I drift off into a deep, blissful sleep.

~ Sixteen ~

I AM WOKEN ABRUPTLY BY A LOUD POUNDING ON THE door.

"Up!" Sil barks. "Today we see what you're made of."

I feel like I could easily sleep for about twelve more hours. I rub my eyes and stretch, then move to wake up Raven. I'd like to let her sleep, but I don't want her to wake up alone.

"Raven," I say, giving her shoulder a shake. "Time to get up."

She lurches upright. "All dark, too dark," she gasps. Her gaze is unfocused as she looks at me. "They'll take your eyes."

"It's okay." I clutch her face in my hands, trying to get

her to focus on me. "You are Raven Stirling. You are real. You are stronger than this."

I can see the change, her cheeks flushing with color, her eyes going from glassy to bright. "Violet?" she says. She glances around the room. "Right. We're safe now, aren't we? No more running."

"No more running," I repeat.

Raven gets out of bed and walks over to the window. I follow and we look out on the vast clearing, surrounded by the thick forest. Frost twinkles on the grass in the morning light. A bird flits through the air.

"It's quiet here," Raven says.

"It is," I agree.

"I like it." She turns to me, a sad smile on her lips. "This is a nice place to die."

I feel like I've been punched in the stomach. "I won't let that happen."

Raven kisses my cheek. "I'm hungry," she says.

I try to keep my composure as we walk downstairs. It won't do anyone any good to collapse into a sobbing heap. Least of all Raven.

Everyone else is already awake. Lucien sits at the dining table, a mug of coffee in one hand, a newspaper spread out before him. It is strange to see him out of his lady-in-waiting garb—he wears a pair of simple brown pants and a gray sweater.

"Lucien," I say raising an eyebrow. "You look . . ."

He smiles wryly. "Yes, it's a change from the usual isn't it? Shocking as it may sound, I don't actually enjoying wearing a dress."

I grin. I'm glad he's in a better mood.

"Eat," Sil says from the kitchen, where she is scooping oatmeal into a bowl for Ash. She shoves it into his hand and starts preparing another one for me, dousing it with a healthy serving of brown sugar.

"How did you sleep?" Ash asks.

"Like the dead," I say. His hair is wet and tangled. I want to run my fingers through it. "Did you bathe?"

He smiles. "It had been a while. I think I needed it."

"Eat," Sil says again, setting a bowl down in front of me. "Then you can take a bath." She sniffs. "You both need it," she says with a glance at Raven.

"Where's Garnet?" I ask, taking a bite of oatmeal. The brown sugar melts on my tongue.

"Outside sulking," Lucien replies. He flips to the front page of the paper and flops it down in front of me. The headline of the *Lone City Herald* reads, ROYAL WEDDING. And under that in smaller print: THE JEWEL'S MOST-ELIGIBLE BACHELOR TO WED.

In everything that has happened, I completely forgot that Garnet was getting married. I even played cello at his engagement party. I shudder, remembering the pain that night, how I nearly died from a miscarriage. I didn't realize a date had already been set for the wedding.

"Oh," I say. "Right."

I've become so used to Garnet's presence. He's like a friend now. It's strange to think that he'll go back to living in the Jewel.

"Will he no longer be part of your Society?" I say. "But he got that tattoo . . ."

Lucien smiles. "I'm flattered you think of it as *my* Society."

"Oh, come on," I say. "*You're* the Black Key."

"It might surprise you to know," Lucien says, "that I am not the first person in the Lone City to think the royalty needs to be held accountable for their actions. It was about two centuries ago—no one remembers it now, and the royalty certainly don't wish to even admit that it happened, but there was a man in the Farm. Bulgur Key. He attempted a revolt on the royalty, formed a secret society, caused a lot of trouble in the Farm. But his reach was not wide enough—he couldn't affect anything beyond his own circle. In the end, he and every member of the Society of the Black Key were executed. And the whole thing was quietly swept under the rug." Lucien taps his chin with a finger. "I felt his Society deserved to live on."

"How did you find out about it?" I ask. "If the royalty tried to hide it."

"The Duchess of the Lake has the most extensive library in the entire city. As you well remember, she allows me to peruse it from time to time." Lucien winks at me and I smile. So the Duchess unwittingly aided the revolution.

"Aren't you at all worried that this time will end like last time?" I ask. Ash gives me a look that makes me wonder whether he was thinking the same thing.

Lucien puts a hand on mine. "No," he says. "Because this time, it won't be one circle fighting within itself. We have something Bulgur Key did not have. We have you."

The oatmeal turns to cement in my mouth. I swallow it down and push my bowl away.

"So what are you going to do about Garnet?" Ash asks. I am grateful for the subject change.

"He wants me to get him out of the marriage," Lucien says. "As if I were a magician."

"You're pretty close," I say.

Lucien smiles. "Thank you."

"He doesn't want to leave," Raven says, staring at the headline. "He likes it here, with us."

At that moment, Garnet bursts in through the door. "Oh, you're up," he says, noticing the newspaper. "Can you convince him to get me out of this stupid wedding arrangement? I can't spend the rest of my life with Coral. She's got a collection of miniature tea sets. What kind of person collects something like that?"

"I imagine she's very lonely," Raven says.

Garnet frowns. "Sure, but do I have to be the one to keep her company? I want to stay. I want to help."

"This *is* helping," Lucien says. "Think about it. This way we can keep someone in the Duchess's palace, someone who will know what's going on there and can report back. Do you know how hard it is to find allies in the Jewel? This is a gift to us, Garnet." He sits back in his chair. "You know, I never foresaw how useful you would be. I only ever meant for you to keep an eye on Violet."

"Thanks," Garnet says dryly.

"I did not mean it as an insult," Lucien says. "You have surprised me, and that is a rather hard thing to do—as you yourself well know."

Garnet sighs and plops down in an armchair. "I thought you were all about freedom and choice," he grumbles.

"I am," Lucien says. "But sometimes sacrifices must be made."

"What did you do anyway, Garnet?" I ask. "You must have owed Lucien a pretty big favor."

"Yes, I'd be curious to know this myself," Ash says. Even Raven has a hint of her old curiosity in her eyes.

Garnet's cheeks turn pink. "Nothing," he grumbles.

"He said some extremely compromising things and got himself into an even more compromising position with a young lady from the Bank," Lucien says with a smirk. "The young lady's father happens to run this very paper." He holds up the *Lone City Herald*. "It would have been a scandal the likes of which even his mother could not have gotten him out of. I saved him from losing his title."

"I don't even want the stupid title anymore, anyway," Garnet protests.

"Well, now we need it," Lucien says.

"You two can discuss this all you want," Sil says. "But she needs to come with me."

She points a finger in my direction.

"I'll do whatever you want," I say. "But please let me take a bath first."

THE BATHROOM IS ON THE SECOND FLOOR.

There is an enormous claw-footed tub, and I fill it with steaming water until the air is sticky and the mirror over the sink fogs up. Then I soak until my fingers turn into prunes. I wash the remnants of soot and dirt and sweat off my body and by the time I'm done, I feel like a new person. I wrap myself in a thick white towel, wipe the steam from the mirror, and stare at my face. I almost don't recognize myself.

The trip through the Bank and the Smoke has left marks—circles under my eyes, a hollowness in my cheeks. Annabelle and Cora would have covered up these imperfections expertly, with creams and makeup. My collarbones stick out more than they used to. But there is a new strength in my eyes, in the way I hold my shoulders and the tilt of my chin. I look at my reflection and can almost believe I'm capable of something incredible.

The closet in my and Raven's room is full of all sorts of clothes, but most of them look like they're for men. I pull on a pair of brown pants that are too big, securing them with a thick leather belt, and slip an oversize woolen sweater over my head. I grab a pair of socks and head downstairs.

Garnet and Ash are sitting at the dining table playing Halma. Lucien is in conversation with Sil in the kitchen, and Raven is rocking herself quietly in the rocking chair.

"You're good for a royal," Ash says as Garnet takes three of his marbles.

Garnet shrugs. "Annabelle taught me," he says. We exchange a glance, and I nod. Annabelle was the best Halma player I've ever met.

"All right, time to get going," Sil says, handing me a pair of worn leather boots. "These should fit you. Let's go."

I lace my feet into the boots.

"Good luck," Lucien says as I follow Sil out the back door.

There is a smaller porch attached to the back of the house. The sky is covered with heavy gray clouds. A light mist clings to the tops of the trees that surround the enormous field. The barn looms off in the distance, its gray wood weathered and cracked. There is a small pond to my right. In between the pond and the barn is a vast garden, row upon row of withered stalks and dried leaves.

Sil marches down the steps of the porch and strides across the field. I have to hurry to keep up.

Dew dampens my hair, making the strands stick to my face and neck. The air is chilly, but by the time we finally reach the tree line, I am flushed and out of breath. Sil stops and stares up at the branches above our heads, a small smile on her face. Then she pats one of the trunks, the way you'd pat a horse or a dog. She wanders through the trees, patting each one. I trail behind her. Sometimes, she stops and runs her hand over a particular branch, or crouches down and picks up a handful of earth, rubbing it between her palms. I wonder whether she's forgotten me completely, when she finally speaks.

"Nature is unselfish," she says. "It only wishes to survive. Humanity inflicts harm on it, digs up the earth, poisons the waters, harnesses rock and metal and stone for its own purposes. We are the protectors. We are the connection between humanity and nature. Nature is always searching for balance." She gazes up at the branches crisscrossing over our heads. "This island has been out of balance for a very long time."

There is a slender birch tree between us. Sil probes its bark with her fingers.

"What are the four elements?" she asks.

For a second, I think she might be talking to the tree.

"Earth?" I reply hesitantly. "Air, Water. And . . ."

"Fire," Sil snaps. "Don't they teach you anything at those holding facilities anymore?"

I choose not to answer that. In the few hours I've known her, I have come to realize that arguing with Sil gets you absolutely nowhere.

"We cannot *create* anything," Sil continues. "We can only call on an element. The island gave us this power. It chose us to be its guardians. You must learn to listen to it. The Auguries are a perversion of nature. When you become one with an element, there is no pain, no blood. Only a deep understanding. You must give yourself up to it." As soon as she finishes speaking, a brilliant green leaf blossoms from the branch of the birch tree that Sil is touching. It flutters in the air for a second. Then its edges turn brown, and the leaf withers and falls to the ground.

"Now," she says. "You try."

I barely hide my smile. Of course I can do this. I've been making leaves grow since I was twelve. Sil picks up a slender twig from the ground and twirls it in her hand.

"Go on," she says. "Let's see what you've got."

I place my hand on a nearby branch.

Once to see it as it is. Twice to see it in your mind. Thrice—

"Ow!" I cry, as Sil hits my wrist with the twig.

"Did I say to use the Auguries, girl?"

"You told me to make it grow," I say, rubbing the spot where it stings.

"Did I? Is that what I said?"

I think back and realize she never actually told me

anything. She just made a leaf grow herself.

"You have to *ask* it," she says.

"How?" I ask.

"Who taught you how to breathe?" Sil says. "It's instinctive."

I put my hand back on the tree.

Once to—

"Ow!" I cry again, as the twig snaps against my fingers.

"Stop using that damned mantra," Sil says.

"How do you even know I'm doing it?" I ask.

"You think I don't know that look?" she says. "You think I can't feel it coming off you, stinking waves of dominance and manipulation? You *reek* of it. Of them."

"Well, you're not giving me very good instructions," I grumble.

"You're not listening to me," Sil says.

"I am," I protest.

"Prove it."

I grit my teeth and place my hand hesitantly on the tree once more.

Um . . . grow, please, I think.

The twig snaps down on my hand again.

"Stop it!" I say. "I'm trying."

"No, you're not," Sil says. "You think I'm a crazy old woman." She cocks her head. "And that's fine. You didn't do anything I didn't already expect you'd do. Azalea didn't understand at first either." She sighs. "But you need to learn. Now comes the hard part."

"What do you mean—"

Suddenly, thick brown ropes shoot up out of the ground,

twining themselves around my feet and ankles and up my calves.

"Stop!" I cry. But Sil has turned and is already walking back to the house.

"Sil!" I shout as I desperately try to free myself. "What are you doing?"

I bend down and see that the ropes are actually roots. She must have done this, called on the tree or whatever it is that she was trying to get me to do. The birch is holding me hostage.

"Sil, you can't leave me here. Lucien!"

There's no answer from the big farmhouse.

"Ash!" I shout again, louder this time. "Garnet! Raven!"

I think I hear a noise from the inside of the house but it's so far away and honestly it's probably wishful thinking on my part. I yank on the roots, clawing at them with my fingernails and pulling as hard as I can, trying to break them. If anything, I think it only makes the tree hold me tighter.

I finally give up, flop back against the birch, exhausted, tears of frustration pricking the corners of my eyes.

If this was meant to be my first lesson, I've most certainly failed.

~ *Seventeen* ~

THE DAY SHIFTS SLOWLY INTO EVENING.

My stomach cramps from lack of food, the oatmeal this morning a distant memory. My mouth is painfully dry and when I touch my tongue it feels like sandpaper. I stuff my hands inside the sleeves of my sweater to keep them warm, but still, my fingers and toes are numb with cold.

I'm no closer to calling on an element than I was when Sil was hitting me with that twig. This feels like a giant waste of time.

My heart lifts when I see a light bobbing toward me. Lucien slowly comes into focus, carrying a lantern with him but no visible signs of food.

"How are you doing?" he says when he reaches me.

"How do you think?" I croak. My throat feels dusty. "When is she going to let me go? This isn't working, whatever she's trying to do."

"Azalea said the same thing," Lucien says.

"Did Sil lock her up like this?" I ask.

"She tied her to a different tree."

"Why?" I ask. "What could she possibly hope to accomplish?"

"The only way Sil knows how to bring out the true Augury is based on her own experience," Lucien says. "For you to comprehend it, she must . . . re-create that experience in you. She wants to break you down. Make you weak. So that this power, whatever it is, will be forced to save you."

"And that's how she taught Azalea? Why would you allow that?"

He shakes his head. "I didn't know. I wasn't here all the time. When I came to see her months later, Azalea was tied up, thin and starving. I was furious. But that was the day she understood. I'll never forget the look in her eyes. I wished I could have seen the world the way she saw it."

Lucien sits down and gazes up at the sky. The first stars are beginning to appear. "Azalea was always so frustrated with me. She thought I could be doing more, helping more people, not just her. But I was selfish. When she died, she said, 'This is how it begins.' She knew her death would spur me to action. And it did."

The phrase shakes something loose in my memory. I see an image of a wild girl with bright blue eyes, her head being lowered onto the chopping block in front of Southgate.

I gasp. "I saw her."

His brow furrows. "I beg your pardon?"

"You never told me how she died," I say. "Was she . . . executed?"

"Yes," he says quietly.

"Lucien, she was executed at my holding facility. She was so . . . strong, so brave. And when the magistrate asked her if she had any last words, she said, 'This is how it begins. I am not afraid.' And then she said, 'Tell Cobalt I love him.' Do you know who Cobalt is?"

A single tear falls onto Lucien's cheek and glitters there like a diamond.

"Me," he whispers.

"What?"

Lucien wipes his face with his hands and turns away from me. Very carefully, he unties his topknot. A sleek ribbon of chestnut hair falls to his shoulders.

"I was born Cobalt Rosling," he says. "In the West Quarter of the Marsh. My father was a very ambitious man—it didn't take him long to discover that his only son was different. I was reading the entire newspaper front to back by the age of five. I excelled with numbers. I loved taking apart the one clock in our house and putting it back together. The magistrate in our area began to take notice of me. He suggested that my father try and find employment for me in the Bank.

"But the Bank wasn't enough for my father. The Jewel was where the *real* money was—not only money, but status. My father hated living in the Marsh. The Jewel pays a premium for ladies-in-waiting. They are the most revered of all servants. But to be a man and a lady-in-waiting, one must

first be castrated. I wouldn't even be considered otherwise."
Lucien runs a hand over the shaved front of his head, then
down the length of his hair. "Of course, I was not aware of
any of this at the time. One day, a few months before my
tenth birthday, my father came home early from work.
There was a small shed in our backyard—my mother had
cleaned it out years before so I could pretend it was my
workstation. I used to make—"

Lucien's voice breaks, and he shakes his head hard as
if trying to rid himself of the memory. I feel strangely paralyzed. I can't imagine a child Lucien. I had no idea he
was from the Marsh, though of course if his sister was a
surrogate he'd have to be. He has always seemed so confident, so cool under pressure, always knowing the right
thing to do.

I never thought about the events that led him to become
a lady-in-waiting. Maybe I didn't want to know. Maybe it
was easier to pretend he'd always been this way.

He looks at the ground when he speaks.

"My father called me into the house," he says. "My
mother was crying. Azalea was only two. The kitchen table
had been cleaned off. My father said I was going to help the
family. I didn't see the two men he'd brought with him until
it was too late."

Lucien tugs hard, three times on his long rope of hair.

"They tied me to the table." He's talking faster now,
the words pouring out of him, and I wonder whether he has
ever told anyone this story before. "They tied me up while
my mother screamed. And Azalea cried, even though she
didn't know what was happening." Lucien digs his fingers

into the earth. "I couldn't move. I felt someone unbuckle my pants and rip them off." His shoulders tense. "And then there was a fire. And then there was a knife."

His head drops into his hands and he sobs, his whole body convulsing.

I don't know what to say. I don't think I could say anything, even if the right words did come to me. My brain is fuzzy. I lay my hand gently on his back.

"Oh, Lucien," I whisper.

He runs his hand over his face again. "He got what he wanted. He sold me to the Jewel in exchange for my family to be moved to the Farm." Lucien finally raises his gaze to look at me. His eyes are red, but there is fire in them. "I should have died. He didn't—he wasn't a surgeon, he had no *idea* what he was doing. I should have died and Azalea should have lived."

"It isn't your fault she died," I say. "Like it isn't Ash's fault Cinder is dying, or my fault that Raven . . ." I can't finish that sentence, so I clear my throat. "This is *them*, Lucien. The royalty. And look what you've done. You've . . . infiltrated their system. Right under their noses. I've only met a handful of your supporters, in the Bank and the Smoke, but you're giving people hope for something better, something different. You are changing people's lives." I squeeze his shoulder. "You changed mine."

Suddenly, a piercing scream echoes across the field.

"Raven," I gasp.

Lucien is on his feet and running, his hair flowing out in a chestnut ribbon behind him.

"Raven!" I yell, leaping up and then falling forward

onto my hands and knees.

She screams again.

"No!" I can't be stuck out here. Not now. Raven is hurt. Raven could be dying. She needs me.

I pull and pull until my knees ache, and still I keep pulling against the hold of the roots. I don't care what happens to me. I'm getting to my friend.

Miraculously, I feel a tiny rip in the roots, the slightest give, and with a mighty yank, I get one foot free. It feels like I might have dislocated my knee joint in the process, but I'm too busy freeing my other foot to feel the pain.

"Let . . . me . . . *go.*" With another agonizing tear, I rip my other foot loose and run as fast as I can across the clearing. I'm sweating and out of breath by the time I throw open the back door of the house. There's no one on the first floor. I fly up the stairs, my feet hammering against the wood as my heart pounds in my throat.

Ash and Garnet are outside Raven's bedroom. Garnet paces nervously. Ash stands staring at the door.

They both look up as I skid to a halt.

"What's happening?" I say.

There is another wail from behind the door.

"Raven!" I cry, lurching forward.

Ash and Garnet are on me in a second, grabbing my arms and holding me back.

"Let me go!" I shout, struggling against their grasp, but I used all my strength fighting the roots.

"Lucien is in there," Ash says. "And Sil. They're . . . they're doing everything they can."

"She needs me." I kick at the door. "Raven, I'm here!"

"You can't go in," Garnet says. There's blood on his shirt. "You don't want to go in there."

My face is wet with tears. I slump forward.

"Oh, please," I whisper, "Don't let her die . . ."

I don't know how long we wait in that hallway. Ash and Garnet let me go eventually, though Ash keeps one arm firmly around my shoulders and Garnet hovers nearby. Every sound cuts through me. Lucien's soothing murmurs. Raven's weak cries. Then nothing but silence.

The door opens.

Lucien stands in the doorway. I don't look at the blood on his hands. I don't look at the expression on his face.

All I can see is the body lying on the bed. *Raven.*

"Violet—" Lucien begins, but I push by him and run to her.

Her skin is damp with sweat. Her eyes are closed, her face peaceful. I collapse beside her.

"Raven?" I whisper. "Wake up. Come on, now." I shake her gently and her head lolls. Tears blur my vision. "You are Raven Stirling and you are stronger than this," I say, louder because maybe she can't hear me, maybe if I can just make her hear me she'll open her eyes. "You've got to wake up now, Raven. You can't . . . you can't leave me." I bury my face in her shoulder. "Please don't leave me."

"She's gone."

Sil is standing by the window.

"She miscarried," she says. "We couldn't . . ." She sighs. "There was nothing to be done."

"Save her," I say, standing up and wiping my nose on the sleeve of my sweater. "Save her like you saved yourself."

"I can't," Sil says. "I don't know how. Only she can save herself."

"No." I say the word with as much force as I can muster. "Someone has to *do* something because she was NOT meant for this. She was meant to be safe and happy. She was meant to grow old and fall in love and have a *life*." So many people have died, and I have borne it all as best I could, but not her. I turn back to the broken, bloodied body of my best friend and I think—no, I *know*—that I would give my life to save her. I would do anything if she would open her eyes and look at me again.

If only someone would help me. If only someone would tell me what to do.

I kneel beside the bed, resting my head on her arm, holding her hand. And then I feel it.

It's like a tiny rustling in the pit of my stomach, like autumn leaves, a small wind stirring inside me. It fills me up, whirling through my chest like a tornado, and with it comes a heat, lovely and warm, a natural heat, like there's a small sun where my heart used to be. I look up and put my hands on either side of Raven's face, and I feel something there, something faint and fragile, a little flutter, a miniscule pulse, and I know she's still there.

The feeling shifts. It starts in my fingers and then spreads up into my arm, a tiny pitter-patter, like drops of rain on a warm summer evening. My skin tingles and Raven's shaking, fluttery pulse gets infinitesimally smaller. She's slipping away.

I close my eyes.

The White Rose is gone.

I am in a place that is at once completely foreign and yet strangely familiar. I know I've never been here before because the ocean spreads out before me, and I have never seen anything but pictures of the ocean. I can smell the briny tang in the air, hear the waves crashing below me. I am awed by the sight of it, this vast beauty of grayish blue.

I'm standing on a jutting cliff. There is no trace of the Great Wall that surrounds this island anywhere. Trees stretch out behind me. But in the center of the cliff is a statue of some kind. It's made of a beautiful blue-gray stone, the same color as the ocean, and it curls up in a spiral, like a wave reaching for the sky. Markings are carved into it, symbols I don't understand.

I take a step forward and it begins to rain. Big, fat, wet drops splash on my face and shoulders, and then the wind picks up and the trees behind me are twisting and writhing, like mad dancers caught up in a frenzy. I think I should be scared, but I just want to laugh, so I throw my head back and release a primal, animal yowl, and the wind yowls with me, and the air lifts up my voice and carries it off to the waves and the earth shivers beneath my feet.

Raven is standing on the other side of the stone statue, but it's like I'm seeing her through a pane of glass—she is slightly blurry. But she is my Raven, the Raven before the Countess stole her and tortured her and left her for dead. The rustling inside me picks up again, leaping and spinning. Its joy is my joy, and I see it now, I see what Sil meant, that we are all connected, that this is a power that cannot be controlled or manipulated because it is part of everything.

Yes, the earth rumbles.

Yes, the wind whispers.

Yes, the ocean cries.

I see Raven mouth my name and I would give anything to have her with me, to touch her hand or hear her laugh.

And as soon as I have the thought, a massive bolt of lightning descends from the sky and hits the monument. Fire blazes up its edges before disappearing, leaving only the faint scent of burning behind. Raven shimmers like a mirage, then disappears.

I open my mouth to cry out, but the rustling fills my throat and the rain beats down harder and I know I have to hold on, to wait, to be patient. So I wait. And I think about every memory I have of Raven, every laugh we shared at Southgate, and all the adventures we've had, how she saved us in the sewers, and saved Ash in the marketplace. I remember the feel of her hand in mine. I remember her kiss on my cheek this morning. I pour out all my love for this girl into the wide-open space. I share it with every fiber of my being.

The world around me reacts. The wind whips my hair about my face, the cliff quakes under my feet, the rain pounds against my back, and for a second it feels as if my body had disappeared. I become the earth, and the rain, and the wind. I am somewhere else, the same place where my music exists, a place without pain or fear or sadness, and I take all those feelings and pour them into one thought.

Raven.

And then she's there, right there in front of me, and her skin is healthy and glowing, and she smiles her old smile, full of warmth and mischief, and she speaks without opening her mouth.

You found me, she whispers in my mind.

I found you, I reply.

Suddenly I'm being pulled, like a giant vacuum is sucking me up and away from the cliff, away from the statue, and everything is spinning and I grab Raven's hand and hold on tighter than I've ever held on to anything in my life. And then I'm pitching forward and I think it must be into nothingness except I feel something soft against my cheek.

I open my eyes.

The first thing I see is a swath of color. My body has fallen over Raven's, the quilt on the bed the only thing I can see. For a few seconds, I lie there, aware of the powerful silence in the room and the even more powerful silence inside me. Whatever I experienced isn't gone—it's more like it's waiting for me to catch up. I take a deep breath and the air tastes different.

I sit up.

The first thing I'm aware of is my body—there's a thrill running through me, a strength coursing in my veins and muscles, but not necessarily physical strength. I feel . . . altered. Heightened.

I look around. The room is a mess, like a twister came through and tore everything off the beds, out of the closets. I'm vaguely aware of the other people—Lucien behind me, Garnet and Ash against the wall by the door, Sil by the window.

Sil. I can feel her presence. It has its own flavor, its own weight. How had I never noticed it before?

Then I turn and focus on the only person who matters in this moment.

Raven's face isn't the face of the healthy, glowing Raven I saw on the cliff. It is sallow and sweaty, and her lips are cracked and dry. Her hair is lank and sticks to her skin in places.

But her eyes are open.

The emotions that rise up inside me are both familiar and unfamiliar, because it's not just me who is celebrating. There is a new part of me, a new awareness, and I know I will never be without it for the rest of my life.

And from outside, very faintly, I think I hear singing. The pond sings, and the wind, and the trees, and there is so much life around me that for a moment, I'm breathless, captivated by it. Then Raven speaks.

"You found me," she croaks.

The spell is broken, and I fall forward onto her chest and cry. I know it's all right, that I should cry, even though I'm so happy. These tears will help her and help me.

"Yes," I say through my sobs. "I found you."

~ Eighteen ~

SIL TELLS ME TO COME DOWNSTAIRS.

I make Lucien promise to stay with Raven, who falls asleep almost immediately. I watch the rise and fall of her chest until I'm sure it won't stop, until I can truly believe she is alive.

Ash and Garnet stay with her, too. They look at me differently now, wide-eyed and wary, confused. I walk silently past them, following Sil, and wonder what it looked like to them, whatever it was that just happened.

I wonder what destroyed the room.

Sil sets a kettle on to boil. I sink into one of the chairs at the dining table. My hands are shaking.

"So," she says. "Now you know."

I nod.

"How are you feeling?"

I shake my head. I don't have an answer to that. It's like I'm feeling everything all at once, a jumble of emotions mixed with something strange and unfamiliar that doesn't quite feel human.

"That's exactly how Azalea looked when it happened to her. Except she didn't have to bring her friend back from the dead." Sil scratches her ear. "Never seen anything like that."

I stare at the grains of wood in the tabletop.

"Did you get turned into a damned mute, girl?"

My head whips up at the word *mute* as the fire under the kettle flares. Sil literally leans back, the fierceness radiating off me in waves. My anger is heat, like the fire—my skin burns.

"Don't say that to me," I say. "Ever."

"All right," Sil says slowly. "But you need to calm down."

I can't calm down. The heat inside me is searing and the more it burns, the higher the flames leap, until the kettle is engulfed in them. I jump up and back away.

"What's happening?" I say. A potted plant on the windowsill bursts from its ceramic home, its roots crawling across the kitchen floor, its leaves swelling up to twice their normal size. The plant is a worm in the pit of my stomach, growing stronger as the roots slither toward me. I shriek and water explodes out of the faucet in the sink—the fire inside me quenched—but I feel like my skin has melted, slipping around on my bones like it might slide off into a puddle on the floor.

"Out of the house," Sil commands. "Now!"

I fly through the back door, the roots veering in their course to follow me. I slam the door on them and collapse on the steps of the porch, holding my head in my hands and gasping for breath. I don't want to touch anything. I'm afraid to look up. I feel like I'm falling down the incinerator shaft again, as if my insides were all mixed up and my stomach had lodged itself in my throat. I grip my neck in my hands, reminding myself that everything is as it should be, skin and bone and muscle. I am whole.

It may be only a minute but it feels like much longer before Sil comes out to join me. She gives me a pat on the back, which hurts more than comforts.

"Don't worry," Sil says. "It's not the first time I've had a plant explode or a fire in this house. Not by a mile."

"I can't . . . I'm sorry," I say. "I don't know what's happening to me."

"Oh, that's plain as day."

"Maybe you should leave me alone. I don't want to hurt you." I don't know what this new power is, but I feel like it's dangerous. Like *I'm* dangerous.

Sil chuckles. "You don't scare me. I know exactly what you're going through, and I've been doing it longer, and if you want to learn how to live without going insane, you are going to have to *listen to me*."

She shoves a mug of tea into my hands. The steam caresses my face as I grip the mug. It's nice to have something normal to hold on to.

"How did I do it?" I ask. "How did I save her?"

Now Sil laughs a full-throated belly laugh, slapping her

hand against her thigh.

"How should I know?" she says. "What, you think we're all the same? Is every tree in the forest out there the same? Every drop of water in the pond? Of course not. Nature made us all different. But you . . ." She whistles through her teeth. "I don't know. Maybe you're some sort of healer. Maybe it was a fluke. Or maybe you just love that damned girl so much."

I sip my tea. It's chrysanthemum, the kind my mother always made.

"What happened in the room?" I ask. "What did you see?"

"A windstorm," Sil says. "Like I said, it isn't the first time things have been broken around here. Four elements, remember. Air. Earth. Water. Fire."

I think about the flames leaping up from the kettle, how I felt them inside me, like I was on fire. I shudder.

"I didn't feel like me," I say. "It was like . . ."

"You give up part of yourself," she says quietly. "You embody the element. It takes some getting used to."

"So what do I do now?" I ask.

Sil stands. "Come with me."

I put down my mug and follow her across the field. Stars dot the night sky. The air is cold on my skin, but it doesn't penetrate the way it did when I was tied to the birch tree. It's like the fire is still smoldering inside me.

Sil stops at the edge of the pond and looks up. The stars twinkle. The moon's light reflects on the pond's surface. I am so aware of the water, its quiet smoothness. I want to touch it.

"You have the power to connect with every blade of grass in this field, every drop of water, every branch on every tree. They will react to you. But, remember, you do not have power over this force. You are only ever its equal. You must be worthy of that. You give yourself to an element, as it gives itself to you."

I bend down and place my palm on the pond's surface.

"You become the water," Sil says.

Instantly, I sense a connection, like my fingers are fluid, malleable, as if they had become the very water beneath them. The feeling travels up through my arm and into my chest, melting me, molding me—it's scary and exhilarating at the same time. Waves ripple out from under my palm and I feel myself rippling, too. The wind stirs my hair and tickles the back of my neck. Everything is so peaceful, still, and yet so full of life. A quiet, thrumming power. I am awed by it. It is so much more than any Augury.

"Look down," Sil says.

I pull away from the pond's surface and my hand feels solid again. I stand and gaze, awestruck, as a tiny patch of white flowers blossom around my feet. But even as I watch, the petals wave at me, opening and closing, and then brown at the edges. In a few seconds, they have all withered and died, leaving behind no trace of their existence.

"Azalea's were blue her first time," Sil says, staring at the spot where my flowers used to be. "Mine were the darkest red I'd ever seen. Like blood."

"Does that . . . what was that?" My voice is so quiet. I don't want to disrupt whatever just happened.

She claps a hand on my shoulder. The gesture is jarring in this moment, even though her grasp isn't that hard.

"That's life," she says.

Then she walks back to the house, leaving me alone. I sit down and press my hand against the grass. Each individual blade feels different to me. Another little white flower sprouts between my fingers, curling and twisting, reaching up toward me, before it inevitably wilts.

Beautiful, I think. It feels like a sigh, a half-formed, yearning thought. Suddenly, hundreds of white flowers blossom around my hand, wrapping their stems around my knuckles and wrist, their cheery white faces fluttering in the light breeze.

I sit there for a long time, listening to the stars and the pond and the grass and the wind. I have never felt so connected to the world around me. Like I am a very small part of something so large it can't be comprehended. It makes me feel insignificant and unique at the same time.

It's odd, but I somehow feel safer out here than I did in the house. In the wide-open space, with water and air and earth free and uncontained, I am calm.

I think of the dirty streets of the Marsh and the filthy air in the Smoke. I remember what Sil said, how the royalty cut up this island and stitched it back together. I see the royalty as a giant spider, ensnaring everything in its web, engorging itself until its body becomes swollen, and still it's not enough. They will never have enough and it's time for them to be stopped.

For the first time since this whole thing began, I start to feel like it is possible. Like I might be able to help the way Lucien wants. I feel so connected to it all, so filled with the power of the elements—maybe I *can* make a hole in their walls, break down the barriers, help unite the circles. I stretch my hand out across the grass and it swells up, growing to reach my fingers. I feel like I am growing, too. The blades tickle my skin.

"Violet?"

I whip around. Ash is walking toward me. The wind picks up.

"I wanted to make sure you're all right," he says. He stops and looks down. "Whoa."

A trail of white flowers lights up the ground. They swarm around his feet, growing over his shoes.

"Is that you?"

I nod.

"What is it?"

"It's life," I murmur. The flowers wither around him. "How is Raven?"

"Still sleeping." Ash sits beside me. "What you did back there . . . it was incredible. A little terrifying, but incredible."

"I think I might be able to help," I say. "I might be able to do what Lucien wants. I think . . . I think I could break down rock and stone. I think I could make this whole pond turn into a tidal wave if I wanted, or coax the wind into a tornado. So maybe I *can* carve out holes in the walls that separate this city."

Ash smiles my favorite smile and slips his hand in mine. "Well, if whatever went on in that room is any indication,

I'd say you can. I think you can do anything you put your mind to."

"What happened?" I ask. "What did it look like, to you?"

"You went very still," Ash says. "I called your name, and Lucien did, too, but your face . . . it was like you weren't there anymore. And then this wind started, slow at first, but soon it was throwing things around the room. I thought it was going to break the windows. Sil shouted at us not to touch you. You weren't affected by it at all, like you couldn't feel it or hear us. But your expression . . . you were so calm and yet . . . strong. That's the only way I can describe it." He hesitates. "What was it like for you?"

I'm frightened by the idea that I caused something so violent without being aware of it. And I don't want to share the cliff with Ash, not yet. It feels too private. But I want to give him some kind of answer.

"I saw the ocean," I whisper.

There is a heavy pause. I can sense his disbelief. I keep my eyes trained on the pond.

"What was it like?" he finally asks.

"Endless," I say.

We sit in silence for a minute. Though it isn't really silence. I can hear the grass growing and the water rippling and the air breathing.

"Do you think," Ash says hesitantly, "that what you did for Raven . . . could you do that for someone else?"

We both know who he's talking about.

"I don't think it works like that," I say.

I don't mention the fact that we couldn't get to Cinder now, even if we wanted to.

"No," Ash says. "I suppose not."

The wind blows a lock of hair into his eyes. He shakes it away.

"I wish there was more I could do," he says. "I wish I was more useful. Four years in a companion house and all I've learned is how to seduce women. There isn't much value in that."

"You have plenty of value," I say.

"Do I? All my life I've only been worth what someone was willing to pay for me."

"I never paid for you," I say. "And you are beyond priceless to me."

Ash cups my neck with his hand and pulls me in for a kiss. His lips feel magnificent—soft and warm and full of life. I could devour him. I want to feel his skin on my skin again. I want to feel all of him in this new body, with these new senses. He pulls back as another wave of white flowers swells up around us and dies.

"You're not bleeding," he says, running his finger down the length of my nose. "Not like you did at the incinerator."

I rub the base of my skull. "No," I say. "And the headaches are gone, too. This is what I'm *supposed* to do. It's the four elements, Sil says—I'm connected to them, somehow. I'm not controlling them, or forcing them, or twisting them to something else." I think about the fiery kettle. "They scare me, though. There's so much power in them. And we never knew. I don't even think the *royalty* knows."

I sigh. "I should probably go back inside. I want to be with Raven."

Ash tightens his grip on my hand. "Sil is cooking," he says. "She suggested that you stay out here for that. Actually, she suggested that you stay out here all night. Apparently, you can do a fair bit of damage in your sleep. Or, I guess Azalea did."

"Oh."

"Raven will be fine," he says. "Garnet and Lucien are with her."

"Right."

"Violet," he says, his fingers brushing my cheek. "I'm staying out here with you."

"Oh no, Ash, you don't have to . . . I mean . . . you probably shouldn't. I don't want to hurt you."

"I know you're alone in this thing, that I can't possibly understand what you're going through. But I can be here with you. For you. That, at least, I am capable of. So here I am." He shoots me a sidelong glance. "Please don't set me on fire in the middle of the night."

"That's not funny," I say.

Ash rolls his eyes. "Sil told me you can't create anything, only affect what's already there. So unless you're planning on sleeping with some matches and a can of kerosene, I think I'm safe." He kisses my temple. "I'll go get some blankets and pillows."

I grab his arm and hold him back. "No," I say. "Stay here with me for a while longer."

Ash inclines his head and settles back by my side. He

wraps his arm around my shoulders and pulls me against his chest. I breathe him in and feel his heartbeat, strong and steady under my cheek, his life and my life and the life of everything around us intertwined in this moment.

We sit like that in the quiet of the night, as white flowers bloom and fade around us.

~ Nineteen ~

I WAKE AT DAWN TO FIND SIL STANDING OVER ME.

She's wearing her signature overalls and a thick woolen scarf. Clutched in her hands is a thin leather portfolio, sheets of yellowing paper sticking out around its edges.

She puts her finger to her lips and jerks her head toward the trees.

Ash is sleeping peacefully beside me. I untangle myself from his arms and the blankets as gently as I can—he sighs and rolls onto his back, but doesn't wake. We slept in the shadow of the barn, so the trees are close by. Sil wanders through the edge of the forest, always keeping the White Rose in sight, until we are a good distance from Ash. On the far side of the clearing, gray light is kissing the treetops, hints of orange and gold peeking out through their branches.

"I didn't want to burden you with this last night," Sil says, holding up the portfolio. "I know you had a lot to take in."

I nod. The air is chilly and I miss the warmth of Ash's body. But at the same time, I can feel the whole world waking up.

Sil stops at a huge sycamore. She groans as she lowers herself onto the ground, resting her back against its wide trunk.

"Sit," she says, patting the grass beside her.

As I do, I become very aware of the earth beneath me, its rich, heavy texture, the roots that live and grow inside it. Somewhere deep below, I think I sense the rush of water. An underground river, maybe?

"You feel it all, don't you?" Sil says.

"There's so much," I say. "How are you not . . . how can you . . . live normally?"

She barks out a laugh. "I don't."

The sun begins to rise, painting the sky with streaks of pink. Sil puts the portfolio between us.

"You need to learn your history," she says. "When this power came to me, I had no understanding of it. I was terrified. And I was alone. For years I wondered where it all came from, this magic that got twisted into the Auguries. Was it some failed royal experiment? Then Azalea came, and Lucien, and he had access to the oldest library in the entire city."

"The Duchess's library," I say. I remember the Duchess

bragging at dinner one night about how her ancestors built the Great Wall, how it was her *duty* to preserve the literature of their time.

Sil nods. "Lucien has been smuggling anything he could find out of that library for me. Piece by piece, I've put this puzzle together. Or at least, I've done the best I could. The only ones who could truly explain it are long dead."

She opens the portfolio. I pick it up with trembling hands—the pages are very old and I'm afraid that if I touch them they'll crumble to dust. The first page looks to be a map. It's the island, but without the city—there are markers on it that I've never seen. Several red Xs line the coastline. Other areas within the island are circled, with scribbled notes that I can barely make out. "Topaz deposit," one says. "Rich soil," another circle is marked.

I flip to another page. This one is filled with thin, slanted writing. It looks like a list of names, but they are strange and unfamiliar.

Pantha Seagrass
Jucinde Soare

There are twenty names in all. I would guess they are all women—the names feel distinctly female to me. And at the bottom of the page is a note that sets a chill creeping through my chest.

Execution date, March 5, in the year of the Founding.

The year of the Founding. The year the Lone City was formed.

I turn to the next page. It's filled with very crude illustrations—one shows a woman holding what appears to be a handful of flames. Another shows a young girl, her arms outstretched, a massive blue wave cresting over her head.

Other pages are too smudged to read, with only a few words and phrases written clearly.

. . . to stomp out the source at its heart . . .
. . . ours to command . . .
. . . mercy . . . of death . . .
. . . riches . . .
. . . promised . . .

But it's a page near the end that holds my attention. Probably because it is the oldest and yet the best preserved. I have a feeling that when Lucien recovered it for Sil, she took great pains to take care of it. It is almost entirely legible. There is a date at the top that I don't recognize . . . was this document written before the Founding?

I start to read, and the first sentence makes my stomach swoop, like I've missed a step going down the stairs.

The island was called Excelsior, the Jewel of the Earth.

I look up. Sil is watching me with a steady gaze, her silver eyes sparkling in the early-morning light.

"Yes," she says. "This island had a name once. And it was not the Lone City." She nods at the page. "Keep reading."

Legend spoke of its riches—thick black dirt where any crop could grow, lush green trees that sang when the ocean breezes tickled their leaves, wild animals of all kinds, striped cats and brilliantly plumed birds and scaly lizards. But most of all, caverns upon caverns of precious gems. Diamond, topaz, garnet, ruby, emerald, sapphire. All these and more.

The next few sentences are hard to read. I see a reference to the House of the Lake, another to the House of the Stone. Something about alliances, and another mention of riches. The next paragraph is much clearer.

But the island was merely myth. The people of Bellstar—ruled by Lake and Scales—and the people of Ellaria—ruled by Stone and Rose— knew this to be true. Many had tried to find the island. None had succeeded. Those who returned spoke of evil winds that blew their ships asunder, or giant waves that swept their crew overboard to a watery grave, never catching even a glimpse of their destination.

But the royal families were not to be dissuaded. Hundreds of ships were built and the great race began. Which country would find the

Jewel of the Earth and claim it for their own?
    I was hired by the House of the Scales, to work
as a scribe. My father did not wish for me to take
this journey. But I had to see the island for myself.
    Dark days . . .

The rest of that paragraph is faded and smudged. I turn
to the next page.

In the end, it took all four families working
together to conquer the island, its magic so deep,
its boundaries so well protected. But the natives
were no match for the power of the cannon,
the brute force of royal weaponry. I have made
a further account of the attack on the western
shore, though, as it does not portray the royalty in
a favorable light, I imagine it will not live to see
beyond this day.
    The executions took place at dawn. Not a
single woman in the village was spared, for who
knew which of them possessed the strange and
wondrous ability to speak to the sea and the wind
and the earth? They call themselves the Paladin,
guardians of Excelsior. They claim it is their duty
to protect the island.
    The royalty is convinced they will track them
all down, but I am not as certain.

The rest of the page is blurred. My hands are shaking
so violently, I have to close the portfolio to make sure that

I don't harm its contents. My brain whirs as I make sense of everything. The royalty always claimed this island was uninhabited. That was the story. That they found it, settled it, built the Lone City.

They never said there were people here.

"Yes," Sil muses, gazing out at the trees across the field. "They really are a bunch of bastards, aren't they."

"Who were they?" I ask. "Those women?"

"They are our ancestors," she says. "We are descendants of the Paladin. The guardians of this island." Her voice is warm and rich, reverent. She places her palms down on the earth beside her. "This island gives us power, I believe. In return, we were trusted with its protection. But we were lost for so long. They thought they killed us, but our good friend the scribe knew differently."

It is strange to think of myself as descended from an ancient race of magical women.

"Maybe that's what that place was," I murmur.

"What place?" Sil asks. I tell her about the cliff and the monument, where I found Raven and brought her back.

"You saw the ocean?" she gasps.

I nod. Sil covers her mouth with her hand, and for a moment, I think she might cry.

"I knew we were connected to it," she mutters to herself, "but I never . . ."

"What are you talking about?"

"When I was dying in the morgue," she says, "I heard a strange sound, like waves, and I smelled something sharp and salty. I'd never smelled seawater before but I was certain that was it. It called to me. It comforted me." She blinks and looks away. "I wish I could see it. These walls . . . these damned walls have been standing for too long." She turns back to me with a sudden ferocity. "Don't you see? This is *our island*. They took it from us, they murdered our ancestors and claimed it as their own. This is about so much more than the Auction. This is about a race of people enslaved and made extinct. But we are not gone. They couldn't kill all of us, and it's time for them to pay for what they've done."

"And you believe that I can break down parts of their walls?"

"I think that's what you were born to do," Sil says.

We sit in silence for a long while. It's so much to take in. I hold out a hand over the grass and feel the roots in the earth groan and stretch. I welcome their strength. I feel as if I could ask them to shoot up from the ground or dig deeper into the earth and they would. I feel as if these trees had been thirsty for someone like me. The air is crisp and cold and infused with desire. To protect. To be protected. To help.

"You understand so quickly," Sil says. "This place is special. They called me here, I think—the Paladin. Their spirits, if you believe in such things. There is an energy here. I think this place might have once been important to them."

"How did you get here?" I ask.

"That's a long story." She rubs the back of her scarred hand.

I wait. With an exaggerated sigh, she leans back against the sycamore.

"You know how I got out of the Jewel."

"The incinerator."

She nods. "I wandered around those sewers for who

knows how long. I was starving. I was terrified. When I finally made it out, I found myself in the Bank. I'd never been to the Bank before. I had no idea where I was. I hid in an alley behind a shop." Her gaze softens. "That was when I saw my flowers. But I didn't find them beautiful. I was frightened of them, of what was happening to me. I didn't feel in control—how you felt last night but a hundred times worse because I was alone. I thought I was going insane. It began to rain. It rained for days, huge biting sheets of water that wouldn't stop. It was me, I suppose, though I didn't know it at the time. I scavenged for food in trash cans. I stole clothes and bandages for my arm. But I could only go out at night. The wind followed me everywhere. Trees would turn into twisted, gnarled versions of their former selves." She lovingly pats a root poking out from the ground. "I finally had the courage to venture out farther into the Bank. I found a train station and hid on the train. I didn't know where I was going but I couldn't stay in the Bank. The train took me to the very same station it took you."

Tiny red flowers grow up around Sil's knees. She brushes her fingers over them before they wither.

"It was a bit easier for me, not having a wanted fugitive as a travel companion." She shoots me a wry look. "No one was looking for me. Everyone thought I was dead. But I was frightened to be around people. I was dangerous. I didn't know how to explain what was happening, but things would go wrong around me. There's a little town outside this forest. I set a store on fire. A terrible wind came and ripped shutters off houses. A little boy was injured. I had to leave.

"No one knew it was me, of course. No one paid any attention to a dirty, orphaned teenage girl. But I left and came to this forest. I felt drawn to it. For two days, I ate nuts and bark, and drank water from the streams that run through it. But something pulled at me. The deeper I went into the woods, the stronger the pull became. Then I found this old house, rotting away, alone, abandoned. And I knew it was meant for me."

Sil looks across the field at the redbrick farmhouse.

"Why is it called the White Rose?" I ask.

"I named it," she says. "It was autumn when I arrived. There was a garden by the porch, all dry leaves and withered stalks. Nothing had grown for years. I stood there, looking at this abandoned wreck, trying to convince myself that it could become my home, that I could find a safe place within its walls. And then a single rose blossomed from a dead rosebush, right in front of me. It was whiter than snow and softer than a rabbit's fur. And it grew out of nothing. I felt like I could do that, too, I could make something beautiful for myself out of nothing." Sil shakes her head. "What an idealistic fool I was."

"But you did make something for yourself," I say, nodding toward the White Rose.

"Yes, yes," Sil says, as if that were somehow beside the point. "I found I could grow my own food, quickly and easily. I didn't have to steal. I could sell or barter for clothes and supplies. I set to work fixing up this place." She shakes her head. "The power was better here. Easier. It didn't frighten me so much. But I felt . . . isolated."

I try to imagine living by myself in the woods for forty

years, with nothing but a strange and unknown power to keep me company. I think I'd lose my mind.

"Then, about three years ago, this girl stumbles onto my doorstep, with a lady-in-waiting of all people in tow. I knew what she was immediately, of course. But she'd never been to a holding facility—Lucien had whisked her away somewhere as soon as she reached womanhood. He'd been hiding her in various places all over the Farm. Her family might have been elevated from living in the Marsh to the Farm, but you can bet the royalty isn't going to let any Marsh-born girl go untested for surrogacy." Sil's eyes grow distant and I wonder what memory is replaying in her mind. "Azalea hadn't been twisted up like all the other surrogates. I thought I could show her. I didn't want to be alone with this power anymore.

"It took Azalea a long time before she felt it. We didn't know what her scores might have been, but probably not close to yours or mine. She couldn't use all of the elements—she could only connect with Air. She used to have nightmares that tore up the furniture. She started sleeping outside. Said she liked it better out here, anyway." Sil smiles and tilts her head up to the sky. "She had a big heart. She was infuriatingly optimistic. For the first time in a long time, I was happy. I had companionship. So when she started talking about saving the other surrogates and how the royalty needed to be stopped, I told her she should be happy that she was safe. Lucien agreed with me. Just about the only thing we agreed on at that point." She chuckles. "Oh, but Azalea was young and full of hope and had never lived in the Jewel. It hardens you, living in that place. It holds up a mirror and shows you the very worst parts of humanity. It changes people."

I shiver.

"And she thought we could do it," Sil continues, "that we could use the elements against them, the way they used the Auguries against us. That this was what we were meant for. That was at the time when I was looking to the past, learning our history. Lucien would do anything for Azalea, including stealing documents right out from under the Duchess's nose. But I wouldn't hear of any such rebellion and neither would her brother. She was safe, we kept telling her, that was all that mattered." She rubs her forehead. "I forgot what it was to be young. To be full of ideas, to think it is possible to change the world. I was selfish. I didn't . . ." Sil swallows and looks away from me. "I believe she allowed herself to be caught, to be tested positive as a surrogate. She knew it was the only way. She didn't want to live my life, to be stuck on this farm forever with nothing but the wind and the trees for company. She wanted more, not only for herself, but for everyone."

"So that's when you and Lucien teamed up?" I ask.

Sil lets out a hard laugh. "I wouldn't call us a team. More like an unlikely alliance." She runs her hand over the sycamore's bark. "This place mourned when she died. We mourned her together." She looks at me. "And now you are here and we have hope again. Hope for our sisters locked away in the holding facilities." She moves to stand, then stops herself. "What is she like?" she asks.

"Who?"

"The Duchess. I'm . . . curious."

"Oh." The Duchess is so many things, but my last memory of her is burned into my mind. "She killed my friend. Right in front of me." My throat tightens.

"So I created a murderer," Sil muses.

"I don't think you're responsible for everything she is," I say.

"Oh, you can bet your boots I am," Sil snaps. "I told you, her father was damned evil." She rubs the back of her neck. "I know the other one died. The younger sister. Read about it in the paper. Turned her back on the royalty and everything."

"Maybe that was you, too," I say.

Sil frowns.

"Violet?" Ash's voice drifts across the clearing. I stand up, brushing the dirt from my pants. Sil takes the portfolio and hugs it to her chest.

"He doesn't belong here, you know," Sil says. "He's not one of us."

My spine stiffens. "He belongs with me," I say.

"He'll cloud your judgment."

"Like Azalea clouded yours?"

Sil's eyes flash. "Exactly."

"Well, I'm not you," I say. And without waiting for a response, I turn on my heel and march back to the barn, where Ash is still calling my name.

~ Twenty ~

"So . . . you're saying you're descended from a race of magical women the royalty tried to extinguish?" Ash says.

We're walking back to the White Rose. I want to see Raven. But I explained to him what Sil told me.

"Do you have to say it like that?"

"Like what?"

"Like you don't believe me."

"I do believe you," he says. "I mean, it certainly sounds like something the royalty would do—annihilate an indigenous population. I'd like to see those papers Sil showed you."

I doubt there's a chance of that happening, but I don't say that to Ash.

"I've been thinking about something else Sil said," I say. "About Azalea. She could only connect with Air. I was thinking . . . maybe the Augury scores actually do tell us something useful. Maybe because Sil and I scored perfectly on Growth, that indicates that we can access all the elements."

"That sounds logical. Though I'm no expert on the Auguries."

I chew on my bottom lip.

"What's worrying you?" he asks. "If you can control the earth, can't you ask it to bring down the walls? Isn't that what Lucien wants?"

"There's only one of me. This power is incredible, sure, but . . . the walls are so thick. The royalty have guns. They have an army. What if I only get through one wall and find I don't have the strength? Do the royalty even need the walls to protect themselves?"

We've reached the pond. I crouch at its edge and place my hand on its cold surface. I want to feel what I felt last night.

What was it Sil had said? That we must embody the element in order to connect with it.

I become the water.

My skin goes slippery again as I join with the pond. It ripples inside me, glassy and bright. I push out across it, and I am the wave that rises up, high over our heads. Ash gasps, and the wave and I come crashing down, spraying him with a fine mist.

I take my hand away and look up at him, suppressing a giggle.

"Sorry," I say, as he shakes drops of water from his hair.

"You know," he says, taking my hand to help me up, "at Madame Curio's, they liked to keep us in competition with each other, all the time. Book a big client, and you'd get a certain number of points. Master a skill, and you'd get more points. They kept a big scoreboard up in the main hall, with a record for each companion. Earn enough points and get a reward. They didn't want us to be a unified front. They liked keeping us separate."

"Oh," I say, not quite knowing where he's going with this.

Ash senses my hesitation and smiles. "That's what you need. A united front."

"Of what?" Right now, the united front seems to consist of three surrogates, one lady-in-waiting, a companion, and a royal son. It's a pretty ragtag bunch.

"A united front of surrogates." Ash shrugs. "I mean, wouldn't all the surrogates be capable of this power? If you are all descended from ancient warrior women?"

I gasp. Several things seem to click together in my brain all at once. I think about what Sil said earlier, how Azalea could only access Air, not the other elements. I think about the incinerator, how Raven and I put the fire out *together*. We were stronger together.

The highest concentration of surrogates is in the Marsh, in the holding facilities. Four facilities in four key locations, north, south, east, and west.

We don't need to break down the all walls. We only need to get inside one—the Jewel.

"Lucien!" I shout. My feet feel rooted to the earth. I grab Ash's arm. "You're a genius," I say.

"What is it?" Lucien comes storming out of the house, followed by Garnet and—my heart squeezes—Raven. She's wrapped in a thick quilt, and Garnet keeps one hand at her back, as if he were afraid she might collapse at any moment. She looks tired, but healthy. Alive.

"How are you feeling?" I say.

Raven smiles at me, her old smile. "It's like this fog has been lifted. Like a weight is gone. I feel . . . clear. Not the same as before but better." She shoots Garnet an irritated glance. "You can tell him to stop hovering. He's worse than my mother."

"You collapsed on me last night," Garnet says. "I'd like to stay within catching distance."

It hits me then that Raven is no longer pregnant. The threat is gone.

"What did you call me for?" Lucien asks. He's changed back into his lady-in-waiting garb.

"Are you leaving?" I ask.

"I have to get back to the Jewel," he says. "Garnet is coming with me. It would be poor form to miss his own wedding."

Garnet grimaces behind Lucien's back.

"I have an idea," I say. "I don't think I'm enough, on my own. You want me to essentially destroy pieces of the walls surrounding each circle, to integrate the populations of the Marsh and Farm and everything, so that this whole city can fight together. But it will take time to get to each of them. And we don't know whether I'm strong enough. What if I can only break down part of one wall? Or what if I get hurt in some way? Then you don't have anyone to help."

"Violet, I don't—"

"No, listen. I assume you have Society members in each circle, right?" Lucien nods. "So let them take care of their own circles. Fight the royalty where they've set up their puppets, in the Bank and the Smoke and all the rest. Let the circles fight for themselves." I remember the Thief, how well he knew the East Quarter of the Smoke. "Why mix up the circles so quickly? I agree it has to be done, but let's pull out the royal roots first. Then we can all break down the walls together."

"And what about the Jewel?" Lucien asks. "Who will fight the royalty where they live?"

"The surrogates," I say confidently.

He raises an eyebrow. "Excuse me?"

"Ash was telling me about the necessity of a unified front. That's what we need. They have an army of Regimentals. I think we need to fight them with an army of surrogates."

"An *army* of surrogates?"

"There is so much potential locked up in those holding facilities," I say. "We need to get to them, show them what they are capable of. *And who they really are*, I add silently. I think of what Sil said to me earlier, about the Paladin being guardians of this island. "I think it's what we were meant to do."

"How do you plan to get into the holding facilities?"

I frown. "I'm not sure yet. But I know every inch of Southgate. And I know many of the girls there. I think they'll trust me. So you need to bring three girls here, from the Jewel. One from each of the other three holding facilities. The ones with the highest Growth scores. If the Growth score indicates compatibility with the elements, then we'll need the best we can get, the ones who can access the highest number of elements."

"And once I've rescued three more surrogates, and you have trained them in this power, how do you propose to get a whole host of surrogates to the Jewel?"

It comes to me in a flash, the most obvious answer sitting there all along. A smile plays on my lips. "We'll use the Auction."

"Yes," Raven says, nodding.

"I don't get it," Garnet says.

"The Auction," I explain. "The trains to the Auction House. We have to get as many girls on those trains as possible. And then the royalty will unwittingly get us into the Jewel. We won't need to break down that wall. The royalty will bring us inside it on their own."

Garnet whistles through his teeth. "I'll give you credit, that's pretty brilliant."

"The Auction isn't until October," Lucien points out. "That's months away."

I bite my lip. He's right. How long can we risk waiting? I worry again about Hazel being tested. We need to end the Auction before that ever has a chance to happen.

"It's a place to start," Ash says. "Coordinate attacks within each circle with the Auction and the royalty won't know what hit them. I'd suggest the Regimental barracks and the magistrate offices for starters. Maybe even the banks. They can't fight everyone at once, not if they're being attacked from within their own walls."

Lucien shoots him a disdainful glance.

"It's a good idea," I insist.

Lucien sighs. "I suppose you have some surrogate or other in mind to be rescued from the Jewel."

I nod.

"Another friend?" he asks.

"No," I say. "But I think she's exactly what we need."

And I tell Lucien about the lioness.

~ Twenty-One ~

"HOW'S OUR STAR REVOLUTIONARY DOING?" GARNET'S voice is tinny through the arcana, which floats above Raven's shoulder.

She's perched on a pyramid of hay bales. Two weeks at the White Rose and she's changed into a new person—healthier, happier.

"Outstanding," Raven says. "Violet's a natural at this."

I become the air.

I accept the element, dissolving into weightless molecules that scoop up the individual strands of hay littered on the barn floor. They hang there, suspended. I can feel each of their tiny weights. I float them over to Raven, and they circle her like oddly shaped planets orbiting a sun.

She claps. Ash chuckles from where he stands brushing Turnip, Sil's horse, who had been called Horse until Ash started taking care of the animals. Turnip is the nickname he gave to Cinder as a baby.

"She should try embroidery," Garnet suggests. "Or knitting. You know, challenge herself."

"Or maybe she should start collecting miniature tea sets," Raven says with a smirk. "So she and your wife can have little crafts parties."

"I'll have you know, Coral has exactly two hundred sixty-five of those things. Trust me. She's counted. To my face. I had to sit there and smile while she gave me a whole presentation. I mean, it's a ridiculous obsession, but you have to admire her determination."

"Color me impressed."

"I'm going to pretend that wasn't sarcastic."

Raven talks to Garnet more than I do. They love poking fun at each other. I think he keeps her sharp. He reminds her of how she used to be.

"I thought you called for a reason," Raven says. "Anything to report from the Jewel?"

The strands of hay fall to the floor as I release the connection with Air. I want to be fully present for this conversation.

"I haven't seen Lucien since the wedding," Garnet says, "so I don't know what he's up to. My mother has some plan up her sleeve, but no luck getting it out of her—and I can't very well pretend to have a sudden interest in surrogates."

"A plan involving a surrogate?" I say. "But she doesn't have one."

"Yes, but no one in the Jewel besides me and Lucien know that. Oh, and that new companion you guys told me about, since he obviously saw you, Violet."

"His name is Rye," Raven reminds him.

"How is he doing?" Ash asks, putting the brush down.

"Fine, I guess. I haven't talked to him, he doesn't know about the Society or anything. Carnelian is still moping over you, if you can believe it. She talks about you all the time to him. I think she's hoping he'll tell her some quality Ash Lockwood stories. It's sort of sad, actually."

"But what about the surrogate plan?" I say. I don't want to waste time talking about Carnelian. "What could she be thinking?"

"Like I said before, she doesn't confide in me. And I'm trying to play the perfect son, you know, marriage has straightened me out, no more late nights in Bank taverns, that type of thing." He pauses. "But she's definitely up to something. She took a letter to the Exetor last night. Delivered it *personally*. The last time my mother delivered her own mail was . . . well, probably never."

"And the Society?" Ash asks, scattering a handful of feed to the chickens pecking around in their pen. "What are they up to? Any developments?"

"You'd have to ask Lucien about that," Garnet says. "All I know is what I've read in the papers. And that's because I know to look for it."

The Society has been vandalizing royal property, hitting specific targets in the Smoke and the Farm. Mostly magistrate offices and Regimental barracks, like Ash had suggested, though Lucien would never admit that Ash had a good idea. They are finding weaknesses in places where the royalty have their claws in the lower circles. They haven't taken credit for it, though there was one mention of a black key being drawn on the door of a post office. Lucien didn't sound too happy when he told us about that.

Neither did Ash, but I think that's because he'd rather be out with the vandals. I know he's frustrated by our isolation, and his lack of an active role in this revolution. I can see it in his face now and the tense set of his shoulders.

"I'm going for a run," he says. He scratches one of the goats behind the ears and stalks out of the barn.

Ash runs the perimeter of the White Rose at least twice a day. I think it helps him channel all that pent-up energy.

"Was it something I said?" Garnet asks.

"No." I sigh. "He's just frustrated."

"Tell me about it. At least he doesn't have to sit through a lecture on the difference between bone china and porcelain."

"And which do you prefer?" Raven teases.

"Oh, bone china, definitely. Did you know it's the whitest of all dinnerware?"

Raven and I laugh.

"I have to go," Garnet says abruptly, and the arcana goes silent. Raven catches it before it hits the hay bales. She hops off them and hands it back to me.

"What do you think the Duchess is up to?" she asks.

"I don't know. It's worrying that she still talks as if she had a surrogate."

"Yeah," she says. "You don't think she stole one from some other royal woman?"

"I think that would have been front-page news."

"Probably." Raven purses her lips. "I'm going to make some tea. Want some?"

I nod. "I'll be in in a minute."

As soon as she is out the door, I sigh and throw my arms out wide.

I become the air.

Hundreds of pieces of hay rise up as I join with the element. It's exhilarating, the sense of weightlessness Air gives me. It's like flying with my feet on the ground. I soar up to the very top of the barn, bringing the hay with me.

Turnip stamps her feet.

The arcana buzzes in my hand and I release my connection with the element.

"She's on her way to you," Lucien says. Pieces of hay drift down and land in my hair and Turnip's mane. She shakes her head and lets out a snort.

"The lioness?"

"Lot 199, yes."

I hate that neither of us know her name.

"What did you tell her?" I ask.

"I didn't *tell* her anything," he says. "We can't approach this in the same way I did with you. I'll get the girls to you the safest way I can."

"Which is how?"

"My original plan," Lucien says, with a bite of impatience. "I dosed her wine with the serum. In the nick of time, too. I think the Countess of the Rose was about to arrange for her to have an *accident*."

I shudder at his meaning. "So . . . she's going to show up

here and have no idea what's going on?"

"I'm doing my part," he says, "you have to do yours. She'll be on the two o'clock train arriving at Bartlett Station tomorrow afternoon. Look for the key."

"I always do," I say.

IT'S VERY COLD THE NEXT DAY. I WRAP MY SCARF TIGHTER around me and pull down the earflaps on my hat.

Sil gave me a ridiculous pair of goggles to wear, tinted to hide my eyes. Just to be safe, in case anyone is looking for me.

"I want to come," Ash says, as he hooks up Turnip to the cart.

"Not a chance," Sil says from the driver's seat. Ash spares her a cold look before turning back to me.

"I want to come," he says again. "I want to *do* something."

"I know," I say. "But . . . it's too dangerous. What if someone recognized you again?"

"With your pretty face, you can bet someone will call the Regimentals as quick as you can say Halma," Sil says.

"Violet disguised me once," he says. "She could do it again."

"Ash . . ." I hesitate. "That was using the Auguries. I don't . . . I don't want to use them anymore." This is only partly true. I can still use the Auguries, but it's more concern for Ash's safety that holds me back. I won't risk his life.

"Right," he says curtly. "I get it."

"Will you take care of Raven for me while I'm gone?"

"Raven can take care of herself now."

I put my hand on his arm. "We'll be back soon. Maybe . . . maybe you can come next time."

Ash nods, but I know he doesn't believe me. He gives Turnip's flank a pat, and storms off to the barn.

I sigh and climb up next to Sil.

"That companion is getting on my nerves," she says.

"He's not a companion anymore," I say as the cart lurches forward. "I wish you and Lucien would remember that. And he's . . . frustrated. He wants to help."

"How is he supposed to help? Seduce our way into the Jewel?"

"You don't understand anything about him."

Sil laughs.

The ride through the forest is very different from that night Lucien brought me here. The sky is a clear, cloudless blue, the air cold and crisp. My irritation fades, replaced by my excitement at finally being out of the boundaries of the White Rose.

"We need to make a stop first," Sil says.

"Where?" I ask. I'm not sure I realized how stir-crazy I was going, but now that we're out in the world again, I'm bursting with energy.

"I have to run an errand for His Royal Keyness," she says.

We emerge from the wood and I gasp—when I arrived in the Farm, it was dark and I was in a barrel for most of the journey. Now that I can see it . . . there is so much space. I've become used to the wide field surrounding the White Rose, the familiar ring of trees that encompass my whole world.

I'd forgotten how big the real world actually is.

Fields stretch out as far as I can see. We're on top of a hill, and in the distance, nestled in a little dip between hills, there is a small town, chimney smoke and pointed rooftops. A big farmhouse looms off to my right, amid neatly trained rows of yellowing grass. I wonder what will be growing here when the seasons change. My most vivid memory from that fateful train ride to the Jewel is the colors of the Farm. The pinks, the oranges, the greens . . . everything is dull yellow and rusty brown now.

But I still find it beautiful.

"Which Quarter are we in?" I ask.

"The South," Sil says.

"My brother, Ochre, works in the South Quarter," I say. It's nice to feel close to someone in my family, even if it's only pretend. The South Quarter is huge—he could be anywhere.

Thinking of Ochre makes me think of Hazel. Again, I worry about the timing of this plan. We've got to stop the Auction before she can be tested. I wish it wasn't so far away. October feels like ages from now. It's only January.

As we pass through the town, I find it hard not to gape at everything. The people, women in long wool dresses and thick cloaks, men in overalls and big furry hats; the houses, shingled in dark reds and yellows; the grocer's, the magistrate's office, the tool-and-seed store. And then I have to laugh at myself because I lived in the Jewel for three months and saw so many incredible things and now I'm awed by a greengrocer.

We pull up in front of a tavern. A painted sign, carved in the shape of a tree, creaks in the wind. Bold letters on it proclaim the tavern's name, THE WISHING WELL. I smile, wondering whether the owner is a fan of the children's folktale. There is a white square of paper plastered to a signpost out front. I can barely make out the words.

WANTED. FUGITIVE.

The paper is weathered and faded, but Ash's face is still clearly recognizable. It sends a shudder through me. I was right to keep him at home. Sil ties up Turnip.

"Keep your mouth shut and let me do the talking," she mutters. "We won't be here long."

The Wishing Well has a broad wooden porch and a balcony overlooking the street. Strains of music can be heard from behind its windows, which are framed with white lace curtains. Its facade is painted a friendly yellow. It is a very far cry from the taverns I saw on the Row, in the seedy area of the Bank.

The interior is as pleasant as the exterior. The bar is made of dark, polished wood, with three shelves behind it containing gleaming bottles of spirits in all shapes and sizes. A mirror on the wall lists the specials of the day in big, loopy handwriting. Tables are scattered across the pale wooden flooring, only about a handful of them containing customers. A wizened old man on a barstool sips whiskey from a dusty glass tumbler, riffling through the *Lone City Herald*. A man in a striped shirt plays piano in the far corner of the room.

"Sil!" the barman cries, emerging through a pair of swinging doors that lead to, I'd guess, the kitchen. He carries a plate of roast chicken and green beans smothered in almonds. My stomach gurgles. "Be right with you."

He hurries off to deliver the food while Sil and I take seats at the bar. I notice that Sil chooses bar stools as far away from the smoking man as possible.

"He knows he's not supposed to call me that," Sil grumbles.

"Do you have a code name, too?" I ask.

Sil's lips pucker, and her cheeks darken ever so slightly. She ignores me and instead grabs an extra copy of the *Herald* and pretends to scan through it.

"It's been quite some time since last I saw you," the barman says, coming over to us. He pulls a bottle off one of the shelves and takes out two glasses. "The usual? And who's your young friend?"

"No one," Sil says, putting down the paper. "And she's not drinking."

The barman must be used to Sil's bluntness—he nods and pours two helpings of whiskey into the glasses, taking one for himself. Sil downs hers in one gulp.

"Here." She removes a brown-wrapped parcel from inside her coat. "Something to help the Shepherd boy."

The barman's face falls. "Ah, yes. He seems to be recovering well, considering."

"Considering what?" I ask. Sil throws me a sharp glance.

"His grandfather wanted to sell him as a lady-in-waiting," the barman says in a hushed voice.

"But he botched the job," Sil says. "Damn near killed that poor boy."

"How awful," I gasp.

"Yes." The barman eyes me suspiciously and I drop my gaze. He turns to Sil. "Do you have any message from the Black Key?"

"Do I ever come here without one?" she says. Her forehead crinkles in concentration as she recites, "Third from the right, fourth from the left. Westing's Inn. Looks like gin." She nods appreciatively at herself. "That's it. And don't write it down this time. That's missing the whole damned point."

The barman nods, muttering the cryptic message over to himself.

"I'd better be off," she says. She slaps a couple of diamantes on the bar. The two glittering silver coins are engraved with the face of Diamante the Great, the Electress who started the first Auction.

"No charge," the barman says, waving the money off. But Sil leaves it, and we walk out into the cold air. I grab the paper on my way out.

"What was that about?" I ask as we climb back into the cart and start off down the busy thoroughfare.

"Weapons," Sil grunts. "Lucien's got some people making them in the Smoke and shipping them here. But it's hard. Can't make or ship more than a few at a time. Slow going for a revolutionary force made up of farmers and factory workers. And forgetful barmen."

I think about the Seamstress and the Cobbler and the Thief, the only other members of the Society that I've met. Without them we would never have made it to the Farm but . . . while immensely helpful in espionage and escape, they don't seem like the makings of an army. Certainly not one that could win against the united force of the Regimentals.

Sil seems to read my mind. "Not your job," she says, cracking the reins to send Turnip into a trot. "We've got a train to catch."

"What did you give him for that boy?" I ask.

She shrugs. "Powdered red willow bark and clove. Should help numb the pain some."

"What will happen to him?"

"He'll live." She doesn't sound optimistic.

I open the paper and flip through it. There was a party at the Lady of the Light's palace that got a bit out of hand—a few royal sons started throwing fists at one another. The paper notes that "it was a scene worthy of Garnet of the House of the Lake, but marriage seems to have tempered the Jewel's most-notorious bad boy's disposition."

I scan the other pages. There's a birth announcement that sets my teeth on edge. "The House of the Willow welcomes a baby girl. Name to be announced." No mention of the surrogate. Another girl dead because of them.

I turn the page and my breath catches in my throat. The Duchess's face stares out at me. Her dark hair is swept up and studded with pearls, and she wears a dress with a plunging neckline. It's like I can feel her eyes on me, and their cold cruelness sends a chill up my spine. The headline reads, DUCHESS OF THE LAKE GRANTED PRIVATE AUDIENCE WITH EXETOR.

This must have to do with the letter Garnet said she delivered. But what is she up to?

Bartlett Station is about thirty minutes outside the town, in a narrow gully surrounded by hills. There must be a lot of deliveries on this train, because there are about ten or fifteen carts waiting at the station. Several of the men eye me and Sil as they puff away on hand-rolled cigarettes. I'm grateful for my hat and goggles.

I hear the train before I see it—two whistle blows that echo off the surrounding hills. The train, big and black, jetting thick white smoke, rounds a bend. It pulls up to the station with a deafening screech, as men with soot-darkened faces jump off, opening the doors on the boxcars, and haul out crates and sacks and packages wrapped in brown paper.

I look for anything marked with a black key, and find it drawn on a crate being unloaded. I wince as two men drop it unceremoniously on the ground.

"That's us," Sil says.

The crate has two handles on it, but it's quite heavy. As we struggle to hoist it onto the cart, a gust of air rises up, pushing the bottom of the crate so that it thumps onto the back of the cart. Sil gives me a wink.

"Helpful," I say. I wish we could open it now.

"And to think," she says, patting the crate, "this could have been your journey to me. As simple as a few drops of serum and a train ride."

It takes a lot of effort not to roll my eyes. "You sound like Lucien," I say.

Sil huffs.

RAVEN AND ASH COME OUT ON THE FRONT PORCH TO greet us as we arrive back at the White Rose. Ash is in better spirits, to my relief.

"Here," he says, hopping up on the back of the cart

with a crowbar. He pries the lid off the crate. The smell of packing hay and stale sweat fills the air.

The lioness is curled up in the fetal position. She wears a brown woolen dress—I assume Lucien had to dress her in the morgue. She is so thin, almost as thin as Raven used to be, her skin stretched tight over her bones. There are shadows under her eyes, black against her chocolate skin.

Ash takes her gently by the wrists and pulls her up over his shoulder.

"Where should I put her?" he asks.

"In Raven's room," I say. "I'm going to stay with her until she wakes up."

The lioness sleeps for most of the day.

As the sun starts to set, the serum begins to wear off.

The sky is quiet tonight, muted in burnt oranges and faded yellows. I'm staring out the window when she lurches up, gasping. I grab the bucket I brought for this very purpose.

"Here," I say, holding it out and keeping one hand on her back as she vomits. Lucien's serum has a pretty nasty side effect.

The lioness coughs and I hand her a cloth to wipe her mouth. She blinks around unsteadily, like her eyes are unsure whether they want to stay open or closed.

I pour her a glass of water from a jug on the nightstand. "Drink this."

Now that she's awake, I find myself jittery with nerves. This girl is from a part of my life that feels so far away. I don't know how to act around her.

She drinks in silence and hands the glass back to me without a thank-you.

"You," she says, pushing herself up into a sitting position.

"I'm Violet," I say. "What's your name?"

"Where am I?" Her eyes narrow. "How did I get here? What do you want?"

"You're in the Farm," I say. I guess I shouldn't be surprised by her attitude. "I want to help you. And . . . I need your help, too."

I wish I had planned out what I wanted to say better.

The lioness's smirk looks all wrong, too much sarcasm on such a sunken face. "Right. So you kidnapped me? How did you even get here yourself? I thought you were locked up in the palace of the Lake."

I ignore her questions. "You talked to me about power once," I say. "At Dahlia's funeral, you told me that we have more power than the royalty because we make their children."

"I'm glad I made an impression," she says.

"You have no idea the power we actually have."

Air is the easiest element to connect with because it's always present. I release myself into it, embracing the heady weightlessness that comes with joining this element. I push it out, circling the room, slow at first, but then faster until it feels like I'm flying. The lioness clutches the bedsheet to her chest.

I let go of the connection. The room settles. I feel exhilarated.

"What *are* you?" the lioness asks.

"I'm . . ." I'm not quite sure how to answer. "I'm like you. We're the same."

"Are you saying I can do what you just did?"

"Something like that. I hope."

The lioness snorts. "You *hope*? What did you bring me here for?"

"Would you rather be back in the Jewel?" I say.

She hesitates. I can see pain in her eyes. I wonder what memory is playing behind them right now. "No," she says.

"All right then."

"So are you going to tell me why I'm here?"

"Like I said, I need your help. Overthrowing the royalty."

The lioness's dark eyes widen so that I can see the whites all around. "You're serious."

I feel that this moment is crucial. I need her to believe me, and yet I have nothing to convince her here except a circling of wind around a bedroom. How can I explain the truth about the Auguries, and the Paladin, and this island, about who we really are? I take a deep breath.

"There is so much I can show you and tell you. If you're willing. But first, I'd like you to tell me your name."

For half a second, I don't think she's going to answer me. Then she smiles.

"Sienna," she says. "My name is Sienna."

~ Twenty-Two ~

SIL IS MAKING DINNER WHEN I BRING SIENNA DOWN-stairs.

Raven sits in the rocking chair reading a book. They both look up at our approach.

"I remember you," Sienna says, taking a step back. "The House of the Stone, right?"

"My name is Raven Stirling," she says.

"Did she kidnap you, too?" Sienna asks.

"She saved my life," Raven replies.

"They said you were dead. Put on a big show, funeral and everything." Sienna looks Raven up and down. "You were pregnant, weren't you?"

"Not anymore," Raven says through clenched teeth.

Sienna smirks. "They do love their lies, don't they?" She looks at me. "My mistress pretended to adore your Duchess but really she couldn't stand her. Jealous. Talked about her all the time behind her back."

The back door opens and Ash walks in. His face is smudged with dirt and he brings the faint scent of hay and manure.

"Soup smells good, Sil," he says, then stops short when he sees Sienna.

Sienna yelps, taking a step back. "You're—you're the rapist."

"They love their lies," I say, echoing her words. "You said it yourself. This is Ash. He's . . . my friend."

"Pleasure to meet you," he says with a polite nod. I can see him working hard not to seem offended.

Sienna looks back and forth between us. Then something clicks in her expression. "Oh," she says slowly. "I see. What, did you two get caught together or something?"

I feel the heat of a blush in my cheeks.

"Yes," Ash says, "we did."

"They said you did terrible things to her," Sienna says. "The Duchess says that's why she can't be seen in public. Lots of royals offered up their companions to be interrogated by Regimentals. Just to make sure there weren't any more like you."

A shadow of guilt passes over Ash's face.

"The Countess of the Rose didn't have a companion," Sienna continues, "but she wanted one. Too bad she doesn't have a daughter. She was so envious of the Duchess hiring you." Sienna's eyes travel over Ash's arms and torso.

"Apparently, you had quite a—"

"If you'll excuse me," Ash says in a hard tone, before stalking past us and up the stairs. A few seconds later, I hear the water turn on in the bathroom.

"He *is* very good-looking," Sienna says, eyeing me.

"He's more than that," I snap. "And he's not your concern." I point to the dining-room table. "Sit down. There are some things to explain."

Sil, who has been uncharacteristically silent for this whole exchange, brings over bowls of steaming black bean soup and sets them on the table without a word. The aroma of garlic and cooked vegetables is mouthwatering. She walks past Sienna and mutters to me, "I don't like this one."

The food has drawn Sienna to the table, and she digs in as Raven and I sit beside her. Raven shoots me a look that echoes Sil's words. While Sienna eats, I explain as best I can about how surrogates die giving birth, how the Auguries have been twisted from something natural to something that serves the royalty, and how we can potentially use this force against them. I tell her that we have a chance to save all the surrogates in this city.

"Why should I care about other girls?" she says. "I'm here now. You got me to safety. Why should I risk that for people I don't know?"

"Don't go throwing that attitude around here, girl," Sil says, from where she stands with her arms crossed in the kitchen. "And don't pretend like there isn't someone in that circle you care about."

I think of the iced cake, the blond surrogate, who was clearly Sienna's friend, bought by the Duchess of the Scales.

Judging by the look on Sienna's face, she is thinking of her, too.

"If what you say is true," Sienna says, putting down her spoon, "she's dead anyway."

I swallow. The iced cake must be pregnant.

"Don't you want to at least try to help her?" I say. "And what about all the other girls at your holding facility, the ones who haven't been auctioned yet, who still have a chance?"

Sienna shifts in her chair. "You don't know anything about my holding facility," she mutters.

"It was Northgate, right?"

She looks up at me, surprised.

"Dahlia told me," I say softly.

"Who?"

"She came with you on the train to the Auction," I say, frowning. "She was Lot 200."

"Oh." Sienna shrugs. "I didn't know her name. There are a lot of surrogates at Northgate. And she was only a kid."

"That's a lie." Raven's eyes go double-focused. The "whispers," as she calls them, have grown fainter since she's no longer pregnant, but Raven still hears things. "You were mean to her," she says, her voice taking on a dream-like quality. "She was so good at the Auguries, but she was younger than you. That isn't fair. You were supposed to be the best. *You* were supposed to be Lot 200."

Sienna jumps up from the table. Raven comes back to the present. "Don't lie around me," she says to Sienna. "And don't waste your time worrying. It saved your life."

"What did?" I ask.

"She can't have children," Raven says.

"How did you . . ." Sienna's hand drops to her stomach. Raven shrugs.

"It doesn't make you any less of a person," I say to Sienna.

"It makes me less of a surrogate," she snaps.

"Sienna," I say. "You're not a surrogate anymore."

Sienna sinks back onto her chair and stares morosely at her soup.

"All my life has been about one thing. How is it that I never had that power all along? It doesn't make sense. It isn't fair."

I put my hand on her arm. I can feel the bones of her wrist poking out under her skin. "You're capable of so much more. You're part of something bigger than you could have imagined."

"Come on," Sil says, opening the back door. "Enough talk. It's time to show you."

I grab a blanket off the back of the couch, in case Sil is going to do what I think she is going to do.

"Be right back," I say to Raven, who looks quite pleased to be rid of Sienna for the moment.

Sienna trails behind me and Sil warily as we walk toward the forest.

"Where are you taking me?" she calls.

Sil ignores her.

"Are you planning to do what you did to me?" I mutter. "Tie her up out here?"

"It worked for Azalea."

"Yes, but . . . it took a long time, didn't it? And we need her on our side, Sil, not thinking we're the enemy."

"Well, unless you want to try killing your best friend and having this new one revive her, I don't see another option."

She has a point. My experience with this power was so fraught with emotion, so heightened, it created an instant understanding, a sudden connection.

But I don't know how to find it again.

As we pass under the first yawning branches of the trees, Sienna stops.

"Where are we going?" she demands.

Sil puts her hands on her hips and turns around. "You need to learn how to do what we can do. We're going to teach you."

I feel like Sil should reconsider her use of the word *teach*.

"We're not going to hurt you," I assure her, because Sil is looking like she'd very much like to club Sienna over the head before tying her up. "You don't have to be afraid."

I connect with Earth, and roots spring out of the ground, twining themselves around Sienna's legs, up over her knees to the middle of her thighs.

"Get them off me!" she screams, but the roots are too strong. I know. I can feel them. Even as I release the connection, they hold Sienna where she is. "Are you two crazy?"

"Why'd you pick this one, anyway?" Sil grumbles, watching Sienna struggle, with a pitiless expression.

"She was Lot 199," I say. "She's strong."

"She's bullheaded."

"So am I," I say.

"No," Sil says. "You're different. You're . . ." Her nose wrinkles like she's smelled something bad. "Nice," she finishes.

I have to laugh.

Sienna has calmed down and is holding on to one of the roots with a focused expression. I see what Sil meant when she snapped at me that first day, when I tried to use the Auguries. I recognize the look of concentration in Sienna's eyes, and the wrongness that emanates from her makes me queasy.

"What, are you going to change their color?" Sil says with a chuckle. "You can make them purple or green or fuchsia but it won't do any good. You're stuck out here until we say so."

Sienna glares at us. "You people are insane."

"I've been called worse," Sil says.

"Here," I say, holding out the blanket. "Take this. You'll need it."

Sienna looks like she'd rather bite my hand than accept charity, but it's cold, and survival wins out. She snatches it away from me and wraps it around herself.

"So what am I supposed to do out here exactly?" she asks.

"Listen," Sil says. "I know it might be a first for you."

"I'll check on you later," I say.

"I can't believe you're leaving me here," Sienna says.

"Rather be back in that comfy palace?" Sil says. "Remember—if you can't bear children, they'd kill you anyway. Would you rather spend the night outside or end up with a knife in your back, or poison in your wine? Come on," she says, tugging on my arm.

Sienna hugs the blanket tight around her and watches us walk away, her expression furious, her eyes glittering like onyx in the dark.

Twenty-Three

I CAN'T SLEEP THAT NIGHT.

There is a throbbing at the base of my skull, like an Augury headache, and I know it's concern for Sienna.

Ash and I have taken to sleeping in the hayloft in the barn. Sil was right about being able to destroy things in my sleep—that first night I spent outside with Ash, he told me later that he could feel things moving in the earth under us. I told him he didn't have to stay outside with me anymore, but he shrugged and smiled and said he didn't mind.

I'm safe to sleep around now, but the house makes me claustrophobic. I like the barn—it's airy and comfortable, and not so confining. The elements can breathe here. Plus, it feels like Ash and I have our own private space.

I stare at the slats in the wooden roof and can't help thinking my plan won't work.

There has to be a way to get Sienna to connect with the elements, without taking the time to break her down, or whatever Sil is expecting to happen. My toes twitch with worry, pulling against the soft wool blanket we sleep on.

"You all right?" Ash murmurs sleepily. I roll onto my side, and he slides his arm around my waist, pulling me back against his chest.

"I'm concerned about Sienna. I'm worried we don't have enough time. What if Sil's method doesn't work? What if she hates us by the end of it? We need her as an ally. Plus, we still need two more girls, one for Eastgate and one for Westgate. And we'll have to show them, too." I pick a piece of hay off the blanket. "I don't even know how we're supposed to get to the holding facilities."

"Violet, a few weeks ago I was locked in a dungeon set to be executed and you were going to be forced to bear a child that would ultimately kill you. I think we're doing quite well, all things considered."

"Aren't you the optimist."

Ash's breath tickles my ear. "I try."

I hear the familiar hint of frustration in his voice.

"I'm sorry," I say. "I know you want to help."

His arm tenses around me. "I do." He rests his chin on my shoulder. "Listen, please don't think I resent you or . . . it's just . . . everyone around here has some special power. Everyone can do incredible things, except me." He pauses, and when he speaks again he sounds embarrassed. "I hope this doesn't come out wrong but . . . I've been serving women my whole life. I want to do something for myself. I want to be in charge of my own fate."

I roll onto my back and gaze up at him. He's right. It isn't fair for Ash to go from one prison to another.

"I know things, you know," he says. "About the royalty. I know how they think. I know some of their secrets. I know which palaces would be easiest to infiltrate, and which royals hate each other most, and which companions might be inclined to help."

"You should talk to Lucien," I suggest.

Ash lets out a hard laugh. "Lucien would never accept my help. Nor would he think he needs it."

"But if you have information that can help the Society, he'll have to listen," I say.

"So far, all I've managed to do is become one of the Lone City's most-wanted fugitives. I don't see how that's helpful."

"We can't always know what will eventually be helpful and what won't," I say. "Look at Raven. The Countess cut into her brain and accidentally gave her the extra sense that got us out of the sewers. She saved you in Landing's Market. She helped me—" I sit up so fast my head spins. "She helped me understand the elements," I gasp.

"Violet?" Ash asks. I'm staring ahead, not seeing anything, one hand clamped over my mouth.

What if I could go to that place again, the place where I saved her? I don't know what it was exactly, but it was old and rich with the magic of this island—it created an instant connection with the elements. Is it a place where the Paladin once lived? Was the stone statue there something they built?

What if I could take Sienna there? Then she wouldn't need to be tied up outside. She'd understand immediately. I'm sure of it.

"I have to talk to Raven," I say, throwing off the blanket. Raven and I were in that place together. Maybe together, we can figure out a way to get back to it.

I climb down the ladder to the hayloft and out of the barn into the night.

As I cut across the clearing toward the White Rose, I see a figure sitting on the back porch.

"You're awake," Raven says as I join her. She is wrapped in a quilt and holds out one side of it. I sit next to her and drape the thick blanket around me.

"So are you," I say.

"The Countess kept me in darkness for so long. Sometimes I'm afraid to close my eyes. Sometimes I have bad dreams." She shivers and I lean into her. "So. Sienna. She's . . . interesting."

"She had such a high score," I say. "And she seemed so fierce, a fighter, exactly what we need. But I guess I don't know her at all."

"She'll come around," Raven says.

"I hope so."

"Once she understands who she is, she'll have to."

Raven finds the Paladin fascinating. She looks over Sil's portfolio almost every day.

"You don't use the elements, though."

She half smiles. "I don't know if I can. I'm scared to try. My mind is still . . . fragile. It's not the same as it was before. What if I can't control it? What if I hurt someone? What if it consumes me, or twists me even further from myself? It's too risky." She closes her eyes. "Sometimes, though, I go back there. To that place where you found me."

My ears prick. "You do?"

"It has this . . . this pulse. It calls to me." Raven opens her eyes. "It's them, I think. Or the echo of them. I hear the whispers there sometimes. But I can never quite understand what they're saying. I think they might feel bad for me. I think they might know that I've been hurt." She rubs her temples. "I love seeing the ocean. On that map of the island Sil has, the one where all those red Xs are? I think those were some of the places the Paladin lived. I think that monument is something they built."

"I was thinking that, too. Raven, do you think . . . could you take me back there?" I ask.

Raven smiles and holds out a hand, her palm facing up. I reach out to take it, then stop myself.

"Could you take Sienna there, too?"

Her face darkens. "I guess," she says. "I could try."

Our breath makes white clouds in the air as we skirt the edge of the pond and head to the tree line. As we approach, I can see Sienna's figure, huddled against an old spruce. I'm glad I gave her the blanket.

"Who's there?" she calls.

"It's Violet," I say. She rubs her eyes and looks up at us.

"Are you going to let me go?" she asks. "It's freezing."

"I'm going to try something," I say. I sit down next to her, and Raven follows my lead.

"That old witch is crazy," Sienna says.

"That old witch didn't tie you up out here," I say. "I

did." I reach out a hand to her.

"You really expect me to hold your hand?"

"Do you want to stay stuck to this tree for the next few months? I think Raven can show you something," I say. "But we need to be connected." I glance at Raven. "Don't we?"

Raven sighs and holds out a hand to each of us. Hers is warm in mine. Sienna's is still cold.

I close my eyes. For several long seconds, nothing happens. Then Raven's grip tightens and my whole body tilts backward, falling, my heart in my throat, and we are there. Back on the cliff. The ocean cries out a welcome as it crashes into the rocks below.

The scene is different than it was the first time I came here. The trees are barren, black branches against a white sky. Snow falls thick and fast, covering the ground in an ivory blanket and leaving a trail of white on the spiraling, blue-gray statue. The ocean foams beneath us, frothy waves of slate-colored water.

Raven is beside me, and she is my Raven from before. The differences are subtle now that she's recovered so well. But she's plumper. And her hair is short like it used to be. But it's her eyes where the difference is most pronounced. They are bright and sparkle with mischief.

Sienna stands on the opposite side of the statue. She looks different, too. Her hair is loose, not in its usual braids, but tight curls that fall to her waist. Her face is full and healthy, and there is a warmth in her eyes I have never seen before. I wonder whether this place shows us as we were before diagnosed as surrogates. Before the Auguries twisted us.

Sienna stares out at the ocean, a rapt expression on her face. Then she sticks out her tongue and catches a snowflake. Her laughter is silent as snowflakes leap and dance around her.

She circles the statue, making big footprints in the snow. She is giddy, like a child. Underneath her hard exterior, there is a little girl who wants to make a snowman. I can sense it. She always liked the snow.

Time to go, Raven thinks. I can hear her as clearly as if she'd spoken out loud.

The wind howls, and I feel myself being sucked up and away, the dizziness growing painful, until we are back in the real world.

Sienna slumps over. Her back shudders, and it takes me a second to realize she's crying.

The roots release their hold on her. Sienna isn't going anywhere.

She looks up, her face a jumble of emotion. "What was that place?"

"Home," Raven says.

"I felt . . ." She clutches her chest. "I feel . . . everything."

Tears spill down Sienna's face, as she looks around the forest like she's never seen anything like it.

"Look down," I say with a smile.

A patch of brilliant orange flowers has blossomed at her feet. They wither back into the ground as a light snow begins to fall.

I'm still holding her hand. It is as warm as Raven's now. I give hers a reassuring squeeze. I can sense the riot inside Sienna, the struggle to understand the sudden rush of emotion. More flowers bloom and die around her.

"What is it?" she asks, breathless.

"It's life," I whisper.

We sit there in a silent circle as the snow falls softly around us.

Twenty-Four

SIENNA CAN ONLY CONNECT WITH FIRE AND EARTH.

We sit outside the next evening, a large fire burning in a pit surrounded by heavy gray stones. Sienna loves making the flames leap higher and higher. Sil won't let her in the house.

"Fire is the most unpredictable," she told us. Then she added privately to me, "And I don't like the look on her face when she connects with it."

Even now as I watch, Sienna's body is inclined toward the fire. She sits closer than I feel is safe, her expression peaceful but her eyes alight. I'm trying to make a blueprint of Southgate on a sketch pad, to remind myself of every wall and door and what might be the best point of entry. The back hall by the kitchen? The windows of the music room?

The flames crackle and bits of burning embers spray across the stones.

"Sienna," I say sharply.

She blinks and the fire dies down.

"It's fun," she says.

"It's dangerous," I remind her. "Remember that."

"I feel like I could burn all their palaces to the ground." There's a hungry look in her eyes as she says it. "I think I could—"

She is interrupted by a shout from inside the house.

"Stay out here," I tell her and rush through the back door.

Sil and Ash are facing each other down in the living room.

"You can't stop me," Ash is saying.

"This isn't your call," Sil shouts. "It's dangerous and foolish and it could ruin everything."

"What's going on?" I ask.

"I heard her talking to Lucien," Ash says. "There's a meeting tonight, for the Society. I want to go." He turns to me. "I want to *help*."

"A meeting?" I look at Sil. "Where?"

"Not you, too," she says. "You have to stay here."

"I've gone out before," I insist.

"Not like this."

"I'm sick of being stuck here while everyone else helps," Ash says. "I have to do something more. Let me *try* at least."

"And what do you plan to do for the Society, anyway?" Sil asks. "Entertain the female members?"

His face turns crimson. "If you think that will be useful," he says.

"Ash," I say sharply.

"I can't sit around anymore, Violet," he says. "Everyone forgets about the companions. We don't have any powers. We aren't special in any way. But we're still people. We still have the right to fight for our freedom as much as any surrogate or lady-in-waiting, farmer or factory worker."

I think about how hard he's tried to be patient, how accepting he's been of everything that's happening around here. The new surrogate. The elements. The true history of this island. There hasn't been much room for him.

He deserves this.

"You're right," I say. "You should go. And I'm going, too."

"No one is going, and that's final," Sil says.

I fold my arms and stare at her. "Keeping us in the dark won't keep us safe. We have a right to be involved." I hesitate before adding, "Don't make the same mistake you made with Azalea."

A gust of air, so forceful it feels like a solid wall, blasts out from Sil's small frame and hits me squarely in the chest. I stumble back, gasping. Ash grabs my arm to keep me from falling.

"Violet!"

"I'm fine," I wheeze as Sil turns on her heel and marches out the front door, the wind slamming it behind her. I straighten my spine. "We're going to that meeting."

THAT NIGHT, IT IS BITTERLY COLD. ASH AND I BUNDLE UP in our warmest clothes.

Sienna has been allowed inside. She sits on the couch, Raven in Sil's rocking chair by the fireplace. Sienna keeps making the flames leap and roar while Raven's expression becomes increasingly irritated.

"Be careful," I say. "Sil might kill you if you burn this house down."

The flames quiet. "You better tell us everything," Sienna says.

"Of course I will."

Raven reaches out to me. I take her hand and squeeze it.

"Be safe," she whispers.

I nod.

Sil is climbing into the driver's seat of the cart when Ash and I walk out the front door. "Come on," she says reluctantly. "We've got a long way to go. Don't want to be late."

I hop up into the bed of the cart, Ash climbing up behind me.

Sil cracks the reins and the cart rolls forward.

"Where is the meeting?" Ash asks.

Sil pauses, clearly still mad that we are going with her. Finally, she says, "In a town called Fairview, about an hour from here."

I snuggle into Ash's side for warmth. The trees reach out over our heads, stars twinkling through their branches. I want to join with the earth and feel those branches stretching toward the sky.

When we emerge from the forest, Ash sits up straighter. Fields of wheat stretch out before us, stunted stumps poking up from the ground, dormant until spring.

"So this is the Farm," he says. "It's . . . big."

I forget that Ash hasn't seen the Farm before. Just the forest that first night we came to the White Rose.

"Rye is from the Farm," he muses. "Not this quarter, though."

I hadn't given Rye much thought since Sienna joined us. But of course, Ash would worry about his friend.

"I'm sure Carnelian is having a fabulous time with him," I say dryly. "Like Garnet said."

"Carnelian is very lonely," he says. "She wants someone to care about her, to like her best. Her own mother refused to stay alive for her. Those sorts of scars don't heal easily."

I hate when he talks that way about Carnelian. I don't want to feel bad for her.

"She turned you in," I point out.

"I think, technically, she turned *you* in," he says.

"Does that make it better?"

"Of course not. But you don't see her the way I do. You dislike her too much."

"Because she's awful."

"But she has also suffered at the hands of the royalty," Ash says. "You saw how the Duchess treated her. They mocked her. No one wanted to marry her. Dirty blood, the other royal daughters called her. Bank trash. Does she not count as their victim, too?"

I hadn't realized Carnelian was bullied like that. Though I suppose I'm not surprised.

"We can't choose who we free from them, Violet. It has to be all or nothing. Do you think Lucien would ever choose to help a companion?"

"All right," I say. "I understand. But don't ask me to like her."

Ash grins and kisses my temple.

"Do you think we can do this?" I ask.

"Overthrow the royalty?"

I nod.

"I certainly hope so. And it seems worth trying, doesn't it?" He gazes out over the moonlit fields. "We were all going to end up dead, one way or another."

"That's an awfully bleak way of looking at it," I say.

He shrugs. "I'm being honest. I'd rather die fighting the royalty than serving them."

"Well said," Sil barks from the driver's seat. Ash and I exchange a smile.

Slowly, the landscape begins to change. Hills break up the skyline in craggy peaks, bigger than the ones surrounding Bartlett Station. We pass a couple of small towns, sheep grazing in paddocked pastures. Sil turns the cart down a narrow path that leads into a little copse of trees.

"We walk from here," she says as Ash hops off the back of the cart to tie up Turnip.

The town of Fairview is much bigger than the town outside Bartlett Station. Houses slowly spring up around us as we walk, a handful of cottages at first, one-story stone structures with thatched roofs. As we get closer to the center of town, the houses become more uniform, all wooden shingles and peaked roofs. They crowd together, lining the hard-packed dirt that forms the roads, though they're not connected like the row houses in the Smoke. Some have picket fences surrounding them; others have porches with rocking chairs or cats prowling on their steps. The main street is quiet at this time of night. We pass a barbershop, and a bakery, and a used-clothing store. There are no gas lamps to light our way, like the ones in the Bank. Sil stops at a dilapidated storefront. A dusty purple curtain hangs over the glass-paned door.

She knocks once, pauses, knocks three times, pauses again, and knocks once more.

The curtain flutters and the door is thrown open.

A pistol is leveled directly at Sil's face.

I leap back, but Sil seems entirely unperturbed. "Put that away, Whistler, before you shoot somebody."

"Who are they?" the man in the doorway asks. He is hidden in shadows, making it hard for me to see his face.

"Friends," Sil says. "You think I'd bring some random strangers here? Mind you, I told them to stay put, but these two are as stubborn as . . ." Her voice trails off and she clears her throat. "The Black Key knows them," she finishes.

"Have they been marked?"

Sil smirks. "Not yet. But she's one of mine." She jerks her head in my direction. "And he's—"

The man steps forward into the light.

"You're Ash Lockwood," he says.

The man is large, heavily muscled, and covered in tattoos from his shaved head to his knuckles. A thick mustache covers his upper lip. He wears a black sweater and pants, and lowers the gun as he gapes at Ash.

"I am," Ash says. I look at Sil—is this man going to turn Ash in? Was that her plan all along?

"You escaped the royalty," the man says. His tone is almost reverential. "Right under the Duchess of the Lake's nose. How . . ." He shakes his head, then extends his hand. "Pleasure to meet you."

Ash looks as shocked as I feel. I suppose I assumed everyone in the city would be after Ash's head on a spike. But this man looks at him with respect.

He takes the man's hand.

"You can call me the Whistler," the man says.

Ash half smiles. "I suppose it's a little late for a code name."

"Are you going to let us in, or should we stand on the doorstep until a Regimental passes by?" Sil snaps.

The Whistler steps back. "Of course. Come in, come in. We're waiting for one more."

The shop is lit with only a single oil lamp. Sheets of paper line the walls filled with a myriad of designs. A delicately detailed sparrow soars toward the corner of one sheet. A peacock feather, all thick brushstrokes and bold colors, is pinned nearby. There is a sun and moon entwined, and a rustic-looking birdcage. I blush at the outline of a naked woman. There is a small desk by the front door and in the back corner of the shop sits a chair that reminds me unpleasantly of the medical bed at the palace of the Lake.

"The Black Key didn't tell you what this is all about, did he?" Sil asks.

"Not a word," the Whistler replies. "He said call an emergency meeting in the usual spot." He sweeps out a hand to indicate the shop. "But the Printer arrived first—says he has big news, but wouldn't say anymore until you got here.

Go on down. I've got to wait for the newest recruit. He's late. Not exactly starting off on the right foot."

"Come on," Sil says to me and Ash, still hovering in the front of the store. "This is what you've been waiting for, isn't it?"

We follow Sil to the back of the parlor, where murmured voices can be heard from behind a green painted door.

"Who is he?" I whisper, glancing at the Whistler, who's still waiting by the front door, pistol in hand.

"Local tattoo artist. Used to run with a rough crowd; the Black Key helped him out of a tight spot. Knows all the criminals and thieves in the South Quarter of the Farm. The Black Key was wise to have recruited him. They can be remarkably helpful, the dregs of society. And they love rebelling against authority." Sil looks at Ash. "Let's hope they all like you as much as he did."

Then she opens the door.

Twenty-Five

I STARE DOWN AT A LONG SET OF RICKETY WOODEN STAIRS leading to a basement.

The voices are louder, and a warm yellow light emanates from somewhere deep within the underground room. Sil shoos us forward. As soon we reach the bottom of the stairs, the voices fall silent.

We're in a storage area underneath the tattoo parlor. The walls are made of cracked gray stone, and various crates have been piled in one corner, along with scraps of paper and sheets of canvas. A circle of five chairs is set up in the center of the space with everyone else crowded around them. Two of the chairs are empty.

There are so many people here. And people of all ages,

male and female. There's a boy of about fourteen, with a thatch of blond hair and an impish expression. There's an old woman sitting in one of the chairs, knitting what looks to be a baby's sock. And there is a handful of what I'd guess Sil would call the "dregs of society." Men and women with gaunt faces, many of them heavily tattooed, with sharp eyes and twitchy fingers.

A bald man with dark skin and even darker eyes gets up from his chair as we enter the room. His gaze falls on Sil.

"The Rose!" he exclaims, then calls to the room at large. "The Rose is here."

I smile at her code name.

The tension in the room dissipates, the voices picking back up again. Several people come to greet Sil, who nods and shakes hands reluctantly.

"And who are your guests?" the bald man asks.

The blond boy pushes through the crowd. "That's . . . that's Ash Lockwood!"

"Oh, don't be stupid," a girl, his same age, says. Her blond hair is tied back in two pigtails. They look like brother and sister. "Ash Lockwood is in hiding. Or dead."

"Ash Lockwood fought a hundred Regimentals to get out of the Jewel," the boy insists. "He could be anywhere, and I'm telling you that's him."

"If Ash Lockwood really escaped the royalty," the girl shoots back, "he'd never come within five miles of us."

"This is surreal," Ash whispers in my ear. I nod.

A girl in her midtwenties shushes them. She has coppery hair and a willowy figure that reminds me of Annabelle. My heart throbs.

"There's no need to spread more of the royalty's gossip and lies," she says. "Why don't we ask him?"

More people have stopped to listen in on this conversation. The boy looks at Ash through his thick mess of blond hair.

"So?" he says. "Are you Ash Lockwood or aren't you?"

"That isn't polite," the Annabelle-girl says. "And you know the rule about names here."

The boy scowls. The girl twirls one of her pigtails around her finger.

"Please, sir," she says, fluttering her eyelashes. "Are you the companion who was falsely accused and escaped the royalty?"

Falsely accused? My bones soften with relief. They know. They know he is innocent. But . . . how could they know that? All the papers reported the rape as if it were fact.

"I am," Ash says. "Though I can't say I fought a hundred Regimentals." He extends his hand to her. "Ash Lockwood."

The girl turns pink and shakes his hand. The Annabelle-girl blushes, too.

"I told you," the boy says.

"We're not allowed to use names," the girl says, ignoring the boy.

Ash nods. "Yes. The Society of the Black Key has to be protected."

The girl's eyes widen. "Do you know the Black Key?"

A small crowd has gathered around Ash at this point. A woman in her forties pushes forward.

"Did you know a boy named Birch?" she says, grasping his hand in both of hers. "They took him, made him a companion. I don't know where they sent him. He's a beautiful boy, he's blond and tall, with green eyes and . . ." Tears fill her eyes. "Do you know him?"

"My son was taken, too," a man in plaid trousers interrupts. "They made him a Regimental. For the House of the Light. Have you been there?"

A frail woman with wispy brown hair pushes forward. "They took my daughter," she says. "They took her right off the street one day. Do you know where they take the girls? She was only fourteen. The coach that took her was from the Bank." Her eyes fill with tears. "Why would they take my Calla?"

Ash looks distraught. I catch Sil's eye. This isn't fair. He cannot be asked to account for all the royalty's faults, to know everything that happened to these children.

"That's enough," Sil says. "Leave the boy alone. From what I've gathered, we have more important things to talk about." She moves to sit in one of the empty chairs. The crowd shuffles back around, re-forming the circle. The boy stays close to Ash and keeps glancing over at him.

"We'll start without the Whistler," Sil says. "He can get filled in later." She looks at the old woman knitting the sock. "What's the status for supplies?"

"One hundred and twelve handguns, eighty-three rifles," the woman says. "And a countless amount of makeshift swords."

"Still not enough," Sil says. "Not nearly enough now."

"What's going on?" a man in a green jacket demands.

"I thought the plan was to coordinate the attacks and the Auction. We've got plenty of time."

"No, we don't." The bald man stands up. "That's why this meeting was called. I received my shipment of tomorrow's paper late this afternoon." A newspaper sits, folded in half on his chair. He opens it and holds it up.

The headline reads, NEW DATE FOR AUCTION! And underneath it, in slightly smaller print, it says, EXETOR TO MOVE AUCTION TO APRIL.

I gasp. That's only a little over three months away.

"How can they do this?" I whisper to Ash.

"They do what they want," he says.

"Do you think—"

"It might be a coincidence," the bald man announces. "Or they might suspect something. There has been a healthy amount of vandalism recently, some of which was unapproved by the Black Key."

He shoots a look at one of the gaunt, tattooed men.

"How are we supposed to be ready in time?" a gruff man with bushy eyebrows and a gray cap asks. "We don't even know our exact numbers. We don't know who can handle a gun. We don't have *enough* guns, for that matter. How are we supposed to fight an army of Regimentals?"

"The surrogates," Sil says. "You know this. The surrogates will help."

The man scoffs. "I still don't see how a group of little girls is going to help us take down an army."

I bristle, and so does Sil.

"Of course you don't," she says. "That would require having a brain. You're good with weapons but don't try strategy, it doesn't suit you." It's nice to see Sil's attitude being directed toward someone else. She looks around the room. Some of the people look as skeptical as the gruff man. Others seem curious, and still others seem resigned, like they've heard about this plan for a while and are tired of trying to work out the secrets. I'm very familiar with that feeling.

"You're all here for a reason," Sil says. "There isn't a life in this room that hasn't been affected in some way by the royalty. If we want it to stop, we have to do it ourselves. We have to trust the Black Key. But more importantly, we have to trust one another."

"She does a good impression of caring," I mutter to Ash.

"Oh, I think she cares a lot more than she lets on," he says.

"How do you think they knew?" I ask. "That you were falsely accused, I mean."

The boy pipes up from Ash's other side. "The Black Key sent a warning. He said none of us was to turn you in if we saw you. He said you were on our side."

"Well, look at that," I say, giving Ash's waist a squeeze. "He doesn't hate you so much after all."

"I'm sure he was protecting you more than me."

"It's a start."

"Who are you, anyway?" the boy asks me.

"I'm Violet," I say.

The boy's eyes widen. "We're not supposed to use real names."

"Well, I'm not going by anything but Violet," I say. "Ever again. The Black Key will have to deal with it."

Ash barely suppresses a smile.

"We'll have to make do with what we have already," the bald man is saying. "But we need to start training."

"There's a field about an hour away from here," Sil says. "It's quiet and out of the way, deep in a forest. This contingent could train there."

It sounds like she's talking about our forest. But she can't mean the clearing with the White Rose—I imagine there must be another field nearby. And that forest is so thick and huge, it could provide perfect cover.

"That's too far," the gruff man protests.

"Tough," she says.

"You need me to help with the training," he says. "Who else here has experience in combat?"

"A couple of altercations with Regimentals doesn't make you an expert," Sil snaps.

"I'm the only one you've got," the man says.

"No," Ash says. "You're not." He seems surprised by everyone's eyes on him, as if he hadn't realized he'd spoken out loud.

The man's bushy eyebrows rise so high they fade into his salt-and-pepper hair. "What do you know about fighting, boy? I thought they sent you to the Jewel to dance with royal daughters."

A few of the other men snigger. I glare, but Ash ignores them.

"They train us in everything," he says. "I know how to use a gun. I know how to handle a sword. I can help."

My heart swells up with pride. This is what he's supposed to do. *This* is how he can help.

"Prove it," the man insists.

"Of course. Do you happen to have a sword handy?" Ash asks politely.

The man grumbles something unintelligible.

"I know the Jewel," he continues. "I know how they train the Regimentals. If you don't think that's useful information, I suppose I don't need to share it."

"What about the girl?" a voice in the crowd asks. All heads swivel in my direction.

"What about her?" Sil asks.

"Who is she?"

"Where is she from? I've never seen her around here before."

"Does she have the mark of the Key?"

"How do we know we can trust her?"

The chorus of voices rises up. Ash moves to stand in front of me protectively, but I pull him back. I can face this myself. I'm going to have to face much worse before this thing is over.

"My name is Violet," I say. "And I was a surrogate."

The word sets off a fury of panicked murmurs. Several people back away from me. The man in the green jacket whispers something to the woman beside him. She nods her head, frowning at me.

"I've seen firsthand what the royalty are capable of," I continue. "And I want them stopped."

I realize most of them have never known a surrogate. They clearly don't know Sil was one. I've never thought about what the surrogates must seem like to the other circles. Even the boy who's attached himself to Ash's side has taken a step away from me.

"I heard surrogates can kill you with their thoughts," he says.

"I heard they can make you beautiful if they touch you," his sister says, eyeing me eagerly.

"That's a load of nonsense," the gruff man says. "They make royal babies. That's all they do."

I'm sick of this man and his attitude.

"No," I say. "That's not all we do."

I connect with Earth, feeling myself become strong and broad, rooted in the ground. Somewhere deep below my roots, I can sense water.

"Violet," Sil murmurs. The floor begins to tremble, and I quake with it. The crowd gasps and everyone shuffles away from me. Even the people in the chairs have stood and backed up. Ash stands beside me, a strong and steady presence, like a heartbeat.

"I'm not sure this is the best idea," Sil says.

But I am the earth and these people need to see me.

I feel a mighty ache in the center of my chest, and the cement floor cracks open. Several people scream. The Annabelle-girl grabs the brother and sister and pulls them back.

I can smell the water now, its earthy tang.

I become the water.

My fingers grow fluid, my body light and stretchy, and a spray of water bursts from the crack in the floor. It swirls up in a glassy ribbon, bursts apart, then re-forms. It fills me up with a bright, bubbly joy, slippery tendrils circling one another before I release my connection with Water and it sinks back to the river below. The looks on the crowd's faces change from terrified to awed.

I connect with Earth again, and the crack in the floor closes up.

The silence that follows is deafening. It presses against my eardrums with the weight of disbelief and fear.

"Violet?"

I turn and see the Whistler at the foot of the stairs, his hand on the shoulder of a fourteen-year-old boy, his mouth gaping at the place where the water used to be.

But the boy holds my full attention.

I'm staring into the wide eyes of my brother.

~ Twenty-Six ~

"OCHRE!" I LET OUT A STRANGLED YELP AND THROW MY arms around him.

"What are you doing here?" I say.

"What are *you* doing here?" he says. "Aren't you supposed to be in the Jewel?"

I release him. "It's a long story."

He glances behind me. "Isn't that the companion everyone's looking for?"

"He's part of the story," I say.

"How do you know this boy?" the Whistler asks.

"He's my brother," I say. "Ochre, how is Hazel? And Mother? Are they all right?"

"Hazel's going to have to be tested soon," Ochre says.

My heart sinks to settle somewhere around my knees.

"Mother isn't handling it well," he adds.

I shudder. My mother doesn't even know the worst of it.

Maybe the new date is a gift. Maybe Hazel won't have time to be tested.

If I can stop the Auction before Hazel even gets a chance to be diagnosed, she'll never have to go through what I went through.

"Can someone please explain what happened here?" the bad-tempered man says. "Is she some sort of . . . witch?"

I forgot I was in the middle of proving myself to these people. "I'm not a witch," I say. "More like . . ." I try to think of how I can explain it. "Like a conduit. I can call on the elements. This island has been torn up by the royalty. It wants to help. Don't you see? This thing is bigger than all of us." I don't know how much to say—do I tell them about the Paladin and the original conquering of the island?

Many faces are definitely looking at me like I'm crazy. But a few seem intrigued.

"What else can you do?" the blond boy asks.

"I'd like to know that, too," Ochre says. "Is that what they teach you at Southgate?"

"No," I say. "That's what they intentionally *don't* teach us at Southgate. But with all the surrogates working together, we can take on their army. We can get inside the Jewel and destroy it from the inside."

"No one breathes a word about this to anyone," Sil says. "Or the Black Key will hear about it."

"Does the Black Key know about this?" someone asks.

"Of course he knows," Sil scoffs.

"Why didn't he tell us?"

"He doesn't tell anyone a damned thing if he doesn't want to," Sil says. "And look at your faces now. You wouldn't have believed him if he did. You have to see it for yourself."

"It's late," the bald man with the newspaper says. "And we've settled what needs to be settled. Training will start tomorrow night." He glances at me warily. "If the Black Key accepts this surrogate, so will we."

People begin to leave, in twos and threes, spacing it out over time so there isn't a huge exodus from the tattoo parlor in the dead of night. That could easily arouse suspicion.

The Annabelle-girl leaves with the brother and sister. The boy leans over to me as he walks past and whispers, "My name's Millet."

I smile. That's one person on my side.

Slowly, the crowd dwindles until there's only me, Ochre, Sil, Ash, and the Whistler left.

I don't want Ochre to leave, but I know he has to. "You can't tell Mother or Hazel you've seen me," I say. "It's too dangerous."

He nods. "I know."

"How did you get involved in this, anyway?"

"Sable Tersing," he says. "There are lots of boys our age who are angry—we get treated worse than the animals at the dairy. They've started docking our pay for no reason at all. They whip us if we show up even a minute late. We wanted to do something, to push back, and Sable said he'd heard about this Society that was secretly undermining the royalty but we didn't know how to find it. He said he'd heard something about a black key, so we started drawing them everywhere. That's when the Whistler came to see us. Told us we could stop vandalizing and actually do something."

"You can't seriously expect I'd let you fight, Ochre," I say. "You're only fourteen."

"And you're only sixteen," he says. "And it looks like you're in the thick of this thing, whatever it is."

"It's too dangerous," I say.

"You're not Mother," he insists.

"Mother would agree with me."

"Well, it's a good thing she's not here then."

I open my mouth to protest, but Sil cuts me off. "As charming as this family reunion is," she says, "we have to be getting home."

"Wait," Ash says. "There's something I have to do first."

"What?" I ask.

He looks at the Whistler. "I'm going to need one of those key tattoos."

"Does it hurt?"

Ash places his hand gently on his shoulder, where the Whistler put the bandage after he'd burned Lucien's symbol into Ash's skin. The cart rolls over a rut, and Ash winces.

"It's just a little sore," he says.

I'm freezing and exhausted by the time we get back to the White Rose. And I desperately miss my brother. The short time with him only made me yearn for home. It must be nearly three o'clock in the morning, but there is a light on in the living room.

Raven is awake in the rocking chair. Sienna must have gone to bed.

"How did it go?" she asks, putting down the book she was reading.

"I saw Ochre," I say.

She sits up. "What? What was he doing there?"

"Joining the forces of the Black Key."

"How was he? How are your mother and Hazel?"

The arcana begins to buzz. I yank it out of the knot at the base of my neck.

"Something has happened." Lucien's voice is exhausted but tense.

"Are you talking about the Auction?" I say. "I went to a meeting with Sil tonight, they're saying the date has been changed. Do you know why?"

"Someone has betrayed me."

"What?" I gasp. "Who?"

"It will be dealt with," Lucien says. "And the informant only knew a small piece of this puzzle—that the October date would not be safe. But it gave the Electress the very excuse she needed."

"Excuse for what?"

"She wishes for her daughter to succeed the throne," he says. "You and I know the Duchess foiled any plans for her to have a daughter from the last Auction. Now she has another chance. Unfortunately, this means our timetable has been moved up considerably."

"But we still don't have girls from Eastgate and Westgate yet."

"They will be arriving on tomorrow's train. I didn't have

time to vet them properly—I hope they will be sufficient."

"I'm sure they'll be fine." I bite my lip. "Lucien, the people at the meeting tonight . . . they were frightened of me."

"Did you show them your power?" he asks.

"Yes."

There is a pause.

"They simply do not understand you," he says.

"They loved Ash," I say with a grin. Ash makes a face and I can practically hear Lucien rolling his eyes.

"Yes, I'm sure they did."

"He's going to help train them, you know. To fight."

Raven raises an eyebrow at Ash, and he shrugs.

"That's . . . fantastic." Lucien's sarcasm is palpable.

"I'd like to go to more meetings," I say. "I want to know the people I'm fighting with."

"You can discuss that with Sil," Lucien says. "But for now, remember your purpose. Train the other surrogates."

The arcana drops into my palm.

"So," Raven says to Ash, "you're going to be the new major general of the Black Key's army?"

He laughs. "I'm glad I can finally do something."

"You know how to fight."

"Yes."

"Can you teach me, too?"

"I . . ." Ash frowns and glances at me.

"Raven," I say. "Are you sure that's a good idea?"

She levels me with her glare. "I want to be strong. I want my body to feel strong again."

It's her decision. After all she's been through, she's earned it. "All right," I say. Then I let out a huge yawn.

"We all better get some sleep," Ash says. "Especially since it seems we're getting some new additions tomorrow."

As Raven heads upstairs to bed, and Ash and I make our way out to the barn, I can't help hoping that whoever comes tomorrow will be as bold as Sienna, kind as Lily, and smart as Raven.

We'll show all the people in this city.

Surrogates are not just silly girls, to be bought and sold and treated like pets or furniture.

We are a force to be reckoned with.

∼ Twenty-Seven ∼

SIL AND I FETCH THE CRATES FROM BARTLETT STATION the next day at noon.

The two girls could not look more different from each other. I stare down at them as Ash pries the lids off the crates.

One is very tall, with pale skin and long blond hair. Her legs are cramped in the small space. The other is tiny and dark with a mop of brown curls.

We carry them to Raven's room and lay them out on the twin beds.

"I remember her," Sienna says, pointing to the small girl. "I saw her at the Longest Night ball."

"Was she nice?" I ask.

"I didn't *talk* to her."

I clench my teeth but say nothing.

Sienna and Raven wait downstairs—I felt it better for the new girls to see one face at a time. Plus, Sienna isn't the best welcoming committee.

The blonde is the first to wake up. After the unpleasant effect of Lucien's serum has passed, I hand her a glass of water. She gulps it down and looks up at me.

"You!" she exclaims. "I remember you. You played cello at the Exetor's Ball." She looks around the room. "I'm not in the Jewel anymore, am I?"

"No," I say.

And just like that, she bursts into tears.

"Oh, thank you," she says, clutching my sweater. "Thank you, thank you . . ."

Her name is Indi. I take her downstairs to meet Raven, Sienna, and Sil. It's immediately apparent that Indi has one of the sunniest dispositions I've ever encountered—friendlier even than Lily. They look similar, too, with the same blond hair and big blue eyes, but Indi is much taller, taller than Raven. And her skin sags on her bones, dark circles under her eyes.

"It was awful there," Indi says, as Sil puts a mug of tea in front of her. "My mistress would shut me in a closet sometimes when she had company over. Oh, this is lovely," she says, taking a sip of tea. "She'd forget about me and I'd be left there for a whole day. She was young, just married, and she was more interested in pleasing her husband. I heard her tell someone she only bought a surrogate to see what the Auction was like. I started to worry . . . I mean . . .

the Electress's surrogate died and then there was one girl I went to Westgate with and I saw her a few times, at the Longest Night ball and a couple of other parties and then she was gone." She looks around the room, taking in the handwoven rugs, the homemade furniture, the cast-iron stove. "I like this house," she says. "It's very comfortable, isn't it?"

"It is," I say. "I'd better go back upstairs before the other girl wakes up." I look to Raven. "Can you fill her in?"

"We've got this," she says.

Indi is still chattering away as I head back upstairs.

It takes the little brunette another half hour before she wakes. Her reaction is the same as Indi's—violent response to the serum, greedily drinking the water, and then bursting into tears.

Unlike Indi, her tears aren't joyful.

I manage to get her name—Olive—before she starts shouting.

"Where am I? Where is my mistress? Take me back! I want to go back the Jewel." Olive's green eyes are glassy under her thick brown curls. "How could you do this to me?"

Before I have a chance to say anything, she runs out the door and down the stairs. I follow her and she stops short at the sight of the four women sitting around the dining room table.

"I remember you," she says to Sienna. "You broke the rules. You drank champagne when you weren't supposed to. I saw you at the Exetor's Ball." She turns to me, as if I had suddenly become her ally. "I told my mistress and she was pleased, yes she was; she knew I would never do that to her. Be obedient and be rewarded, that's what she always said."

Olive claps her hands to her chest. "Oh, my poor mistress, what will she do without me?"

"She'll survive," Sienna snaps. "And so will you."

Indi shoots her a look. She gets up and puts her arm around Olive.

"It will be all right," Indi says. "I think they're trying to help us."

"I want to help my *mistress*," Olive says with a giant sniff.

"You don't have a mistress anymore," I say gently.

"Yes I do, she's the Lady of the Stream and she needs me!" She collapses into sobs on Indi's arm.

"We need to show her. Let's get this over with," Sienna says. "Maybe when she goes to the cliff she'll understand."

"I've never been on a cliff before," Indi says, stroking Olive's hair and glancing around as if it might be hidden under the sofa or behind the loom.

"I want to go back to the Jewel," Olive moans.

I'm surprised by Olive's reaction, and her complaints are unsettling. I'd never imagined any surrogate who'd spent any time in the Jewel actually defending the royalty. "You're right, we should show them now," I say to Sienna. "Raven?"

Raven is hunched over, holding her head in her hands.

"What's wrong?" I say, hurrying to her side.

"She's been twisted up," she says, speaking to her feet. "Not the way I was but . . . she believes their lies. She loves them. It hurts."

I put my hand on her knee. "We can wait. You don't have to take us there now. It's all right."

Raven's head whips up. "Of course I can take you there.

It's better there anyway." She rubs her temple. "I wish she'd stop crying."

We take Olive and Indi outside to the pond. The chill from last night has lifted; the sun is dazzling in a cloudless blue sky. It's almost warm.

Ash is running laps around the field—he's not wearing a shirt, and his back muscles ripple as he runs.

"Who's that?" Olive asks, her tears stopping for the first time.

"He's someone you'll meet later," I say. Indi's eyes are glued to Ash's retreating form.

"Let's do it by the pond," Sienna suggests.

"Where are you taking me?" Olive asks. I keep a tight hold on her hand and am glad that Indi seems to have the same idea.

"What a charming house," Indi says, looking back at the White Rose. "And the air here . . . it's so clear. Clean." She takes a deep breath.

We stand in a circle at the edge of the pond. Raven takes Indi's other hand as I take Sienna's. Olive tugs against me.

"What is she going to do?" she asks.

"We're going to show you who you really are," I say.

"So stop trying to fight it," Raven adds. "Because you can't."

She closes her eyes. Sienna and I do the same.

I hear a faint shriek from Olive as the cliff pulls us to it.

This time, the trees on the cliff are caught in a windstorm, their branches shaking and creaking as the wind howls. Dry brown leaves fly in the air around us. I've never felt this space so charged. I see Olive and Indi, on the far side of the spiral statue, and they have that same look on their faces that Sienna did when she first saw the ocean, a mixture of awe and reverence.

We stay here for a few minutes, letting the power of this place soak in. When we return, Olive and Indi look down and see flowers—dark green and lemon yellow—around them.

"What was that place?" Indi asks, bending down to stroke her flowers. Even as they wilt under her touch, new ones bloom.

"What did you do to me?" Olive asks, stepping backward. "I feel . . ." She clutches her chest. The trail of green flowers follows her. "I don't . . ."

The arcana begins to buzz in the knot in my hair.

"I'll be right back," I say to Raven and Sienna. "Stay with them."

I run back to the house, ripping the arcana out.

"Lucien?"

"It's me," Garnet says. "I need to talk to you." His tone is urgent, like it was the night I first heard him on the arcana. "There's something I thought you'd want to know. My mother received a delivery late last night."

"What was it?"

"A surrogate."

My heart plummets. "How could she have gotten another surrogate? The Auction hasn't happened yet."

"I don't know. I saw a girl arrive. She was handcuffed and blindfolded. And Dr. Blythe came to the palace this morning." He sighs.

"Does Lucien know?"

"I've been trying to get in touch with him. I expect he's fairly busy, now that the Auction date has been moved."

"So you heard about that, too."

"Yes. It's like a bloodbath here. Hardly any of the surrogates from last year's Auction are left alive. Everyone knows the Electress wants her daughter to rule. The Auction has been moved up, making it more likely she'll have one. So any surrogate who is pregnant with a girl is essentially useless."

"They're killing their *own* surrogates?"

"Yes," Garnet says grimly. "And you're not safe if you're a surrogate carrying a boy, either, because you can bet some rival House is going to try to take you out."

I shudder. "This is going to be harder than we thought."

"It was always going to be hard," he says. "I've never . . . it's like . . ." He lets out a growl of frustration. "I see them all now. The surrogates. I never noticed them before. Except now I see *her*, in every one of them." I know he's talking about Raven. "I see you in them, too," he adds quickly. "They're all people now, frightened girls who are paraded around on leashes and locked up in medical rooms. It's disgusting."

I press a hand to my mouth, a smile spreading beneath my fingers. It's incredible how much he's changed since the first time I saw him, drunk in the Duchess's dining room.

"How is everything at the White Rose?" he asks. "The last time I talked to Lucien he said he was sending you some new recruits."

"I think one of them is going to be . . . difficult."

"I've got to go," Garnet says suddenly. "I'll let you know if I find out anything else about this new surrogate.

Mother's keeping her under tight lock and key. And tell
Raven I said hello. Sorry I couldn't talk to her today."

"I'll tell her," I say. "And take care of yourself."

"I always do."

The arcana drops into my hand.

～ Twenty-Eight ～

ASH LEAVES FOR HIS FIRST TRAINING SESSION TONIGHT.

Raven goes with him.

I like the idea of Raven fighting even less than the idea of Ochre, but Ash makes a good point.

"She wants to be able to defend herself," he says. "After all that she's been through, I think she deserves that." He kisses me lightly. "Do you honestly think I'd ever let anything happen to her?"

After dinner, Indi, Olive, and I go walking on the grounds. I'm hoping Olive will feel her connection to the elements more strongly. She can connect with Air and Water, but she doesn't seem to have any interest in them.

"I want to sit by the pond for a while," Indi says as we

pass by the body of water. Indi, as it turns out, can only connect with Water.

I nod, and Olive and I continue to the forest. I remember that first night I came here. How Lucien told me to trust my instincts and how foolish I felt. I don't feel foolish anymore.

We walk in silence until Olive says, "I want to go back to the Jewel."

"You can't," I say. My mind is racing. There must be some way to get Olive on our side. "I was born in the South Quarter of the Marsh. You are from the East Quarter, aren't you?"

"Yes," she says.

"I have a younger brother and sister," I say. "Do you have any siblings?"

"Six older brothers, and one younger sister."

"Would you want your sister to be diagnosed? Taken from your home and sold?"

She shrugs. "My family would get some money, if she was."

"They stop paying once you're dead," I say.

"My mistress wouldn't kill me," she says. "She needs me. And now she thinks I'm dead."

"She'll buy another surrogate," I say. "Does that seem right to you?"

Olive hesitates, and I see a way in. She doesn't want to be replaced.

"They've moved the Auction up. She could be getting a new surrogate in a few months." Olive's mouth puckers. Her eyebrows scrunch together, forming a dark line across her forehead. "No, my mistress—

"Your mistress wants a child and she'll do anything she can to get one. We've got to stop the Auction," I say.

I can see her processing this, the crease between her eyebrows deepening "Stop the Auction," she says.

It's not exactly how I'd like to convince her, but my choices are limited at the moment. We don't have the time.

"And then I can be with my mistress," Olive says.

I don't answer. My heart is heavy in my chest. I don't like manipulating her like this, but what choice do I have?

We continue our walk and head back to the house, passing Indi, who is sitting by the pond, her face a mask of calm. Little white-tipped waves ripple out from beneath her palm.

I'm about to sit beside her when the arcana begins to buzz.

"Excuse me for a second," I mutter, hurrying into the house.

Sienna is in the kitchen doing the dishes. Sil sits in the rocking chair by the fire, sipping a whiskey. I yank the arcana out of my hair.

"Hello?" I say.

"Something's happened," Lucien says.

Sil sits up and puts down her drink.

"There has been . . . an arrangement. An engagement is about to be announced."

"I don't see how that's relevant," I say. "Who cares about a royal engagement?"

"It is between the Duchess of the Lake's daughter and the Exetor's son."

I stare at the arcana. "The Duchess doesn't have a daughter."

"I don't know how she did it," Lucien says, and it feels like he's talking to himself. "How she managed to convince him or threaten him or . . . no one knows what happened to end the Duchess and the Exetor's engagement—and believe me, the Electress has had me try very hard to find out. But whatever the cause, the Duchess must have something over him. Something very big. The Electress is furious, of course."

"But, Lucien," I say again, "I don't understand. The Duchess doesn't have a daughter."

"Garnet told you about the surrogate?"

"The one she stole? Yes."

"No one knew you were gone. The Duchess claimed she was keeping you sequestered after the alleged rape. So she replaced you, quickly and quietly. I can't find any records of any surrogate vanishing from a holding facility. And all the royal surrogates—well, the ones who are still alive—are accounted for."

"So where did this surrogate come from?"

"I don't know. But the Duchess has done something that hasn't ever happened in the history of the Auction. She has bartered an engagement *before* the child is born."

"So . . . her surrogate is pregnant?"

"It would appear so."

"But she only got her yesterday!"

"The Jewel is seething," Lucien says. "Many of the royals feel this is unfair. Many are angry with the Duchess. And now that the Auction date has been moved, Houses are lashing out at rival Houses' surrogates worse than ever. Old alliances are being broken. Ladies-in-waiting are feeling the strain, and it's worse for the lower servants, the footmen and the maids."

"Well, that's good for us, isn't it?" I say. "Those are the people we need on our side."

"We don't need them dying," he says.

"Of course not. That's not what I meant."

Suddenly, Ash bursts through the front door, Raven on his heels.

"Violet," he says, panting.

I leave the arcana hovering in the air, my immediate thought that Raven has been injured. But she steps aside to reveal another figure I hadn't noticed at first.

"Ochre?" I practically tackle him with my hug. "What are you doing here?" I turn to Ash. "You shouldn't have brought him. He shouldn't know about this place."

"Violet." Ochre looks pale in the moonlight. His big brown eyes are dark shadows. "They took her. She's . . . she's gone. I tried to get in touch with someone from the Society, but they moved me to a different dairy and I didn't know anyone. I barely managed to get to the training tonight. I thought maybe you'd be there. They *took her*, Violet!"

"Slow down," I say, leading him over to sit at the dining table. "Who's gone?"

He slumps into a chair. "Hazel," he says miserably.

My heart turns to stone. The very air around me seems to freeze.

"What?" I whisper.

"Regimentals came to the house. Mother said there was a doctor with them. They wore a crest on their jackets—a blue circle crossed with two silver things, like spears or something. And they just . . . took her away."

His head drops into his hands as my stone heart thuds into the pit of my stomach.

A blue circle crossed with two silver tridents.

The crest of the House of the Lake.

It's my turn to sink into a chair.

"Lucien," I call to the still-hovering arcana. "Did you hear that?"

Lucien's voice is grave. "Yes."

I think other people are talking, but their voices sound far away. I can't focus on what they're saying. My head pounds, one thought repeating over and over.

They took Hazel.

Hazel is the stolen surrogate.

The Duchess of the Lake has my sister.

Acknowledgments

CHARLIE OLSEN, AGENT OF AGENTS, THANK YOU FOR another year of incredible support and encouragement. You are my sword in the darkness.

To my editor, Karen Chaplin, thank you for your unbelievable patience and spot-on wisdom as you guided this story. I am so grateful to be working with someone who loves this world as much as I do—and who handles my rambling emails with such grace.

Huge thanks to the whole team at HarperTeen, particularly Rosemary Brosnan and Olivia Russo. Big hugs to the design team for another stunning cover. And to the lovely ladies at EpicReads, Aubry Parks-Fried and Margot Wood—your humor and enthusiasm are such bright lights in this industry. Lyndsey Blessing, thank you for taking Violet out into the world and making sure she was so well received.

Jess Verdi, I have still not figured out the words that will express how thankful I am for your presence in my life. I'm working on it. You've been there through each bump in the road and celebrated all the good stuff. You've read every word and cheered me on when I needed it, or told it to me straight when things weren't working. I don't know how I got so lucky to have you as my friend, but I'm so glad I did. Verveine.

A massive vat of thanks to my beautiful betas on this book, Caela Carter and Corey Ann Haydu—you always know when to push me and when to rein me in. And to Alyson Gerber and Riddhi Parekh, thank you for being amazingly supportive.

I have to thank the staff at Harlem Tavern, especially Bryan, Maria, and Istvan, who saw me through the initial drafting of this project with well-timed jokes and Sauvignon Blanc. Thanks for always telling me to get back to work.

Jill Santopolo, Maura Smith, Jonathan Levy, Rory Sheridan, Erica Henegen, and Matt Kelly, you have all influenced me, supported me, laughed and cried with me, and just generally been some of the best friends a girl could have. I am eternally grateful.

And to my wonderful family, both Ewings and McLellans, thank you all for the encouragement this past year. It has meant more than you could know. Special thanks to Ben, Leah, Otto, and Bea.

To my parents, I think the dedication for this book says

it all. You always believed I could do whatever I wanted, and you never once tried to steer me onto a "normal" path. You always embraced me for exactly who I am and that is a rare and precious thing. I love you guys.

And to Faetra. I miss you every day.